I owe a debt of gratitude to my children who encouraged me to write this story. Having gone through a divorce in 1991 in Bellevue Washington, I would see my children every other weekend and for two weeks during the summer months. Their visits were the highlight of my weekends. I would pick up my children on Friday evening and we would go and have dinner and then watch a movie. When it was time for bed my children would ask me to tell them a story. At first I would read to them, but as time went on I began to tell them make believe stories. We would spend countless hours talking about ghosts, murderers, creatures from another world and everyday people. On Saturday we would go for long hikes, play basketball or visit friends. Once Saturday evening rolled around and it was time for bed my children again would ask for me to tell them a story. I loved spending time with my children and they meant the world to me. Sunday would come and it was time for my children to leave. I would stand outside my house and watch their mother drive them away. I would wave and wave until I no longer saw them. My heart was empty those Sunday evenings but I also knew that two weeks later we would start the process all over again. After many years of doing this my children asked me to write a book. Finally, I took the time and pieced together a murder mystery.

I also want to thank all of my family whom I love and who encouraged me to finish this book once I started it. They all mean the world to me and I will always be mindful of that.

MURDER AT THE
LOG HOUSE RESTAURANT

BRAD L. EPPERLY

Murder at the Log House Restaurant
Copyright © 2010 by Brad L. Epperly

Borderline Publishing LLC
305 N. Steelhead Way
Boise, ID 83704
www.borderlinepublishing.com

ISBN 978-0984366903 (Paperback)

Printed in the United States of America on post-consumer recycled paper

CHAPTER ONE

It was a chilly August evening in Swan Valley, Idaho. The weather forecast was predicting light snow in the surrounding mountains. The brisk wind made it feel like late November instead of late summer. Perhaps for this reason, the Log House Restaurant was unusually busy for a Wednesday evening. The food at the Log House was simple; steak, potatoes, soup and salad and for dessert, a piece of apple pie, with or without vanilla ice cream. Not much variety, but after all you're sixty-five miles from Jackson Hole, Wyoming, and around forty-five or so to Idaho Falls. If you wanted something a little classier you could spend the extra hour or so and do a little traveling. Most of the guests at the Log House were there because they just enjoyed a great day of fly fishing on the Snake River and now were ready to sink their teeth into a nice 10 or 14 ounce rib eye.

The Log House does make a great rib eye and the beer is always ice cold. The restaurant is full of rustic charm, had room for about forty or so hungry visitors and tonight every seat in the house was occupied making the owner very pleased. After all, most full houses were on the weekends and a little extra money now or then never hurt anybody. Yes, if tradition held true, the tips should be as large as the fish that got away on the river that day. Most owners do not split the tips with the staff, but Lynn was not your typical owner. She makes sure that every tip is placed in a pickle jar conveniently located by the cash register, and when the doors are locked for the evening, she counted the tips and splits them into thirds, one third for her, one third for the cook and one third for me the waiter.

The Log House Restaurant was designed and built by Lynn seven years ago. It has a charm that brings the customers back year after year. Built out of logs, it made one feel they had just left civilization and had stepped directly into the wilderness. The outside porch that surrounded the front of the restaurant added just the right touch of ambiance. The slanted roof, two chimneys and spacious windows allowed the imagination to wander. The only constant reminder that civilization was just a stone throw away was the traffic that would occasionally pass by on Highway 26.

Upon entering the restaurant, the allusion continued. Placed neatly on each wall are several pictures of the mountains and the wild animals that live therein. Each table and chair in the restaurant was made out of the finest wood available, with tabletops covered in fine glass. Placed under the glass of each table are thousands and thousands of stories told through the pictures of fish and of those who have caught them.

Opposite of the entrance door, a large corkboard hangs on the south wall. Above the board is a sign that simply reads; "Fish caught during the month of..." It was at this point in the sign that the letters of the month were removable and the current month was always neatly displayed. It was only natural for the first time visitor, as well as many others who had been to the restaurant countless times before to pompously place their pictures there or to stare enviously at another's prize catch. To further enhance the excitement; at the beginning of each month the pictures on the board would be removed and the best one would make its way to one of the many tabletops, where it would be placed under the glass for years to come. It was like magic as the board would slowly fill up with new pictures of fishermen and women and the fish that they had caught.

On each table was a small business cardholder and placed in each holder were cards that proudly portray the name of the restaurant and its mailing address for all of those who have no current photo, but plan on mailing one to Lynn as soon as they develop their pictures. It is interesting to note that although Lynn received thousands of photos yearly, she still prides herself by spending a little time each week to look through all of them, placing a few of the chosen photos under each tabletop. Thus when customers return the next year, they excitedly look to see if their photos have been smugly displayed.

Each day before the restaurant opens for business, the tabletops are set with four placemats made out of paper. On each placemat, is a picture of a fish, magnificently jumping out of the river and while doing so is proudly declaring; "Catch me if you can." Placed on the wall behind the cash register is a large wooden frame that is empty. Engraved below the frame is a silver plaque that has the words:

"The one that got away!"

If you carefully look at the empty frame, you can plainly see an impression made by a very large and beautiful fish. It absolutely leaves you wondering where the fish might be now.

What makes serving food in the restaurant simple is a pair of swinging doors that separate the kitchen from the dining area as well as a small, four foot wide by two foot high window without glass. The window is suitably placed twenty or so feet away from the swinging doors and allows me as the waiter to quickly clear the dirty dishes from the table and place them through the window so that the cook can stack them for later cleaning.

Perhaps the item that I like the most about the dining area is how easy it is to serve the customers. Everything from the table arrangements to where the cash register sits is conveniently placed allowing me ample time to serve the customer as well as join in their hearty conversations. It is so fitting that after a wonderful meal and at least an hour of chatting with other patrons, as the customers prepare to leave the restaurant, the final thing they see is on the left hand side wall of the main entrance. It is a beautiful wood framed saying

"May your memories of this day,

last you a "Life-Time"

Three of us work at the restaurant. Lynn really does most of the work though. When she first started out, she hired an ex-con to be her cook. Upon their first meeting, he introduced himself simply as "Hammer." Honestly, I don't think anyone but Lynn and Hammer even know his given Christian name and without having to write his given name on a paycheck every two weeks, she would probably have forgotten too. The last person hired, is of course me, Billy Lee, to be her waiter.

CHAPTER TWO

We had nonstop customers all night and they for the most part were in good spirits. I was quite amazed at how much they were tipping. On most nights we would average around fifty to one hundred dollars each. On Fridays and Saturdays we would make up to one-fifty and sometimes two hundred dollars in tips. This was good money for one who left Denny's and great money for one just out of prison.

Hammer came out of the kitchen wiping his hands on an old dish towel. I quickly whispered to him,

"If things keep up at this pace, we will have our best tip night ever."

With a grin, he said, "Great, I planned on buying some new fishing gear and some clothes."

"Not a bad idea. I think I will do the same."

As he picked up a tray of empty dishes, he said, "The customers appear to be in a good mood tonight."

"Yes, they are. Most of them have told me that they had a great day of fishing."

For the most part, the fishing on the Snake had been tremendous all year long, but the last two weeks had been stupendous. The water flow being released from the dam was perfect for fly fishing. The weather, for the most part, was cooler than normal, but this made for exceptional hatches. The fish had plenty to eat and were jumping.

As the waiter at the Log House, I was able to talk to all of the customers. This gave me the opportunity to discover where the fishermen had been during the day and what they were using for bait. In addition, I had the privilege of talking to the customers about where they were from and what other places they planned on fishing in the future. It was truly a dream come true job. Basically I served a little food to a bunch of people who did nothing but talk about fishing, travel and fun.

The evening went by quickly and it was around 10:20 p.m. All of the customers had come and gone. Hammer opened the swinging kitchen doors and yelled at me, "I'm going to go outside to empty the trash. I will be back in about fifteen minutes. Do you think you can handle everything without me?"

"Of course I can, I do ever night, don't I?"

He began to snigger. "Yes, you do."

Picking up several bags of garbage, Hammer headed out the rear kitchen door. I looked around for Lynn, but she was nowhere to be seen. I made the decision to lock up a few minutes early and was in the process of walking over to the front door when a late straggler came into the restaurant.

"We have turned off the grill for the night, but if you want a cup of coffee I would be happy to get it for you."

He was a strange looking man who had large eyebrows and a nose larger than normal. He wore a black leather jacket and hat. If I had to guess, I would say he was in his early to mid-fifties. Without a word, he pushed me aside and went and set down at one of the tables that I had cleaned just moments ago. Then he barked out in a deep demanding voice,

"Come here."

This ticked me off, so I slowly walked over to him. When I was about two feet from the table, I stopped and stared at him. He quickly glanced around, reached into his jacket and pulled out two items,

"Listen, take this envelope and appointment book and hold onto them for me."

Then he grunted, "Bring me a damn cup of coffee while you're at it."

I didn't take kindly to his attitude and began to turn to walk away. He reached out and forcibly grabbed my arm,

"Have you forgotten something?"

"No."

He waved his left hand in disgust, leaned towards me and with his right hand pushed a manila envelope and small black appointment book into my apron pocket. For a second time, he grunted in a demanding fashion.

"Now go get my coffee."

I wanted to tell him where to stick his stupid envelope and book but it was late and I just wanted to finish up for the night. I intentionally walked leisurely to the coffee pot and began to pour a cup of coffee. When unexpectedly I heard a large screech in the parking lot, two doors immediately slammed and within a split second two masked men entered the restaurant brandishing pistols.

As they entered, they shouted at me to get down on the floor. I thought they were going to rob us, but instead ran up to the strange man at the table and screamed,

"Where is it?"

The strange man at the table calmly smiled,

"I have nothing. I don't know what you are talking about."

Without warning, the taller of the two masked men slapped the stranger across his face and yelled, *"Don't lie to us!"*

As he spoke I could detect an accent. From all of my TV watching his accent appeared to be from a South American country, possibly Colombia or El Salvador. It was very distinct and had a certain poetic rhythm. I felt certain if I ever heard it again, that I would recognize it instantly.

The strange man fell back from the slap. Blood straightaway began to spurt from his nose and lip. The masked man slapped him yet again. He hit him so hard this time that the strange man spun to the ground. The masked man shouted even louder, *"Tell us where it is!"*

The eccentric man who now was on his knees and apparently dazed from the two powerful blows, continued to be defiant. "I don't know what you're talking about."

This infuriated the masked man, who had already hit him twice. He turned to the other masked man. *"Search him! Search him now!"*

The second masked man grabbed the stranger by the throat and hefted him up. He searched his pockets and roughly patted him down. When he had finished he let go and the odd man fell to the ground. He turned to the first masked man and in perfect English said, "He has nothing."

This further angered the first masked man, who once again shouted, *"This is your last chance, tell us where it is!"*

I began to fear for this bizarre man and was about ready to say, "Is it this envelope that you are looking for?"

But as I made a sudden move to speak, the strange man glanced my way and shaking his head boldly declared, "I threw it out the window twenty miles back. You'll never know where."

With that the taller of the two masked men, the one who had already severely stuck the strange man twice howled, *"Then you are no use to us."*

He promptly aimed his pistol at the strange man and shot him in the chest. The two masked men looked at me and the taller of the two shouted, *"Stay there or you'll be next!"*

They then ran out the front door and jumped into their car. During all of this commotion, Lynn was no where to be found and Hammer when he heard the gun shot, raced back into the restaurant by way of the back kitchen door. He burst through the swinging doors in time to see two men hop into their car. Continuing to run, Hammer exploded out the front door to get a better look at them, nevertheless they sped off. It was dark outside and the parking lot lights were not very bright. But he did his best to glance at their license plate as they drove away; all he could make out was 1J 24. He knew there were more numbers but was unable to discern what they were. Taking a moment, he made a mental note that the car looked like a green Ford Taurus. Then, he hurriedly returned to the restaurant to see how I was doing, fearing that I might have been shot and robbed.

I, on the other hand, sprinted over to the man who was shot. I thought about how my father had died just four years earlier and felt like deejay-vu. I fell to the floor and grasped him. I placed his head unto my lap,

"Hang in there. I will get some help for you."

"No, too late for that, it is now up to you to reveal the truth. Tell no one about the envelope and book that I gave you. Keep them safe, use them both to reveal the truth."

"What truth? What are you talking about?"

As I held him, his blood was seeping out of his jacket onto the floor and on to my apron. His face was very pale and with each breath that he took, his eyes would slowly open and close.

Gasping he struggled to speak, he said, "You'll find out, but be careful many lives are at stake. There are two people I have not yet discovered. You must discover them."

Again I said, "What are you talking about?"

He slowly raised his finger to his lip,

"Hush someone is watching."

I awkwardly looked around and saw no one.

"Man, what are you talking about? I see no one."

His eyes portrayed the deep pain he felt as his body began to slowly tremble. It took great effort on his part, but he clutched my arm with his hand and in a faint whisper said, "Remember 9…3…9,"

He paused for a second to take a deep breath of air and then continued… "14."

Again he stopped. But this time he started to cough. I continued to hold him tight.

"Hang in there, you're going to make it."

His grip on my arm was slowly weakening. Only with great effort did he begin to whisper again, "Remember 9…3…9."

He paused for a moment and coughed, and then continued…"14."

He coughed several more times. With each cough, blood flowed freely from his mouth. I did not know what to make of what he was telling me. I exclaimed,

"If this is a phone number you are leaving out some digits!"

He was about to answer me, when his body began to violently shake. I held him tighter.

"Not yet man, it's not your time to die."

He turned his face towards mine. With great effort he held his eyes open. I gazed deep into them. Again, I saw the same agony in his eyes that I saw in mine when I lost my father. It felt like I was peering deeply into his soul. I knew this strange man had performed something very important, something worth dying for. It was so apparent that he wanted to tell me so much more. I slowly placed my head next to his mouth. He began to whisper for the last time the following words, "You must reveal the truth."

His body made one last quivering motion. His eyes shut for the last time. I knew he was dead.

At that moment, Hammer rushed back into the restaurant and shouted, "Are you okay?"

I screamed back, "Call 911 and get some help here immediately."

Hammer didn't move but looked at me and asked, "Are you okay?"

"I'm fine, but I am afraid this poor man is dead."

Hammer raced over to the phone and called for help. About a minute after he made the call, Lynn appeared and not seeing me asked him, "I heard a loud noise, what has happened here?"

While still sitting on the floor I said to her, "This man has been shot by two masked men."

Lynn hearing my voice looked down at the floor where I sat holding the dead man. She saw blood all over him as well as on me. She let out a horrific squeal and began to panic.

She ran right into the table next to where I sat. Hammer sprung towards her and took hold of her arm, "It'll be okay Lynn, calm down."

He then escorted her to a table away from the dead man. He pushed a chair out from underneath the table and had her sit down. She began to sob as her whole body started shaking. Hammer said, "Let me get you some water."

He rapidly went over to the counter where the coffee and water sat. He poured a glass of water and brought it to her. She took the glass of water from him and gulped it down. She said, in a distraught voice, "I went upstairs for just a moment to use the bathroom. I heard such a loud bang and thought maybe you had dropped a stack of dishes. I finished what I was doing and came down to help cleanup. I saw Billy sitting on the floor with blood all over. I can't handle this."

She squealed again.

Hammer immediately sat down next to her and held her hand. Meanwhile, I continued to sit on the floor holding unto a complete stranger who died just moments ago in my arms. It seemed like an eternity, but the local sheriff finally arrived on the scene. About ten minutes later an ambulance and two deputy sheriff cars pulled into the parking lot as well.

CHAPTER THREE

The first person to arrive was Sheriff Rick Thompson. He came in with his pistol drawn. We explained that the shooters had already left heading northeast towards the dam. He holstered his pistol and came over to me. He wanted to see if the stranger had a pulse. After verifying that the stranger was indeed dead, the sheriff lifted the stranger from off of my lap and kindly laid him down. The sheriff held out his hand and assisted me in getting up.

"Billy you look terrible, I want you to go and clean up, but be careful not to disturb any evidence."

I carefully went to the kitchen area to clean off the blood that was all over my hands, apron and clothes. Meanwhile the sheriff surveyed the area and then walked over to the table where Lynn and Hammer were sitting,

"How are the two of you doing?"

Lynn was still quite pale and looked like she was about to pass out. Hammer responded, "I'm fine, but I'm very concerned for Lynn and Billy."

"I understand, but please tell me what took place here?"

Hammer continued, "There's not much for me to say. I was out back dumping the garbage when I heard what sounded like a shot. I raced into the restaurant's kitchen and then straight out to the dining area only to see what looked like two men jumping into a car parked in our parking lot. I watched them head towards the dam and then raced back into the restaurant to see how Billy and Lynn were doing."

The sheriff turned to Lynn. "Where were you during this time?"

"I was upstairs in the bathroom. I thought I heard a banging sound and thought that perhaps Billy or Hammer had had an accident with the dinner plates. I came downstairs into the dining area to find Billy on the ground holding a dead man. They both looked like they were drenched in blood and I began to scream."

Sheriff Thompson was taking notes on everything they had to say. When Lynn stopped, he asked, "Did either of you see the two men who did the shooting?"

Hammer and Lynn both said, "No."

"Do either of you know this man who is lying here on the ground?"

Again they responded with a, "No."

"Excuse me for a moment, I have to call this in." he said,

The sheriff took a moment and contacted the dispatch assistant at the state police office located in Bonneville County. He gave his report and asked for the state police to be on the look out for any suspicious car that may have two men aboard who were armed and extremely dangerous. The dispatched officer asked, "Do you have anymore information on the car or the passengers in the car?"

He responded, "No."

The dispatch officer groaned, "Man do you realize that could just about be anyone and everyone driving the freeways tonight?"

"Yes, I know, but that's all we have to go on for now. I have a dead man here and any help rendered will be welcomed." He then signed off.

While the sheriff was interviewing Lynn and Hammer, I finished washing the blood off of my hands and removed the apron, pants and shirt that I had on. The manila envelope and appointment book that the strange man gave me fell out of my apron pocket, so I quickly picked them up and ran upstairs to get a clean shirt and a pair of pants. While I was upstairs, I placed the items under my pillow. In my closet was a stack of writing paper so I snatched several sheets and proceeded to write down the numbers that the strange man gave me. Sitting on top of my nightstand was a book that I had been reading on fishing so I folded the piece of paper and placed it in the book as if it were a book mark. The other sheets I laid down on the nightstand next to my book. I glanced around the room for just a second and proceeded to run back downstairs to talk to the sheriff.

When Sheriff Thompson saw me return to the dining room he anxiously asked,

"Billy, I want you to take a moment and describe to me what just took place here."

I began, "I was just about to lock the doors when this stranger came into the restaurant. He ordered coffee and I went to get it. Before I knew it two men wearing masks barged into the dining area with guns in their hands. They looked over at me and ordered me to get down on the ground. To tell you the truth, I thought they were going to rob us."

"So why did they just shoot this man and not both of you?"

I was going to tell the sheriff about the conversation that the two masked men had with the stranger just before they shot him. After all, he was rude and I had no idea who he was and what he was doing in our restaurant so close to quitting time. I opened my mouth to speak and then stopped, I thought of what he told me, "Tell no one."

These three words caused me to reflect on what all of this could mean and what about the envelope and book? The old man must have known about the two masked men following him. Matter of fact, he gave me the items so quickly and then so roughly ordered me to get him some coffee, it was just as if he expected them to enter into the restaurant moments after he did. It now appears he wanted to get me away from him so that they would not question me about the items he gave me. Furthermore, just when I was going to speak to try to help the stranger out, he glanced at me and shook his head in such a way that I knew he wanted me to be silent. Then the old man defiantly told the two masked men that he threw the items out the window. He knew that they were going to kill him and yet he gave up his life to protect the items he gave me. Now for some unknown reason, I knew I must not tell the sheriff anything.

Sheriff Thompson was somewhat impatiently waiting for me to speak.

"Yes, what is it that you have to say about the events that just took place here?"

I peeked over at Hammer and then Lynn,

"Like I said, I really know so little, except that this old man came in here in a hurry and demanded coffee. As I was getting it, the other two men came in and ordered me to the ground. I really thought they were just going to rob us. I had no idea they were going to shoot him nor do I know why they did it. In fact, once they shot him, I thought for a moment they were going to shoot me. They didn't and boy I am so glad they left in such a hurry without hurting anyone else."

The sheriff looked intently into my eyes and asked, "When you were holding this man on the ground, did he say anything at all that might help us catch these two individuals?"

Again I quickly decided to withhold some information from the sheriff and said, "No he didn't say anything at all except to tell me he was in pain."

As I said this, I quickly glanced at Hammer and Lynn. They both appeared to be relieved that I knew so little. I contemplated to myself that Hammer may have heard the stranger whispering to me, and possibly Lynn as well. But I definitely knew that Hammer was too far away to hear what he was saying. He had just returned from the front parking lot when the strange man was whispering his last words. As far as Lynn overhearing anything, I didn't think so. She was nowhere to be seen. By her own account she was still upstairs in the bathroom and even if she was coming down the stairs or in the kitchen all she would have heard would be faint sounds from the dying man. Yes, I was rather convinced that I was the only one who could have heard what he said in its entirety because he was speaking in such a soft whisper.

Sheriff Thompson was about ready to ask me another question when the ambulance and two deputy sheriffs arrived. He quickly excused himself and went out to the parking lot to give them some direction. As he did so, Hammer and Lynn both came up to me and gave me a big hug. They told me how glad they were that I was not hurt. They said they would be there to support me if the sheriff had any other questions. I thanked them and then just gave them each another hug. As I did so, I had a strange feeling come over me. What was it about me and death? I now have had two people die in my arms. That in it's self, must be a rare experience.

The first was my father and it drained my soul for three years. The second a complete stranger, yet for some reason, this second death has actually aroused my curiosity. What was so important about a manila envelope and appointment book that someone would be willing to die to keep it out of someone else's hands? And why would a dying man's last request be for me, a complete stranger to him, to find out *The Truth,*" truth to what? And if I did find out the truth, what would he expect me to do with it? And the numbers he gave me are they someone's phone number, if so, he left a couple of digits off, not to mention area code? But for now, I have decided to tell no one what I knew until I had a chance to look at the appointment book and open the envelope to see what may be inside.

CHAPTER FOUR

I'm twenty-three years old. I was born in a small town by the name of Nampa, Idaho, which is on the western side of the state and close to the Oregon state line. After just a short stay of only two days in the hospital, my family brought me home to Caldwell, just a few miles away. My father would always joke with me about the limited stay in Nampa. He said, "You cried so much that the doctors requested that I take you from the hospital early." For seven years we lived in Caldwell, which can be best described as a rural farming community. Boise, the capital of Idaho, is about thirty or so miles away. As a little kid, that was like a million miles away. Anymore, it is just a short drive. I liked going there though because it is so different and we called it going to "the city."

When I was seven, my father had the opportunity to start and own his own business in Eastern Idaho, so off we went to Idaho Falls. The city itself was small, but it was about three times the size of Caldwell, so it was more exciting than Caldwell. It is a beautiful city and actually does have waterfalls in the city park, hence the name Idaho Falls.

I had an uneventful eleven years in Idaho Falls. I did manage to graduate from high school, but even then my teachers told me that I would never amount to much. The only redeeming grace about my experience in Eastern Idaho was the time I spent with my father fly fishing the Snake River.

One day, after months of planning, my father and I scheduled a trip to fish the Salmon River just north of Sun Valley, Idaho. As we were preparing to go, my dad received a phone call that he was needed at his store. He told me it would take about an hour or so, so I offered to go with him and help him out. As we arrived at the store there appeared to be a lot of turmoil. A disgruntled customer who had been caught shoplifting a week earlier at the store was demanding to speak to my dad.

Now my father was very charismatic and handled everyone he met in an extremely sincere and friendly manner. Thus he freely approached the angry customer and asked, "Can I assist you?"

The customer whirled around and looked at my father, "Are you Jerry Lee?"

"Yes, I am. What can I do for you?"

The customer snarled, "Are you the owner of this store?"

"Yes, I am."

The expression on the customer's face grew distorted and angrier than it already was.

"I was a navy officer training at the nuclear power plant in Arco. But, because your store had me arrested for shoplifting, I have lost my job. I have nothing left to live for."

Without another word he took from his jacket a revolver. He aimed it directly at my father's chest and pulled the trigger three times. I heard three loud bangs. I hopelessly watched as my father clutched his chest. Then just as quickly, his knees buckled, and he fell awkwardly to the ground.

I immediately rushed to my father's aide and sat next to him. I lifted up his head from the hard cement sidewalk and placed it gently into my lap. As I did so the disgruntled customer aimed his gun at me. It appeared that he was going to shoot me as well. But he suddenly stopped and instead of shooting me, he placed the gun to his own forehead and pulled the trigger. He lurched back a step or two and dropped to the sidewalk. As he fell, his head crashed into the cement. His body quivered for just an instant and then he was dead.

I turned to the other people who were there and cried out in agony, "Please, someone call for help!"

One elderly employee rushed into the store and called 911. While the ambulance and police were being notified, I held my father close to me. It was obvious that he was struggling to breath. With the saddest eyes I had ever seen he turned his gaze to me.

"I'm so sorry about this, I feel I have ruined our trip to the Salmon River."

I gently stroked his forehead and in a sorrowful whisper cried out, "Dad, I don't care about the trip. I love you."

His voice became fainter, "Son, promise me you will take care of your mother."

Again in even greater despair I replied, "Dad, you are not going to die."

He took a deep breath and then groaned, "Son, please always remember, how much I love you."

He barely whispered the last three words, and then died.

My heart was distraught, my friend, my confidant, my father, was now lying dead in my lap. The days before and after my father's funeral was an extremely difficult and overwhelming time for me and my mother. Upon hearing of her husband's death, she wept uncontrollably. She ate nothing and talked to no one, including me. She basically gave up on life. Her devastation was so complete that she passed away two weeks later. The doctor told me that she died of a broken heart. In a sense, she willed herself to die.

I was now alone in Eastern Idaho, the only family member I was aware of lived in Southern California. I thought of moving there, but instead at the age of nineteen, I sold what little was left of the business, packed my bags and moved to Boise. I held several menial jobs, from being a night clerk at the Holiday Inn to a part time waiter at Denny's. For three years I just barely eked out a living and for three years I had not once touched my fishing pole. It was at this point in my life when a Boise prison guard entered into my life. His name was Del Montgomery. He just happened to be the Captain of the Guard at the prison. He was around fifty-three years old, was a very kind and intuitive person. It seemed to me that he knew I was hurting inside.

He would come by the restaurant several times each week. He had a habit of showing up during my shift. After several months of visiting the restaurant, he was about ready to leave when he turned and asked me, "Do you like to fish?

The word fish brought back some painful memories, but I raised my head and responded, "My dad and I would make weekly trips to the South Fork of the Snake to fish. Once maybe twice a year we would go to places like Yellowstone, or to the Madison River in Montana."

He then asked, "Would you like to go fishing with me one day?"

Tears welled up in my eyes and as I lowered my head, I softly said, "No…., no thanks. But, Del, thanks for asking."

Now Del was an incredibly optimistic person and was not used to people telling him no. In fact a no to him just meant that there was more to the situation and he adopted the attitude of, 'What more do you need to know?' Consequently, he kept on visiting the restaurant and I kept on serving him his traditional ham and egg breakfast. Finally, after two months of nonstop asking me about myself and my goals in life, he asked me to go fishing again. I told him the story of my father and how it came to be that he was murdered in front of me. How I felt it was my fault that he had died.

He told me that it was not my fault, bad things happen in life. That unfortunately this disgruntled customer whacked out and shot my father and then himself. I stopped him in mid sentence,

"Del, there is one major thing you do not know about this story. Indeed I have not shared this with anyone. I have had no time to share it with anyone. I tried once to tell my mother but she was never the same and up until her death would not listen to anyone. I tried once to tell a local doctor but I couldn't. And to be honest, I am not certain why I am telling you this. But,

Del, the customer that shot my dad was arrested for shoplifting at my father's store. It was I who had him arrested, it should have been me whom he shot, but instead he shot my father. When he aimed his gun at me, I didn't care. He had just taken from me my best friend and he might as well kill me. But he didn't. Perhaps, he just wanted me to suffer. I don't know what his intentions were that day, but I do know that I am suffering inside now. How can I ever, ever let the pain go?"

Del took a deep breath,

"Man, that is a heavy burden to bear, and I'm certain that anything I say at this time will feel insincere. So for now, I will say nothing, but I will be back tomorrow."

He then did something he had never done before, he gave me a huge hug and walked out the door. I knew he would be back, and I knew he would have something positive to say, but for now, I just wanted some space to think.

The following day on my way to work, I was pulled over by a Boise City Policeman. I knew I had not been speeding so I decided to get out of the car and talk with the officer,

"Sir, I don't know why you are pulling me over, what did I do wrong?"

When he saw me walking towards his car, the officer pulled out his pistol and yelled, "Son, don't move, put your hands above your head and slowly backup to my car."

Pulling out his gun greatly startled me. I didn't know what to do. But after a moment of sheer terror, I did as he ordered. When I got to his car, he opened the backdoor.

"Please get in, and watch your head."

He did not handcuff me, search me or even read me my rights. Instead he closed the door behind me. He proceeded to contact another pair of patrolmen who were only two blocks away.

"Car 457, where is your location?"

"We're two blocks away sir."

"Good, please come to Fairview Avenue and Maple Grove. I'm parked on the south side with lights flashing."

While we were waiting for them to come, he asked, "Where do you live Billy?"

I thought it was strange that he knew my name.

"Here you go officer, here is my driver's license."

He shook his head,

"No, that won't be necessary. I just need your address so that I can have your car removed from this busy street. I will have some other patrolmen drive it back to your place of residence."

I still found this to be very strange indeed. I had no idea why I was pulled over or why he was going to have my car towed back to my apartment complex but I did as he said and told him my address. He wrote it down on a piece of paper.

Just then another police car pulled up. He indicated to the other officers to take my car and park it at the address that was listed on the piece of paper that he handed to them. They said, "Sure thing Sergeant."

And off they went. I began to be unsure of what was taking place when a beautiful Silver BMW pulled up. Out popped Captain Del. He said to the sergeant, "Great work, I will take it from here."

Del escorted me from the back of the police car to his car and off we went. I muttered, "What's going on here?"

"Don't worry; I have already made arrangements with your boss for you to have the day off. You and I are going fishing."

"Fishing???"

"Yes fishing, so sit back and enjoy the ride."

For the next forty minutes we drove in silence. Finally we reached a beautiful spot located along the Boise River. I looked at the water and turned to Del,

"I don't think I can do this."

"Sure you can, and I am going to show you how."

He grabbed two brand new fishing poles and handed me one.

"This is a gift. If you catch the first fish, I will throw in the reel as well."

He seized me by the arm and escorted me down the riverbank. We hiked for about two minutes towards a large rock sitting out in the middle of the semi-swift river. Where the current flowed past the rock, a perfect pool of water formed for the fish to feed in. He pointed to the pool.

"That's where we're going to fish."

It was identical to what my father use to do when we fished together. My dad knew how to read the water and where the fish would be feeding. And now Del was doing the exact same thing. I stopped and in almost a pathetic whine said, "Do you know how much that cop scared me when he pulled out his gun and asked me to backup to his car?"

"I am sorry about that, but it felt like the right thing to do at the time. You see, when I was just a kid, my father taught me that when you get bucked off your horse that you must get right back up on it and ride it again. I know that you were hurt when your dad died, but if he was here right now he would tell you to get back up on that horse. Therefore, I'm saying to you, go out there and catch that first fish. You know where to place your fly and you know how to make it float. You just have to get back up on that horse. It has been long enough. It is time for you to show me and your father you know how to survive."

I couldn't speak, I just wanted to cry, but I had cried enough over the years. I took the fly pole and I stripped out some extra line. Doing my best Norman Maclean imitation, I gently whipped the fly back and forth about three times and then released the line. I aimed about six feet in front of the rock. The fly landed perfectly on top of the water and it began to drift downstream around the rock and straight to a pool of foam that was forming behind the rock. Instantaneously the fly was devoured by a trout that was just waiting for its next meal.

I set the hook and the trout was now mine for the taking. I knew that if I gave it too much leeway that it could possibly slip off. I had to keep the tension just tight enough. The trout was a fighter and without delay took off upstream; he jumped twice and then darted back downstream.

It became a personal battle between me and the fish. If he fought hard enough perhaps he would escape. On the other hand, if I played it right, I would begin to wear him down and slowly bring him to shore. For about six minutes the battle waged on. But it was just like yesterday; I knew what to do and when to do it. If he darted away from me, I would give him some extra slack. If he charged towards me I would immediately bring in the extra line to keep it tight. Then just as quickly as it began, the trout surrendered. Proudly, I brought him to shore since it was better to come in with a fish and a story than just a story about a fish.

During this entire time Del was shouting words of encouragement. He exclaimed, "That might be the biggest trout I have ever seen caught out of that hole! And I have been fishing here for years!"

He then bent down and keeping his hands in the water unhooked the fish. It was a beautiful twenty-one inch cutthroat, close to three pounds. He looked at me,

"I bet you want to release it don't you?"

Breathless, I said, "Yes, this one is for my dad."

I then sat down and cried for about eight minutes. Throughout this time, Del kept silent. He would take his fly pole and cast upstream, but I knew he wasn't trying to catch anything. I knew and he knew that he had just caught me from a three year fall. That I was now back on the horse, and from this time forward I would learn to master that horse.

I stood up and turned towards him, "Thank you, Thank you so very much."

He smiled. "You really do know how to fish. I have never caught one on my first cast."

I looked at him and began to laugh. It was the first time in years that I really laughed. For the next three hours we fished and talked about life.

"Would you be willing to come to the prison to teach some of the guards how to fly fish?" he asked.

"I know so little about fly fishing, but if you want me to, I would be more than pleased to do so."

"Next Tuesday then at six thirty."

For the rest of the afternoon, we just fished. Neither of us said another word until it was time to leave.

CHAPTER FIVE

Hammer was an ex-con who went by the name of Hammer, not so much because he looked like a hammer, but because he looked like a nail that was struck by a hammer. He wasn't very tall, about 5' 10" or 5' 11", but weighed a good 220 pounds. One might envision a fat, dumb man, but in Hammer's case he was neither fat nor ugly, he was all muscle and remarkably, very intelligent. He served time in prison for first degree assault. He and his mother were being abused by his stepfather and one day he just went berserk and broke every bone in his stepfather's body....literally. At the time this happened, he was only twelve years old. The judge, not very lenient on him, sentenced him to eight years. Six years at St. Anthony Juvenile Detention Center in upstate Idaho, and the remaining two years to be served in the State Penitentiary in Boise.

In the juvenile detention center, Hammer was a terror. Even though he was only twelve, he could take on anyone there, including all of the eighteen year olds. In fact, one day he was found thumping on three of the meanest and oldest ones there at the same time. The guards however liked him because he basically beat up the ones that they couldn't touch. Allegations often surfaced that the guards would simply turn him loose on any juvenile who was causing them grief. He was their enforcer and they enjoyed watching the fear in the other juvenile's eyes when they would threaten any unruly person with a visit from the Hammer. But good things can last only so long and upon reaching his eighteenth birthday, was sent off to Boise to serve the rest of his time. .

At the state penitentiary in Boise, the inmates not knowing of Hammer's previous reputation or moniker, decided he would be an easy target. They were wrong. On his first day there, several inmates joked with him about how he would become someone's bitch. Hammer, not interested in any sexual relationship with another man, decided to set the stage right from the start. The first thing he did was identify who the biggest, meanest son-of-a-bitch was and the following day, broke his jaw. As he stood over the helpless inmate he proudly declared, "I am the Hammer and no one messes around with me." He served two weeks in solitary confinement for his actions. Upon his release from confinement, he found the second meanest bastard and broke his nose and arm. This led to another month's worth of confinement, but the message was sent out loud and clear. He was a serious force to be reckoned with.

Hammer made no friends and had no plans on ever doing so. But, like most lost causes, there always is a ray of hope and that hope came in the form of Captain Del and me, Billy Lee. Now, I do not want you to get the wrong idea or anything. I wasn't sent to prison for any criminal offense. I was there to do a presentation on fly fishing.

Up to this point in time, Hammer had no interest in any prison activity. But, when he heard about the class that was going to be taught, he actually went out of his way and approached the guard on duty and asked him if he could attend. This surprised the guard because he knew of Hammer's reputation of being a recluse. Indeed, Hammer, had not even spoken more than ten words to him in the entire seventeen months that he had been there. The guard told him that he would take it up with the Captain who was actually responsible for making arrangements to have the class taught. The Captain, upon hearing Hammer's request, was very pleased. He immediately saw an opportunity to reach out to a prisoner whom up to this point in time seemed like a lost cause.

The Captain approached Hammer and began to speak, "I hear you are interested in learning about fly fishing?"

"I am." Hammer anxiously replied.

The Captain looked him over, trying to figure out why all of the sudden interest in fly fishing when he never cared about a single thing.

"If I let you attend, I would expect you to follow-up on all of your duties during the week and I would expect you to take an active role in preparing yourself for your future release from prison."

Hammer paused for about two seconds, and then earnestly blurted out, "It's a deal."

The Captain was elated because he believed that once Hammer made a promise it would be kept. Hammer was, if nothing else, true to his word. Sure enough, during the following week, Hammer completed all of his assignments and even went out of his way to speak to a few of the other guards that he knew would be attending the class.

Tuesday evening rolled around and at six thirty, I was invited into the prison grounds and there with nine guards and one prisoner named Hammer, taught the vital elements of fly fishing. During my two hour presentation, Hammer was quiet as a mouse. He took notes on everything I said. Finally, when my time was up, the guards all came up to me and shook my hand, they each personally thanked me and left. Hammer on the other hand raced up to the captain and inquired if he could take just an extra thirty minutes to ask me some additional questions. The captain was pleased with his interest in the class, but he turned to me and spoke earnestly.

"You do not have to do this if you do not want to?"

I looked over at Hammer and saw in his eyes a sincere interest. I turned back to the captain and thoughtfully replied, "Oh it's quite alright. This should be a lot of fun."

Again I turned my attention to Hammer. "By all means, ask away."

There was something about his sincerity and personality
that made me like him instantly. He on the other hand was so
thrilled about my willingness to stay late and answer his
specific questions that he bonded to me. Together we became
instant friends. He asked me question after question about fly
fishing. He wanted me to explain to him how much fun it
would be to actually catch a fish. I answered each question and
did my best to describe the thrill of catching a fish. It was at this
point that I surprised myself. I found myself telling him,

"Upon your release from prison, I'll take you over to
Eastern Idaho and we'll fish the South Fork of the Snake. We'll
be able to fish to our heart's content."

The captain joined in, "You only have six months left to
serve of your two year sentence. This is your opportunity to
make the best of your remaining time here."

Hammer nodded his head enthusiastically in agreement,
and then looked over at me. "Will you please write?"

"I promise you that I will, but you must promise me that
you will listen to the captain. Furthermore, you must promise
me that you will do exactly what he says. If you do this, I will
take you to the South Fork of the Snake."

He let out a loud shout for joy and darted towards the
captain. With great excitement he asked, "Do you think it
would be okay if I kept in contact with Billy by mail?"

"Yes I think it would be okay. Matter of fact I will
personally mail the letters if you adhere to all of the rules and
become a model prisoner".

Now when Hammer smiled, he became very pleasant to
look at. After hearing what the captain had to say his smile
must have been a mile long. He bobbed his head up and down
in agreement, "I will do whatever it takes from this moment
forward."

He reached out grabbed my hand and shook it so hard that
I thought for a moment he was going to break it. My faced

grimaced in pain. When he saw the pain in my eyes he quickly let go.

"I'm sorry about that, sometimes I don't recognize how strong I really am."

He then quickly turned around and skipped off towards his cell.

I took my left hand and began to rub my sore right hand as the captain approached me.

"You might have just changed his life forever. I can only hope that he will follow through on all of his promises. He has a lot of potential, if it can only be funneled in the right direction."

Joking, I retorted, while still rubbing my hand, "Not only potential but a hidden amount of strength. He almost broke my hand shaking it."

The captain laughed. "Yes, that he does have as well.'

He then placed his arm around my shoulder and escorted me to the main prison gate.

Just before I left the prison, he turned to me, "Thanks again for showing us the fine art of fly fishing."

And that is how Del, Hammer and I became friends.

CHAPTER SIX

During the next six months, Hammer wrote me faithfully every week. He kept his promise with the Captain Del and became a model prisoner. All of his assignments were done on time. He spent extra hours in the prison library preparing himself for his May 1st release date and life on the outside. He finished the necessary courses to obtain an associate's degree in business and even assisted other prisoners in their day to day activities. I, in return, kept to my promise and wrote him back every week. In each letter we talked about the excitement of fly fishing. We further discussed in great detail what it will be like for him to catch his first fish. His desire to learn how to fly fish saved his life. He spent hours at a time practicing casting in his cell, with a fictitious fly pole. Captain Del worked very close with him and within a six month time frame he was prepared to leave prison. Together, we counted the remaining weeks until his release.

Over those six months Del and I fished at least once a week. We visited various locations along the Boise and Owyhee Rivers. Each trip brought me great pleasure. I found myself being released from the imaginary prison I had created and looking forward to each day with a new found awareness.

Eventually May 1st arrived and Hammer was paroled. I met him at the prison gate with Del and off we went for a bite of lunch. As we ate, Del gave us some important advice on how to stay out of trouble. Furthermore, he told us if we ever needed anything to just call him and he would be there for us. We thanked him for his friendship and took off to Eastern Idaho to fulfill the long awaited promise I had made to Hammer.

Idaho is a large state and the trip from Boise to Idaho Falls was approximately three hundred miles. We started off heading east on Interstate 84. We climbed a little bit in elevation as we headed towards Mountain Home, a very dry and hot looking area located in the high desert area east of Boise. After passing Mountain Home, we drove for several miles before entering some very beautiful farm land and then passed several dairies before entering Jerome. The smell from the dairies was unusually strong and Hammer grabbed his nose.

"God, couldn't you wait until the next rest stop?"

"Not me. That's the dairies."

He looked at me as if I was stupid.

"Billy, I know that. I was just kidding."

I realized that we were just getting to truly know one another. And his sense of humor was more intact than mine.

Continuing past Twin Falls, and about fifteen miles east of Burley, the freeway splits off. Interstate 84 continues southeast to Salt Lake and Interstate 86 heads to Pocatello. We took I-86 east and continued to gradually climb. The traffic was less congested as fewer cars take I-86 than the ones heading to Salt Lake City. The scenery was very peaceful as we drove along the Snake River for several miles past Massacre Rock State Park. We then buzzed by a small city called American Falls about seventeen miles west of Pocatello.

Just before reaching Pocatello, we passed the J.R. Simplot fertilizer plant. The stench was equal to if not worse than the smell of the countless dairies we had passed earlier in the day. It was my turn to accuse Hammer of passing gas. He got the joke immediately and began to make loud noises with his mouth. It was obvious to me that he enjoyed being free. During the trip, we talked about the future and how we both planned on making the best of it. He explained to me that his stepfather was always abusive, and how he would beat him and his mother constantly. There was not a single day that went by that they did not receive some form of abuse from him. That on the day he finally struck back he had had enough. He did not mean to cripple him the way that he did, but he could not stop himself.

When the judge sentenced him to eight years of prison, he felt betrayed. It was his stepfather that should have been sentenced and not him. This made him so angry that he just shut down. He would do everything in his power to disobey authority. His stay at the St. Anthony Juvenile Detention & Youth Rehabilitation Center was nothing but a big joke. The guards treated him like a bulldog and would only show him any attention if he would enforce the rules. He did manage to obtain his high school diploma there, but other than that, there was nothing else it offered him.

His transfer to the Boise State Penn was no better. He felt he had to establish himself quickly and that is just what he did. The only person who seemed to care was Captain Del. His own mother never visited him while in St Anthony or in Boise. In fact she never even wrote. She just took off and disappeared. To this very day he has no idea where she is.

He told me how he had always lived near the Snake but not once had he the chance to go fishing. He never knew his real father and his stepfather could care less about him and his desires. When he heard about the class on fly fishing he felt an immediate need to know more. He approached the guard and the rest is history. He told me about how Del would always encourage him to do better but until that day there was no reason to change. What we talked about during that class gave him hope. The fact that I was willing to take extra time to talk to him directly made him my friend for life.

It was amazing how fast the time flew by as we chatted. Before we knew it, we were heading north on I-15 to Idaho Falls. We were still climbing in elevation until we were at about 4,900 feet high. From Pocatello to Idaho Falls, we passed by several farms, the Blackfoot Indian Reservation, the city of Blackfoot, part of the lava beds formed by ancient volcanoes and finally into Idaho Falls, getting off of I-15 at the Broadway Avenue exit and into downtown Idaho Falls.

We were looking for a place to buy some food before heading north to Ririe where we would be spending the night. There was a small grocery store across the railroad tracks called the Jiffy Mart, so we decided to stop and get some soda, chips, bread, meat and other items to get us by during our fishing trip.

This was the first time that I had returned to Idaho Falls in nearly four years. The town had not changed, it was still the same old city. It brought back some sad memories, but I knew that was the past and I had a new hope for the future. We finished our purchases and climbed back into my old red Toyota Camry and off we went to Ririe.

We drove down Yellowstone highway until we came to another fork in the road with Rigby to the north and to the north east, Highway 26 and Ririe. We went through Ririe past a small convenient store that my dad and I would always stop at to buy some flies and snacks. The road continued on for several miles through beautiful farm land full of wheat and potatoes. About five miles past Ririe, we took a left towards a small place called Hi-C Hot Springs. There were several open areas just past the hot springs in which we could camp out for the night. One spot was particularly beautiful. It was next to a rock that the local climbers would scale during the day. It made for the perfect campsite. Hammer set up the tent while I made a small camp fire. Together we unloaded the food from 'Old Red' and roasted some hot dogs.

The night was very chilly. It was early May and it was quite typical for the weather to be in the low 30's this time of year. As we prepared to call it a night we heard a couple of coyotes howling off in the distance. The sky was clear and the stars were shinning brightly. Hammer looked up, "God, it sure has been a long time since I have seen the stars. There so brilliant and vibrant out here. I definitely missed the beauty of the outdoors."

"I know how you feel. It has been a long time for me too."

For the next thirty minutes we watched the stars. Each passing moment they grew brighter until the Milky Way was clearly visible. Without saying another word that night, we got into the tent and both of us slowly drifted off into a deep sleep.

CHAPTER SEVEN

As the sun rose the next morning, we awoke and prepared for a day of fishing. We grabbed a couple of Pop Tarts and some jerky and off we drove to our first spot of the day. It was an old farm house that my dad had shown me when I was growing up. I always had luck fishing here and felt it would be a great spot for Hammer to cast his first fly. As we walked across the farmer's field and approached a spot where the trees nestled next to the water, we found the small path that led to the water and then began our slight descent to the water's edge. It was almost like the last time I had visited; with one obvious exception, several trees had been chopped down. Not by man but by a pesky beaver that must live somewhere near by. I could see his or her, or for that matter, their teeth marks at the base of several stumps that jetted out of the ground.

As we waded quietly into the river, I felt as if I had never left. For just an instant I sensed the presence of my father. I took three deep breaths and said a silent prayer. With new found energy, I proceeded to show Hammer where to cast his line, explaining how he would want the fly to drift down river by floating it on top of the water. I made it clear that if the fly went under it would be harder to see, but sometimes the fish here would hit a wet fly as well as a dry fly. Stepping back to his left, I watched him unhook the fly from his pole, holding it lightly for a few seconds and then slowly releasing it from his grip. He began his first cast by flicking his wrist twice, and then with a gentle toss, let the line go. The fly plopped down on top of the water and gently floated downstream. He watched with great glee until the fly reached the end of its float, and then smoothly started the whole process over. It was apparent that all of his "practice" was time well spent.

I watched him as I am sure my father use to watch me. I was proud of the fact that I had somehow helped him find himself, the same way my father and then later Del helped me. It was on his fourth attempt that he had a strike at his fly. He quickly jerked the line back, a little too fast in all the excitement, missed the fish but caught the tree directly behind him. He shouted with joy, "Did you see that? I almost had him."

"Good first catch!" I shouted back. "You're supposed to catch the fish though, not the tree!"

Hammer surprising laughed and said. "At least I caught *something*. Let's see you do any better."

I began to chuckle and directly remembered the countless times that my father had told me to be a little more patient when setting the hook. I waded back to shore to untangle his line from the tree. It was at this point that I took a few moments to coach him on the fine art of knowing when to set the hook without jerking the fly out of the mouth of the fish.

Again, he flicked his wrist several times and let the line soar across the sky, placing the fly lightly on the water. I complimented him on how well he did in casting out the fly. He told me that his success was due to all the hours of practice in his cell. This time, as the fly floated down river, we could detect a sudden silver movement in the water. The fish took the fly. As Hammer successfully set the hook, he now had the opportunity to land his first fish. But just like I did the first time I ever went fishing, he horsed around a little too much with the line and the fish was able to wiggle off the hook and safely swim away. It didn't seem to matter to him one bit. He had hooked his first fish and even though the fight was short lived; the thrill would fill his memories forever.

Yet again and with great patience, I coached him on how to gently work with the fish once you have him on the line. I explained the need to keep the line tight, but not so tight that you rip the hook right out of the fish's mouth. I went on to explain how if the fish took off up or down river that you might have to release some extra line in order to keep the fish on. We talked about all of the possibilities and then he tried for a third time. Again, his cast was perfect and the fly floated down river. Just then, we both saw a flicker of silver down in the water and the fly suddenly disappeared. Hammer set the hook at the right moment. He had yet another fish on his line, but just like before, his lack of experience showed and the fish got away. It didn't matter to him or me, we knew it was going to be a great day and the fish were biting.

For several hours we fished this particular spot in the river. Hammer had several hits and several on the line, but it wasn't until his tenth or eleventh try that he had one on, that he finally figured out how to successfully battle the fish and bring him in. Hammer, in his excitement, grabbed the line with leaving the fish dangling in midair. Hammer stood there for a second with a rather perplexed expression on his face.

"What do I do next?" he shouted.

I calmly went over and gave him a slap on the back out of pride for his first true catch of his life. I then showed him how to unhook the fish while keeping it in the water. Since we were using barbless hooks, it made it easy for me to unhook the fish.

I raised the fish up out of the water to show Hammer. It was a beautiful cutthroat. It had stunning orange markings underneath its gills and was about thirteen inches long.

"Do you want to keep him or release him?" I asked.

Without giving it a second thought, he blurted out, "No, just like me, I want to release him. I want to watch him swim free."

Upon hearing these words, I tenderly placed the fish back into the water and effortlessly let go. At first the fish just sat there, then, with a rapid dart it was gone. Hammer had caught his first fish.

CHAPTER EIGHT

We spent a couple of more hours fishing this particular spot. It was close to noon when we chose to drive upriver to the Swan Valley Area. The mountains surrounding the valley still had a healthy snow pack and the day was actually quite chilly. We decided to stop at the local gas station to get some hot chocolate. As I parked the car, Hammer turned to me, "Let's stay here for the summer. Maybe we can find some work or a place to stay and just fish every day."

What he said made sense and I echoed out my agreement, "Sounds good to me. I'll ask the gas station attendant if she is aware of any openings in the area."

We found the hot chocolate and a couple of doughnuts towards the back of the store. As we were paying, I asked the clerk, "Do you know of any jobs in the area?"

She thought for a few seconds, "No, but you may want to drive to Idaho Falls; they should have plenty of opportunities there."

Thanking her, we began to leave when the customer behind us, perhaps the ugliest woman I had ever seen before in my life, moved toward us, "I know of two openings. If you wait for me to get my stuff, I will explain the job to the both of you."

We agreed and waited outside for her. Soon, she exited the store and approached us. Looking us over, she said, "I own a restaurant here in Swan Valley. This morning my cook and waiter both quit. They called me about a half hour ago and told me they were both going to Seattle together and wouldn't be back. If you want the jobs, you can have them."

I was ecstatic, "I was a waiter at Denny's in Boise. I planned on calling them today to quit."

She smiled. "Great,"

Turning to Hammer, she asked, "Do you know how to cook?"

He paused for moment, "A little bit in prison."

The lady frowned for a second or so, and then proceeded to cautiously look him over. "Can I trust you?" she asked.

He confidently responded, "Of course, if you can't trust an ex-con, who can you trust?" He said this with such a sly grin that even I wondered if I could trust him. She continued to study him a little longer and then broke out in laughter.

"My restaurant is very unique and is up the road about three miles from here. For obvious reasons, I call it the Log House Restaurant. Look, I need someone for tonight. If you are willing to start today, you both are hired. I'll pay you three hundred a week and give you free room and board. We will split all of the tips equally and there will be just the three of us. Your hours will be from four to eleven, six days a week. We will have Tuesday's off. I am open from May 1st to October 31st of each year and spend the rest of the year traveling."

Then with a grin she continued. "Wait until you see the restaurant, I designed it specifically with fishermen in mind." When she said that, she had us, hook line and sinker. We both shouted out at the same time, "We'll take it."

"Good. Now let's get going. We have only an hour until we open. Follow me, boys."

Hammer and I raced over to 'Old Red' and followed her to the Log House Restaurant. As we arrived, we knew instantly why she called it the Log House. The building was made out of logs and was exceptionally beautiful. Pulling a set of keys from her pocket, she unlocked the front door.

"By the way my name is Lynn. And you are?"

"I'm Billy and this is Hammer" I replied.

We shook hands and she opened the door to the restaurant. She was absolutely right about her place being unique. Upon entering, Hammer and I both fell in love with the place. She quickly showed us around and then took us upstairs to our rooms. As she was about to go back downstairs, she stopped and looked at both of us, "Both of you smell like fish, so take a quick shower and come on down to help me. We open in thirty-five minutes."

She gave us both a nice smile and went downstairs. We both raised our right hands into the air and hi-fived one another. It was a dream come true for two young men who basically wanted to enjoy a summer of fishing in perhaps the prettiest area in the world.

We quickly showered and returned to the kitchen where she explained her menu. One choice and one choice only. It made cooking, cleaning and serving very simple. She proudly said, "Most of my customers are regulars. They come back every year if they live far away and at least once a month if they live nearby. I even have a few customers who live here locally and they come every week."

We were anxious to get started, so I asked, "Do you mind if I make two quick phone calls?"

Showing me the phone, she said "Have at it."

I called up Denny's in Boise and asked for my boss Larry. He came on the line and I told him that I was quitting and that he could send my last paycheck to the Log House Restaurant in Swan Valley. He immediately had a few choice words for me, but what the heck, I didn't care, I was starting a new life and leaving Larry behind was a good first step. I then called Del on his cell phone. He answered, "Hello"

"Del, it's me Billy, I've got so much to tell you!"

"Whoa Billy, slow up, first tell me, how are the two of you doing? Catch any fish?"

"We've had an awesome day. Hammer caught his first fish. We both have fallen in love with the area. What we plan on doing is staying here for the summer and part of the fall. We have been offered work as well as room and board at the Log House Restaurant. It is an amazing place, you have to see it."

"I know the place. I've eaten there in the past. Know Lynn too…*uugly!* You know, this is actually great news. I was concerned that it might take a little while for Hammer to get a job, but this sounds like a great opportunity for him. I also know that you will be a good influence on him. I can only imagine how much fun it will be to have the opportunity to fish every day."

"That's right; we plan on going out every chance we get."

"It sounds like you have a plan. I'll make arrangements for a parole officer to visit Hammer once a month. Furthermore, for your information, I personally will plan on coming out that way a couple times this summer. Perhaps you can show me a few of the good holes?"

"Sure thing, but for now I have to run. Talk to you again real soon."

"Okay Billy. Take care and keep fishing"

I hung up the phone with a smile and put on an apron. The Log House Restaurant was opened for business.

CHAPTER NINE

The parole officer visited Hammer as arranged and we stayed in touch with Del weekly. Del even made it out to fish with us twice, once in early June and again in late July. We took him fishing to the Farmer's Field and The Great Feeder canal, two of my father's favorite places to fish. So essentially May, June, July and most of August went by with Hammer and I enjoying early morning fishing and late afternoon work. We took advantage of our Tuesday's off and visited the sites such as Jackson Hole, the Tetons, and Yellowstone. Life could not have been better for two young adventurers.

There were times we offered to help Lynn on Tuesday with the shopping, but she insisted on doing it alone. She would always say, "Six days a week is hard enough on young minds. If I didn't own this restaurant I certainly wouldn't work a seven day work week."

As far as our ability to perform our work duties, Hammer became a very good cook. Granted, all he had to make was a few items, but each passing day gave him great confidence. For me I had become a very reliable waiter. It was easy taking orders.

"How would you like your steak cooked?" was perhaps the hardest thing I had to remember about the menu.

Possibly the most exciting thing that happened all summer long was a boating accident. It took place August 23rd on Palisades Lake. One of our regular customers named Keith Smith came into the Log House and ordered a cup of coffee. He seemed to be very upset. I stopped what I was doing and walked up to him, "Can I help you with anything?"

"I wish you could but there is nothing anyone can do at this time."

"What do you mean by that?"

"Oh, it's nothing, your better off forgetting about what I just said."

Then with a forced smile, I asked, "Maybe a good day of fishing will change everything. I plan on going out early in the morning. I'm going to do a little lake fishing. Do you know any good spots?"

"Yes I do, I have heard from several of the local fishermen, that they are catching quite a few fish towards the east bank of the lake."

He placed down a twenty dollar bill, "Thanks for the information." He then turned to leave.

"What about your change?" I yelled out,

Without looking back, he said, "Keep it, you'll need it more than I will."

As he walked out of the restaurant, I wondered what was bothering him, but soon I got busy with other customers and totally forgot about our conversation.

The next day Hammer and I had a couple of hours to do a little fly fishing. We took 'Old Red' and headed towards the dam. Some fellow fishermen had told us that there were some good size trout trying to make it up Palisades Creek. Up to this point, we had not done any fly fishing on small creeks and thus decided to give it a try. As we were driving towards the creek, we found a perfect spot to park the car on the side of the road. We pulled over and began to get our fishing gear ready when out of nowhere we saw Sheriff Rick Thompson speed by with his siren blaring. About two minutes later we heard some more sirens and saw an ambulance and three additional police cars race by. I took the car keys out of my waiters and headed back to the truck.

"Bag fishing; let's see what is going on." I said.

We rapidly returned to "Old Red' and followed the blinking lights. They led us to the top of the dam where we saw the police cars and ambulance. We promptly parked alongside of Sheriff Thompson's police truck and hopped out.

The Sheriff was busy yelling directions to several men who were in three different boats.

"Continue combing the area for any signs of a body. You might find it floating anywhere from the base of the dam to the spill way." They waved back, and off they went.

Running up to the Sheriff, "What's going on?" I asked.

He pointed out into the lake about four hundred yards or so.

"See that object out there?"

We looked and saw a capsized boat that was freely drifting in the water. "Do you mean the boat out there?"

"Yes, the person that was fishing on that boat about an hour or so ago phoned into the sheriff station. He told them that he was having motor problems and his boat was taking in water. He was quite concerned and feared he would have a difficult time staying afloat. Dispatch radioed me to see if I could help. I straightaway radio the forest service to see if they could send someone out immediately to assist him. The forest service radioed back that they would get someone right on it. It was just about twenty minutes ago that they radioed me indicating that the boat had capsized and they couldn't find anyone in the water. I stopped what I was doing and raced up here to lend a hand. It appears we may have to get the divers out to search the lake. Now, you two boys get about your business because I have things to do."

We thanked him for his information and asked, "Can we help?"

He didn't seem to hear us as he walked off to his truck.

The next day it was all over the news that a fisherman had supposedly drowned in the lake. No body had been found at this time but divers from the sheriff's department would continue to search the lake. It was further reported that the man who was missing and presumed drown was possibly a Mr. Keith Smith from Blackfoot, Idaho. Two days later a picture of Mr. Smith was published in the Post Register, a local Idaho Falls paper stating that it was his boat and he was presumed drowned in a fluke boating accident. When I saw the picture I recognized Keith immediately, and remembered our conversation. For several days it was the main topic of discussion on whether or not his body would ever be found. Many fishermen told stories of strong currents on the bottom of the lake and that the body could be anywhere by now.

CHAPTER TEN

After the murder in the Log House dining room, the remainder of the evening dragged on. Lynn, Hammer and I had to basically sit around the restaurant and answer the occasional question that was thrown our way. We waited for the sheriff and his deputies to take pictures and rope off the crime scene. The sheriff also informed us that we would have to close the restaurant for the next several days so that they might dust for prints, study tire tracks, and even see if the two assailants left foot prints or other incriminating evidence behind. It was finally two in the morning when we were permitted to head upstairs to our rooms.

Sheriff Thompson gave us some final instructions. "Remember to stay out of the dining room area until further notice."

Turning to Lynn, he said, "I am sorry about the inconvenience, but we will try to be done in three to four days. Perhaps there are some other things you can do? Look at it as if it was a vacation and not a crime scene, just a little time off."

"Yes a little time off with no pay, unless you plan on compensating us for our inconvenience." Lynn growled at him.

"I wish I could, oh by the way, try not to go to far away. We will need to interview you all again tomorrow morning."

"Don't worry, we'll be here." The sarcasm in her voice was readily apparent.

The Log House Restaurant was not only built to serve hungry customers but also has a place for the staff to live. A wooden stair case with oak handrails leads from the back part of the kitchen directly to the second floor in which there are four private rooms. The rooms consist of three bedrooms and one reading/recreational room. All bedrooms have a nine foot ceiling with a gorgeous wooden fan placed directly in the center of the room. Every bedroom has a bay window with solid wood frames and foot stool. The rooms are spacious and have there very own private bathroom, king size bed, two night stands and a dresser with six drawers. They also have a walk-in closet that has shelves built into one side for shoes and other odds and ends. All the material in the closets and bedrooms are made out of the finest cherry wood. On the walls of each room are various mountain paintings. You immediately have the feeling that you are spending the night at a luxurious hotel in Sun Valley or some other mountain retreat. The bathrooms are large with a walk-in shower and tub. They also have side by side sinks with large wrap around mirrors. Several lights are placed above the mirrors making the room bright and easy to see.

The three of us left the sheriff and his team to do whatever else they had to do. We were tired and ready for bed. All I could think about once I entered my room was sleep, so I plopped down on the bed. I wanted to check out the envelope and book, but was too tired, and it could wait until later. My eyelids were heavy and within minutes I fell fast asleep. It must have been a couple of hours when I heard someone creeping into my room. Whoever it was, they were looking for something. I slowly reached over to my bedside lamp and as quickly as I could, turned on the light. To my surprise I found the strange man who had been shot just last night standing in my room. I heard his dying words, I saw the sheriff check his pulse, I cleaned his blood off of my hands, I saw them haul him away in the ambulance, he was dead, yet here he was standing in my room.

He was not startled when I turned on the light, instead, he was pleased. He held his finger up to his mouth, "*Shhhh!* I came back to talk to you about the stuff I gave you. Did you tell anyone about it?"

"No."

"Good, can you tell me where you put them?"

"They're here under my pillow."

"Can I have them?"

"Of course, they're yours."

I reached under my pillow and the items were not there. Someone had been in my room and took them. I looked at him in great despair,

"There not here; someone has taken them!"

His calm demeanor changed. His face grew distorted and all twisted. He looked at me in great disgust, "I told you to keep them safe. How can you get to the truth if you do no have them? You have let me down, and now I have died in vain. I spent the last five years gathering up information so that this wouldn't happen, and you in a matter of one night lost it all for me."

He sprang unto my bed and began to choke me. I tried to fight him off, but I was still under the covers and couldn't do anything with my legs. It was as if they were tied together. His hold on me was tight and I could barely breathe. I had to loosen his grip and cry out for help or die. So with all of my remaining strength I took my left thumb and jabbed it into his right eye. This caused him to momentarily loosen his grip from around my throat and provided me with the opportunity to let out a large scream.

"Hammer! Hammer! Help me! Help me!"

Just as quickly as I screamed, he again placed his hands around my throat. I could yell no more. I was just about to give up when all of a sudden the door slammed open and the bedroom light was turned on. I heard Hammer's voice.

"Billy, Billy, what is it? Billy, Billy, wake up, you're having a nightmare."

He came over to my bed and shook me.

I finally awoke and in doing so threw a wild punch, but fortunately it just hit him in his arm.

"Hammer, grab him before he leaves." I shouted,

"Grab who? There is no one here."

"Grab the strange man who was shot last night."

"Billy, wakeup, you're dreaming, there's no one here."

It was at this point that I realized I had been dreaming. Sweat was pouring down my forehead, and I was as pale as a ghost. Still half awake I sat up.

"Are you sure there is no one here?" I asked.

"Sure as sure can be."

I paused for a moment and took a couple of deep breaths.

"Let me go and get some water for you."

He got up from the side of the bed, went into the bathroom and filled a glass that was sitting on the counter top with water. He then brought the glass of water back to me. I was fully awake by now. My heart was not beating as fast as it was just a few minutes ago.

"That must have been some dream you had."

"It was."

Sitting down on the bed, he said, "Well, tell me about it."

Just then Lynn came in, she looked around the room and then at me,

"What is all the fuss about?"

"Oh, Billy here has had a nightmare. He must have been screaming for about two to three minutes before I could get him to wake up."

"Oh my poor boy, it must have been tough to see that stranger get shot. Is there anything I can get for you?"

"No, I'm alright now, just had a bad dream."

Hammer jumped in, "Tell us about it."

I was just about ready to do so when Lynn reached out and took a hold of Hammer's arm,

"No, not now, it's still early. Lets all get back to sleep. He can tell us about it in the morning."

"You're no fun Lynn, but I guess I can wait until later"
Hammer complained

She looked at me, she asked, "Are you sure there is nothing
we can do for you?"

"Yes, I'm sure, I will be okay. It was just a rough night,
having that old man die in my arms just brought back some
bad memories."

They both nodded, and she said, "Go back to sleep Billy, try
to get some rest."

She escorted Hammer towards the door and they both left
my room. Hammer stuck his head back into the room and
smiling said, "Get some sleep old buddy; we will have lots to
talk about later."

He then turned off the light and shut the door to my room.

I could hear them talking in the hallway.

"Let him be, it has been a very hard night and he needs
some sleep."

"You're right; I'll leave him alone for now."

"Good, now get to bed."

"Goodnight Lynn."

"Goodnight Hammer!"

They both went their separate ways. I listen for a moment
longer and heard their bedroom doors shut.

Boy what a dream that was. It felt so real. He was so mad at
me for not keeping the envelope and book safe, I thought with
a deep sigh.

Just then I had a sinking feeling, I hastily reached under my
pillow and began to panic—they were not there.

How can that be? No one knows that I have them and
surely no one knew that I placed them under my pillow.

I started to get up and as I did so, I saw them both on the
floor next to my bed. *They must have fallen out while I was
dreaming.* In a soft whisper I cried out, "I must take better care
of them."

Quickly I sprung out of bed, grabbed the envelope and appointment book and went over to my dresser, yanking opened the bottom drawer. I put them both underneath my socks and exercise clothes. For a moment, I glanced around my room, seeing and hearing nothing I returned to my bed and drank the rest of the water that Hammer gave me. It took awhile but soon I was deep asleep.

Chapter Eleven

Around 11:00 a.m. that morning, I finally woke up. The weather outside was sunny, so I hurriedly got out of bed to use the bathroom, took a shower, brushed my teeth and combed my hair. After preparing for the day, I made sure that the envelope and book were still safe. I checked out the book and sheet of paper that I had written on, all was fine. Then for the first time since moving into the Log House, I locked my bedroom door. It felt strange to pull the key out of the lock and put it into my pocket. I felt awkward as I headed downstairs for some breakfast, but it felt it something I had to do. Not that I didn't trust Lynn or Hammer, I just felt it was something I had to do deep inside for some reason.

Hammer and Lynn were already up and drinking a cup of coffee. When Hammer saw me he stood up and walked over to where I was standing.

"How are you doing today? Did you have anymore bad dreams?"

"Leave him alone!" Lynn shouted.

"I just what to know how he is doing," he yelled back.

She was about to say something when I interrupted them. "I'll tell you how I'm doing, I'm starving. What's for breakfast?"

Lynn smiled. "That's my boy, bacon and eggs coming up."

I turned to Hammer and with a slight nod of my head whispered, "We'll talk later." He nodded back and went outside for some fresh air.

I finished eating breakfast and returned to my room and proceeded to unlock the door. It must have been the feeling of doing something important that made me look around to make sure no one had followed me up the stairs before entering my room. After feeling secure I entered my room, shut and relocked the door. Curiosity was killing me; I had to know what was inside the envelope and book. I went to the dresser drawer and took them out. The envelope was a manila envelope, about four inches by six inches. It was not sealed except for the little metal clip that would fasten into the hole provided on the outside jacket of the envelope. Gently, I unfastened the clip and opened the envelope and shook the contents out. A sheet of paper fell out and fluttered to the floor. I bent over and carefully picked it up and unfolded it. The following words were neatly typed on the paper.

Obtained information
Will take place this Saturday!
Must not go any further because they know too much about me!
Delays will make it impossible to stop the threat!
If unable to deliver message, then all is for not!

Seventeen sparrows went abroad
Four seasons past without a struggle
Yet thirty-four Knights failed in their flight
Because three fair maidens were nowhere in sight
Twice the king he was but nothing did he possess.
Until the bells tolled out the midnight doom.

The paper made no sense to me whatsoever. I immediately thought of some kind of special code. Perhaps the book will explain it further. But before I opened the book, I decided to write these words down on a separate piece of paper, just in case I should lose it or misplace it. I went to my nightstand and took out one of the extra sheets I had placed there the night before. Very cautiously, I rewrote the note word for word on two separate sheets of paper. I took one copy and folded it three times and placed it into my wallet. The other copy I taped to the backside of my nightstand. It was sitting next to the wall and the only way anyone would find it was if they moved it away from the wall. I felt it would be safe there for the time being.

I took the original sheet of paper, refolded it, and was about to place it back into the envelope when I noticed something taped to the inside of the envelope. It appeared to be stuck to the rear of the envelope, so I reached in and gently removed the tape. As I did so a small key fell out. It was just an ordinary key, but the way it was taped to the inside made me feel like it had great importance. Wanting to hide it, I decided to place it on my key ring next to my car key. For a replacement key, I removed an old apartment key from my key ring. With immense care, I taped the apartment key to the inside of the envelope. I finished by placing the letter back into the envelope and then replaced the metal clip into the hole and sealed it shut. The envelope looked like it had never been opened.

I turned my attention to the small appointment book. It was the exact same size as the envelope, four inches wide and six inches in length. To my surprise, as I opened it, there were no addresses or phone numbers. The book was basically empty. As I looked a little closer, I noticed on the bottom of each page various letters, numbers or characters written down. There must have been about twenty such characters per page. I took another sheet of paper off the nightstand and carefully copied each page. When I had finished, I had the following characters:

```
KLUDJI9ETNHHXCS24L9NEMJDUIOPWTDARFSDR42LKU?>JD
U7DHC#VK*JNVMBC&AVXF%$GDHTYEO6RT*@DGALDAEWS
QDSD?FSCVDGFTRYN?UI#?OJPOLKWGJNMGHFYB*R67YHDG
ACBL9?D5DGSFLCVER2D*GCFHA,7%#GNMJFKOI2K{LDEU8,W
JNMS6MSU*JH2J#MNSNHEDKHKDUIEK+^&893OREPLYDJKD6
27DIKD,M*CKCFODWIDKFJHDPI;Y&@KOELTKDHIE0PELDKO$
R@U*FJULEYD7E6WGSDTGREHWYSH3R2DA&TP%DRZXYPL
RTY$GHDJKODM$3HDEKG
```

For several more minutes, I studied the appointment book on the off chance I had missed something. When I finished, I took the book and envelope and carefully placed them back into my dresser drawer. I then proceeded to study the sheet of paper on which I had written all of the characters. It was useless. What I had written down was nothing but a jumbled mess, so I folded the sheet of paper and put it into my wallet, alongside the first sheet of paper with the strange poem. It felt like I had somehow been asked to be a private eye, or perhaps a spy. I acquired a letter with a weird poem and a book with characters that made no sense. Not to mention a key that could unlock just about anything.

As I was thinking what all of this could mean, I heard Hammer enter into the recreational/reading room. I thought, *Should I involve him with this or not?*

Instantly I blurted out, "Without a doubt, Hammer needs to be involved!"

I knew that I was in way over my head and could use some help. Hammer had become a trusted friend over the past ten months and I strongly felt I could trust him with my life. Therefore, it was a simple choice when I decided, there and then, Hammer would be involved with everything I knew, so I unlocked my door and left the key in the doorknob where it had been for the past three and a half months.

I went to the rec room and sat next to Hammer. The rec room was another area that Lynn had created with her ever-present need for comfort for her and those she cared about. The reading/recreational room, divided into three parts, has reading side, the recreational side and the entertainment side. The reading side has five book shelves full of the best novels ever written with several comfortable chairs for sitting. In the middle of the room is a ceiling fan that is place directly over a new ping pong table. The far side of the room, where Hammer spent most of his time, had a large fifty inch plasma television set connected to a Bose Stereo Sound System surrounded by two Lazy-Boy chairs and a wrap around sofa; a coffee table placed conveniently placed between the furniture and television set. Lynn had all of these rooms specially built when she designed her restaurant.

Chapter Twelve

As for Lynn, the owner, who is in her mid to late forties and looks like she's sixty, is perhaps one of the ugliest women that ever visited the State of Idaho, or for that matter, any state in the entire country. She has never married even though she wears a wedding ring. She tells the customers that her husband died years ago while fishing the Snake.

She likes to tell everyone that her husband hooked the largest cutthroat in the river and while trying to bring him aboard their boat, he slipped and fell into the water. Now mind you, all he had to do was throw the fishing pole away, but he couldn't. After all, he had the largest fish ever hooked on the Snake and come hell or high water, he was not going to release it. As she continues the story, a tear forms in her eye and she sadly claims, "And that was the last time I ever saw my husband."

This of course is just a bunch of bull, but it appears to be good for business.

Lynn further explained her life history by telling everyone that she was an only child born in West Virginia and both of her parents worked the coal mines. When asked why they had only one child they would simply say, "The doctor dropped our baby on the floor and she turned out so ugly we did not dare have another."

I could only imagine how this must have torn away at Lynn's self esteem, but just the opposite happened. She knew she was ugly and just decided to make the best of her situation. She continues the story by telling everyone that she was well liked in school and even became the class president. But, two weeks after graduating from high school there was a tragic accident in the mine and both of her parents died.

Lynn was awarded a large settlement by the mine for her parents' death, setting up a trust fund for her and provided her with thirty thousand dollars a year to live off of for the rest of her life. However, the shock took its toll on her. To her credit, she never lost her sense of humor, but she did lose her focus and she wandered the countryside for nearly twenty years. I can't really blame her, she had money coming in and she just went from place to place throughout the country looking for something. Whether it was acceptance from others or just a place to forget about her past was the true question. I personally feel she was looking for a place to belong. She told me it was by chance that she wandered into Eastern Idaho and felt in her heart that somewhere near here would be her home forever.

She did several small jobs in the Idaho Falls area for nearly a month, and then one day out of the clear blue decided to float the Snake. Her guide took her by car to the base of the Palisades Dam and from there he launched his boat into the river with just him and her aboard. They floated the river for nearly three hours. Not once did she fish, instead she enjoyed the beauty of the scenery, the mountains, the trees, the cloud formations, even the other people fishing and floating the river. Twice she saw deer and on one of the bends in the river she saw a mother moose and her two calves feeding along the river bank.

She told me how she saw all types of birds, from eagles and ducks, to geese and even some pelicans. As her mind wandered that day, she was struck with a powerful thought, *I know nothing about fishing but I do know something about cooking. What would it be like to have in this peaceful valley, a restaurant? One that is comfortable, inviting, full of charm, and provides each fisherman at the end of the day something simple to eat.*

Thus the dream to build the Log House Restaurant was born.

CHAPTER THIRTEEN

Sitting next to Hammer in the rec room, I noticed that he had just turned on the weather channel to check out the weather in case we had the opportunity to fish later that afternoon. I began to speak, "I have something very important to ask you."

He looked at me, "Wait just a second; they're about ready to give the local forecast."

The forecast was for the next seven days called for sunny warm days with little to no chance of rain. Temperatures would be in the high 80's and the lows in the mid 40's. When the forecast was finished, he switched off the set.

"Fire away."

"Well, you see, last night when the sheriff asked me if I had heard anything, I decided to not tell him everything. I also did not share with him what the strange man told me."

He clasped his hands. "I knew it, I could tell by the way you said it, that something was up, so continue on."

"Well, the strange man gave me something just before he was shot." I said

"What did he give you?"

"He gave me a small appointment book and a manila envelope with a key and a letter inside it. Hammer, I do not want to say anything more for now. The sheriff said he was going to come back to ask us some additional questions. When he is done, let's go for a drive and talk."

He shook his head in agreement, "I also withheld information from the sheriff."

"You did? How?"

"When I heard what you had to say, I felt something was up. I guess you can say that I have come to know you quite well and I sensed you were not telling the whole truth. There for a moment, I thought of telling the sheriff what I had seen when I ran out into the parking lot. But felt there must be a very good reason why you were withholding information. You see, Billy, I noticed part of the license plate. I also think the car they were driving was a green Ford Taurus."

"Great, we're both in up to our necks in this one."

"Yes, kind of exciting isn't it?"

He looked at me with a silly grin. I looked back at him and thought about what he had just said. *Kind of exciting isn't it?*

I pondered these words for a moment and then retorted, "It really is!" Furthermore, I don't plan on saying anything else until the sheriff tells us more about the strange man who died in my arms last night."

Just then Lynn yelled up the stairs, "Boys, come on down, the sheriff is back and wants to ask us some more questions."

We hustled downstairs and into the dining area to talk to the sheriff. He started off saying, "Listen it is very important that we find out everything that took place last night. I want the two of you to take some time and think real hard. Try to remember what you saw and heard. If we are to catch these two individuals, we need some help and you may provide the information we need. Now, Billy, it appears you were in the dining area the whole time. Surely, you had to hear or see something?"

"No, sheriff, the guy sat down and ordered some coffee. A few minutes later, the other two came in yelling and waving guns. I was scared and hit the ground like they asked me to."

"Okay, so they came in and asked you to hit the ground. Did you get a good look at them?"

"No, not really."

"You can't describe anything about them at all?"

"Well, one was taller than the other."

"Okay, that's a start. So tell me, which one was taller than the other? Was it the one who did the shooting?"

"Yes, the one who did the shooting was taller. Not by much, but he was taller."

"Can you give me an estimate on how tall you thought he was?"

"I would say he was about two to three inches taller then you are."

"Good, and the second man?"

"Oh jeez, I just don't know, perhaps the second man was about your weight maybe smaller."

"Alright, and how big were they?"

"I would say they were both very well built and appeared to be in good shape."

"Why do you say that?"

"Well, they weren't fat, and when the taller of the two slapped the guy, he gave him a bloody nose. The second time he slapped him, he knocked him down. The second guy must have been fairly strong as well since he lifted him up by the throat with just one hand and started patting him down with the other. I just assumed that this would take a great deal of strength to do so."

"Yes, continue."

"They yelled at him and then shot him."

"What did they say?"

"Couldn't really tell, maybe something like, '*He's no use to us.*' "

"Very good," said the sheriff. "You see you have already told me so much more than you did last night. For example, you told me they hit him, not just once but twice. You also said you saw the smaller of the two lift him up with one arm. Thus you must have been watching. You also said that the smaller of the two patted him down. So they must have been looking for something. Did the strange man have anything on him that they may have taken?"

"No."

"So, you have described a person about my height and I am around six feet tall. The second man was about two to three inches taller; therefore he must be around six feet two or six feet three inches tall. Now, I am in good shape. Tell me, how much bigger or smaller than me would you say they were?"

"I would say that they were about your build."

"Good, now we have height and possible body size. I'm forty-six. Were they younger than me, or older?"

"I can't tell you that because they wore masks."

"Alright, that's okay, what about their hair, eyes or skin color?"

"Hmm, let me think about that for a moment. If I had to guess the smaller person was white and the taller person appeared to have brown skin. I really couldn't tell you for sure, because the masks they wore appeared to cover their entire face."

"What about their hands, could you see anything there?"

"Maybe, maybe not, I'm quite sure they had gloves on and they were wearing jackets, I assume because it was so chilly out."

"Can you tell me anything about their voices; were they hi-pitched or low-pitched? Did they speak with any kind of drawl or accent?"

I paused for a second here. I gave the impression to the sheriff that I was thinking about his question, when in reality I was debating whether or not to tell him about the taller person's accent. Instead I continued, "Sheriff, their voices were normal, just like yours or mine. I hate to say this, but I couldn't really hear very well because I was so scared."

Hammer butted in, "It's okay to be scared. God knows I would have been."

The sheriff looked over at him as if to say, "*Shut up; it will be your turn soon enough.*"

"I understand you were scared," said the sheriff, "but once the men left the restaurant you got up and went over to the dying man, why?"

"To help him out, I just couldn't leave him there."

"Good, and as you did so, you saw that he was bleeding and still alive?"

"Yes, I did."

"So what went through your mind at this time?"

"The first thought was that the ground must be very hard, so I set down next to him. I gently took his head and placed it in my lap."

"Why did you do this?"

The sheriff seemed very insensitive, I said with some disgust in my voice, "Because it was the right thing to do!"

The sheriff, picking up on my anger, raised his hand as if to calm me down, said, "I'm not trying to be nasty; I'm trying to get to the bottom of the truth here."

When he said truth, my mind raced back to last night when the dying man said, "You have to reveal the truth." Just what did truth mean and where was it taking me? And now since I have involved Hammer, him?

The sheriff continued, "Most people when they see a dying person for the first time, kind of panic, why didn't you?"

I thought of my father and how I rushed to him when he was dying, I then turned to the sheriff and peacefully replied, "My father died in my arms after being shot by a distraught person. I guess when I saw this strange man lying down on the ground bleeding to death it brought back some harsh memories. However, it was the right thing to do, show a dying man some compassion."

As I told this to the sheriff, I was amazed that I was calm and had a feeling of strength inside of me. The feeling of guilt that I had carried for so many years was gone. I had my dear friend Del to thank for this new found strength. He provided

me the tools to deal with tragedy in my life and to handle it
effectively.

As I was thinking of Del, the sheriff again interrupted my
thoughts. "So what did this man tell you?"

"All he said to me was he was in pain."

"That's what you told me last night."

"That right, that's what I told you last night. So please tell
me, what is so hard about accepting that?"

The sheriff rubbed his chin a couple of times.

"Look, Billy. In my business, I have seen several people die.
One thing that they have all had in common is that they all
have had some kind of message to deliver before they died.
Like, tell my wife I love her, or tell the cops that I was shot by
my brother-in-law. I guess what I am trying to get at, is did this
person say something that might seem innocent to you, but be
very important to us in finding his two killers?"

Again I said, "No, if he did, I didn't hear it."

The sheriff looked at me. His gaze told me that he didn't
quite believe me. He said basically what I had been thinking.

"Billy, I'm sorry I seem so persistent in this, but I have been
a sheriff here for around seven years. I can't help but feel that
there is something useful he said to you that you are either
deliberating not telling me or that you might have forgotten
due to the nature of the situation. But for now, you have done
well. You have at least identified them as two men around six
feet to six feet three inches tall, with normal to muscular builds.
You also said you felt that one of them might be white and the
other brown, why?"

"Because Sheriff, when they came in I did see a small
portion of their neck area and I would say the smaller of the
two appeared to be whiter than the taller person."

The sheriff triumphantly declared,

"See, when you take a moment to reflect you really can give
us valuable information to go on. So, I will talk to you again
tomorrow. If you remember anything between now and then,

and I do mean anything, please call me anytime day or night. Here is my cell number," he said as he handed me a business card.

The sheriff stood up for a moment and stretched his hands high into the air. He asked Lynn for a glass of water or juice. She went to the kitchen and poured him a glass of pineapple juice. She then returned and handed the juice to him. He sat back down and took a couple of sips from the glass of juice and wrote some notes into his book.

"Thanks for the juice. Now Hammer, it's your turn. Tell me what you saw and heard?"

"Well, I was out back when all of a sudden I heard a loud bang. I ran in and saw two men in the parking lot jumping into a car."

"What kind of car?"

"Not certain. Perhaps a Chevy, maybe a Ford, I really don't know much about cars."

"Did you see the color of the car?"

"No, it was just too dark outside."

"What about the license plate?"

"Didn't see it. They were just too far away."

"Hammer," said the sheriff, "Is there anything you can tell me about the conversation that went on between Billy and the dying man?"

"No, nothing, I rushed back in to see if he was hurt. I saw him on the ground and asked him if he was okay. I recalled him saying that he was fine and that I should call for help. I rushed over to the phone and called 911."

The sheriff quickly scanned the area. "Where is the phone?"

"Next to the cash register."

He walked over to the cash register and then walked back to where the man had died. It was about thirty feet.

"Far enough," said the sheriff, "That it would be difficult for you to clearly hear any conversation that may have taken place between Billy and the dying man."

He then turned to both of us, "Okay guys, that will be enough for now. Let me talk to Lynn alone for awhile. Stay close by, and if you think of anything, even the smallest item, jot it down and call me immediately."

He handed Hammer a business card. He accepted the card and placed it into his wallet. We were about to leave the room when I stopped and said, "We will stay in touch, and if we think of anything else that might be useful we will call you immediately. Is it alright if we go fishing and perhaps later tonight to Idaho Falls for dinner and a movie?"

"That's a great idea," responded Lynn, "The restaurant will be closed anyway. This way, the two of you can take sometime to relax."

The sheriff gazed over at Lynn and then back to us.

"Yes that is a great idea, have fun and stay out of trouble. I'll be back tomorrow morning to talk to the both of you again."

Hammer and I left the dining area and went into the kitchen. We both paused for a moment to see if we could hear Lynn and the sheriff talking. We could and we heard Lynn in somewhat of an angry voice say to the sheriff, "You're awful hard on those two boys. They didn't do anything wrong."

"Calm down Lynn, I'm not hard on them; I'm just doing my job."

She snapped back, "Yes I know, but it has been seven years that I have known you and you haven't changed a bit. Your always doing your job, so cut them some slack would you? They're good kids."

"Okay, okay" said the sheriff, "I just want you to know that I think they both know more than what their telling me. So let's drop the subject of them and find out about you, what can you tell me about last night?"

She calmed down and we could hear no more, so we quietly exited the kitchen and bolted to 'Old Red'. We were both grateful to have a little time to ourselves.

CHAPTER FOURTEEN

We started west on Highway 26 towards the Swan Valley bridge. We crossed the bridge and took an immediate left onto a dirt road. We drove several miles past the waterfalls where a lot of the locals like to swim. We had been there several times before to swim and chat with the girls. We continued to drive for another mile or two and then parked 'Old Red' in a small turnout.

We put on our waders, boots and the rest of our fishing gear. In case someone was watching, we wanted to look the part. We began to hike down the trail to the edge of the river. As we were walking we started to talk.

"Hammer, this is what I know so far. I was given a small appointment book from the strange man. When I opened it, all of the pages appeared to be blank. The closer I studied it; I began to notice some small characters on the bottom of each page. For the most part they were just letters and numbers. I took a sheet of paper from my closet and copied them down."

I reached into my wallet and took out the paper with the characters and handed it to him.

He studied it carefully for a moment before saying anything.

"This makes no sense what so ever."

"Yes, I agree, and that bothers me a lot. Here is a guy being beat up right before my eyes. I was about to tell the two masked men that I had his book. However, he must have known what I was thinking about doing because he glanced at me in such a way that I knew I had to keep still. He was willing to die to keep it a secret and that is what makes me feel that we have really stumbled onto something very important here. Last night, the man also gave me a manila envelope. I opened it this morning and found a letter and a key that was taped to the inside."

I handed him the letter with the poem on it and he handed back to me the sheet of paper with the strange characters. I placed it safely into my wallet while he read the poem. When he had finished he glanced over at me.

"It sounds like whatever is going to happen will happen this Saturday. It also seems like he knew they had figured out who he was. He must have been desperate to give this information to someone he didn't even know. Why didn't he just drive to the police?"

"I was wondering the same thing. Perhaps he knew they were so close to catching him that he took a chance and tried to hide in our restaurant. He must have known that he had to get rid of this information as swiftly as possible, and forced it upon me."

"What about when you were holding him, did he say anything then?"

"Yes he did, he said that it is now up to me to reveal the truth. He told me to keep the book and envelope safe and to use them both to reveal the truth. I asked him what truth, and he said that I would find out. He also told me to be careful because many lives are at stake. I think he was somewhat delusional at that time. As I spoke to him to find out more, he told me to hush because someone was watching us. I looked around and saw no one. Now, I realize that I am telling you, but I need some help and I trust you. He also whispered to me the following numbers, 9, 3, 9, and 14."

Hammer gasped, "Sounds like some phone number or maybe a zip code."

I shook my head up and down to concur. "I thought about a phone number, but not a zip code. You know it appeared to me that he may have deliberately paused at the end of the first three numbers and then continued with 14. I'm not certain, but I think that was what he was trying to accomplish."

Hammer pondered what I had just told him.

"Should we share this with Lynn or the sheriff?"

"I'm not certain. I suppose we should. After all, the sheriff does need information to catch these two killers. But I can't help feeling inside that there was a reason he came to our restaurant. If he wanted to go to the cops it would have made more sense to keep on driving until he reached a police station."

"Yes, good point, but maybe he didn't realize that they were so close behind. Perhaps he felt he had sometime."

"I have thought about that, but he gave me the info so quickly. I feel he knew they were there, yet still he stopped."

"Billy, I think we should call Del. He might be able to give us some insight on the whole thing. I would also like to ask the sheriff about the man who died. I want to know who he was and what he was up to."

My eyes brightened, "That's a great idea. Let's drive back and ask the sheriff what he knows about the man that died. Once we discover more about him that should make our decision whether or not to tell the sheriff, easier."

He nodded his head in agreement. As we turned around to walk back to the car, he abruptly stopped.

"Don't we have time to at least fish for a few minutes?

"I wish we could, but I have a hunch that we may not be able to fish for awhile," I chuckled.

As soon as I said this, a gust of wind swept down the valley and took hold of the paper that Hammer was holding. The mysterious poem blew into the air and towards the river. Before we could even move, the paper was halfway across the river, when just as sudden as it had started the wind died down and the paper drifted into the river. We both watched as it floated on top of the water and then abruptly disappeared.

"I'm really sorry about that. I thought I had hold of it, but the wind just came out of nowhere."

"It's okay, I made an extra copy of it and we still have the original. Let's get going before it's too late."

We hiked back up the trail to 'Old Red'. Upon reaching my car, we took off our fishing gear and placed it in the trunk. We sped off to find the sheriff. We drove down the dirt road back to the main highway and crossed over the Swan Valley Bridge. It had only been an hour since we left and we hoped that by returning to the Log House Restaurant we might still find him there.

As we were driving along, I spotted the sheriff's truck with his lights on. He had apparently pulled over a car for speeding. I drove by and did a u-turn and pulled in behind his truck. We quickly hopped out and started to walk up to the sheriff. He was in the process of giving a ticket to the other driver when he noticed us coming. He stopped what he was doing and said to the driver, "This must be your lucky day. I'm going to let you off this time with only a warning. But rest assured that the next time you speed through here like that, there will be hell to pay."

The man in the car gracefully said, "Thanks, I appreciate it. I will do my best to keep to the speed limit."

The second I heard his voice, I thought it sounded familiar. It sounded like the masked man's voice from last night. The accent was identical. I hurriedly moved by the sheriff to take a good look at the driver. As I did so, he stared back at me. We made eye contact and then he drove away. As he drove away I looked at his license plate. I noticed the number was 1J 24897 and that his car was a green Ford Taurus. The sheriff turned to me, "If you had not pulled up I was going to give him a ticket. He was doing at least seventy-five through here and the speed limit is only sixty. So what can I do for the two of you?"

"Who was that man?" I asked.

The sheriff looked at me somewhat quizzically, "Do you know him?"

"No, not really, but I think he has been into the restaurant before. You work so long as a waiter and you begin to know everyone in these parts."

"That's true, the same goes for me. You see so many people that after awhile you start to recognize the regulars. I thing he is just some local fisherman. I have seen his car before, but basically that's all I know of him. Have the two of you remembered anything else about last night?"

"No, we haven't, but we were wondering, do you know the name of the man who was shot last night?"

He again looked at me somewhat puzzled, "Why do you want to know that?"

"We were thinking that perhaps if we knew anything about him it might help us remember more. You know kind of a connection of some sort."

"I see something that might trigger a thought or two. For now I don't know. He had no identification on him. We're currently doing a background check on the car he was driving. If I hear of something, I will let you in on it, but remember, it will be confidential."

Hammer jumped into the conversation. "Yes we understand, you don't need to worry about us, we can keep a secret."

The sheriff looked at him and then back at me. "Is there anything else?"

"Yes you said you wanted to speak to us again tomorrow. Do you know what time?"

"Does it matter?"

"Yes it does. We would like to try to do some fishing. It would be helpful to know when you plan on coming by."

"Sounds fair to me. I will be by at noon."

Just then his radio blared. "I have to be off for now, you two stay out of trouble now," he said as he walked away.

As he jumped into his car, he took the radio off the dash and responded to the call. A few seconds later, he drove off, seemingly in a hurry.

"Hey Billy, let's go call Del. He might have some connections that could help us with this mess."

"Alright, but let's drive to Idaho Falls to make the call. I want to have complete privacy."

We took off towards Idaho Falls. As we were driving, I said,

"Did you notice anything strange about the car the sheriff had pulled over?"

"Yes, I did. It was a green Ford and the license plate looked familiar."

"Did you here the man talking to the sheriff?"

"Of course I did. He sure had a thick accent didn't he?"

"Sure did. Just like the masked man who shot the stranger. If I had to make a bet, I would say that they are one in the same. Same accent, same car type, similar license number."

"Wow! Why didn't you tell the sheriff?"

"For the same reasons you didn't. What do we really have to tell him? That you and I think he just pulled over the killer? What evidence do we have? After all, we have told him that we know nothing."

"That's right; we have pretty much kept everything to ourselves."

For the second time that day Hammer said, "Kind of exciting isn't it?"

I thought for a moment and then blurted with more enthusiasm than I had done earlier that day, "Yes, it really is and I wouldn't trade it for anything in the world. What do you think stops us from solving this case? We know more than the sheriff. We have just had the opportunity to see the potential killer. We might be able to make the news. Better yet, obtain a reward if there is one. Fishing has been great this year, but I would like to catch the killer red handed, wouldn't you?"

Hammer gave his typical grin, "Me too, this will be the best catch of the year and we should have a lot of fun while we are at it. But, Billy, we must be careful, after all they have already killed someone and I know from experience what desperate people can do, and it isn't pretty."

We continued to talk until we made the outskirts of Idaho Falls. We saw a Stinker gas station and pulled in for some gas and to use a phone.

I called Del on his cell and asked him if he would be willing to keep what I had to say confidential and if he would be willing to work with Hammer and I.

"Are the two of you in some kind of trouble?" he asked.

"No, we're not, but there was a murder at the restaurant last night and we need some help."

"Yes, I heard about it on the news here in Boise. I am glad that you have called. I'm going to visit the two of you this weekend to see how everything is going."

"That would be great, but before you leave Boise, we need to see if you can obtain some information for us. We need to know about the man who was killed last night. It may be important and we feel it will shed some additional light on solving this case."

He interrupted me. "If the two of you have additional information that is important in solving this case, you both need to share it immediately with the local authorities."

"Yes Del, we know that. But you're going to have to trust us on this one. Hammer and I both feel that there is more to this shooting then meets the eye. We want to see what we can discover on our own."

Again he interrupted. "Billy, you can't take the law into your own hands."

"We're not going to. You have been there for us before and we need you to be there again. We both think we have seen the killer but have no proof at all. Furthermore, we have some very important clues that might be useful."

He was about ready to interrupt for the third time when I said, "You have to do this for us. Find out all you can for us. Now when are you coming here?

He finally gave in and said, "Okay, you win. I can see the two of you have made up your minds to become some kind of superheroes. I will do all I can; call me on my cell tomorrow around three in the afternoon. I will leave for Eastern Idaho about five p.m. and should be there by ten tomorrow night. I have booked a room at the Red Lion Hotel in downtown Idaho Falls for Friday and Saturday night. I want to see the two of you when I get there. Remember, this is not a game. Do I make myself clear?"

"Plain as day Del, we will be there, but don't please tell anybody what you're doing. We have a hunch that it will be nice to have you as a silent partner in this. Whatever is going to happen is supposed to happen Saturday night."

"How do you know this?"

"I'll tell you Friday. Meanwhile we have a lot to do between now and then." At that moment Hammer tugged at my arm.

"Don't look now, but the man the sheriff pulled over for speeding earlier today is parked across the street. He appears to be watching us."

"We've got to go, but will talk to you tomorrow," I said, quickly finished my phone call with Del.

Del was about to ask another question but I hung up the phone. Without looking in the direction of the Ford Taurus we filled 'Old Red' with gas and drove off.

I headed west on Highway 26 towards downtown Idaho Falls, often called I.F. by the locals. Hammer said, "Just keep driving. I will occasionally glance around to see if we our being followed."

As we left the Stinker Station, the green Ford Taurus began to follow.

"He must think we know something, otherwise there would be no need to follow us."

"Yes I agree, what should we do now?"

"Play it cool man, you're with the Hammer. You'll be okay."

"Oh I'm not worried about that, but whatever is going to happen will happen soon."

"That's true and for tonight there is nothing we can do, so lets get a bite to eat and go to the movies. You know, Billy, if we act normal, they may think we don't know anything. After all, we're just two young men who are hungry and haven't had a Thursday night off in the past four months."

"Sounds like a plan, but I want you to place this dollar bill in the glove compartment box. Tear a very small corner of it and place it on Washington's face. When it is time to head home, we'll check it out."

"Oh, you want to see if they rummage through your car while we're at the movies. Sounds like a clever way to do it. Where did you ever come up with this idea?"

"To be honest, I just thought of it now. Seems like a good way to discover just how much of a suspect we are."

The drive from the station to a local restaurant called Smithy's Pancake House took only fifteen minutes. We looked over the menu and wanted something that did not have red meat in it. After all, serving steaks six days a week does ware a person down. Once we saw the menu, we both ordered the fried chicken dinner. Dinner was served with soup or salad, mashed potatoes, four pieces of chicken and dessert. It was relaxing to have someone wait on us for a change. The waitress was polite, brought us plenty of water and deserved a huge tip.

When we finished, we drove to the movie theater. It really didn't matter to us which one we watched. We just wanted a few hours to unwind. The movie ended around eleven p.m. We walked out of the theater and headed for 'Old Red'. We both studied the parking lot and the green Ford was nowhere to be seen. We climbed into the car when Hammer said, "Drive around for awhile to see if we're being followed."

I agreed and started off heading west on 17th Street. Hammer was about to open the glove compartment box but stopped. He whistled out loud, "It looks like they don't trust us."

"Why?"

"The corner of the dollar bill is sitting on the floor mat."

"Great!" I exclaimed, "It looks like we're going to have to be more careful than I thought. We have to figure out what all of this means and we need to do it soon. Let's head home and get a good nights rest. The sheriff will be by around noon and we can answer any additional questions he may have for us at that time. When he is finished we'll pretend to go fishing and establish a plan of attack for this weekend."

The drive home took almost an hour. On the way, we discussed the strange letter and all of the weird characters. We assumed something was going to happen Saturday because the poem said so. We did not know where or when, but we were going to do our best to be part of whatever it may be. We arrived at the Log House and I parked 'Old Red' in the usual spot. As we were opening the doors to get out, Hammer said, "Its sure is gloomy out tonight, by the way its twelve o'clock, the midnight hour."

"Yes it is, and all good little boys should be in bed by now," I replied.

We started toward the door when out of the blue I shouted, *"That's it. I think I now know part of the puzzle!"*

Hammer grabbed my arm, "Tell me."

"Not now, later when we go fishing, I need a little time to see if I am correct."

He began to complain, but instead said, "Okay, I understand."

We unlocked the back kitchen door and headed upstairs to bed. When we got to my bedroom door he stopped, "Good night, Billy," and then jokingly said,

"Be sure to call me if you have any bad dreams."

"You'll be the first to know." I said, slugging him in the arm.

And from there, we went our separate ways.

I took a moment to brush my teeth and get ready for bed. Once I finished, I went to the nightstand, turned on the lamp and reached behind it for the paper I had taped there earlier. After obtaining the paper I began with the last sentence, it read, "Until the bells tolled out the midnight doom." When Hammer said it was gloomy outside and that it was twelve o'clock the midnight hour, it made me think that the poem might be full of some kind of numerical message. Thus the message read the midnight doom; or in other words, the number twelve. Could this be the time that something was about to happen?

I decided to study the rest of the poem. I took a blank sheet of paper and wrote down any corresponding numbers. The first sentence read, 'Seventeen sparrows went abroad'. That had to be the number seventeen. The second sentence read, 'Four seasons of struggle past without much time'; the number 4. The third sentence read, 'Yet thirty-four nights failed in their flight', yet another number, 34. The fourth sentence read, 'Because three fair maidens were nowhere in sight'. The number 3 stood out. The fifth sentence read, 'Twice the king he was but nothing did he possess'. The number 2 jumped out. And finally the last sentence, 'Until the bells tolled out the midnight doom'. The last number, 12.

I had the following numbers: seventeen, four, thirty-four, three, two, and twelve. I pondered for several minutes the meaning of these numbers. My first impression was a silly one, but I thought to myself, *Perhaps I should go and buy a lotto ticket. After all, I have five numbers and the last one, twelve, could be the Power Ball.*

However, I knew that this was not what the code was trying to tell me. I stared at the numbers every which way possible. For some unknown reason I felt 12 might be a time frame because it said midnight, but the other numbers made no sense.

Glancing over at the alarm clock by the side of the bed, I noticed it was already past one-thirty in the morning. It was time to call it quits for the night. Hopefully with a few hours rest, I would have more success figuring it out later. Not wanting to leave the papers unattended for the night, I took them and folded them both. I then placed them in my wallet next to the sheet with the strange characters. I opened the nightstand drawer and placed my wallet inside. For a moment I thought about shutting the drawer, but quickly changed my mind and place my wallet under my pillow. If someone wanted it they would have to wake me first.

Having placed my wallet in a secure place, I walked over to the dresser drawer to check on the manila envelope and appointment book. The drawer was firmly shut so I opened it and checked underneath my clothes. Both items were right where I had left them earlier in the day. This brought me great joy, so I went back to my bed and hopped under the covers. Once comfortably in bed, I reached over and turned off the light and within minutes, I was fast asleep.

Chapter Fifteen

During the night I slept well, but woke up and gently rolled over a few times to see what time it was. My clock said four twenty-three. I was about to roll back over when I felt a hand press against my mouth and at the same time, the lamp light was switched on. To my utter amazement, the strange man who had died two days earlier was back in my room. He removed his hand from my mouth, sat down on the edge of my bed and began to speak. "How goes the search?"

"Look, I know I am dreaming this time. You're dead." I said.

He smiled. "Yes I am, but I thought you might need some help. What questions do you have for me?"

"Well to begin with, you could tell me what you whispered to me. Was it a phone number or a zip code?"

This odd man shook his head slowly, "I can only help you with what you already know."

I complained, "What good are you to me if you can only help me with what I already know? I mean get real, if I know it, then why would I need your help?"

"Because you may think you know it but really do not know it? For example, you think the number twelve in the poem stands for the time of day when something is going to happen, yet in reality it does not."

This statement startled me; he appeared to be able to read my mind.

"Wait a minute, how do you know what I am thinking?"

Again he smiled, "Because I am really you and you are really me."

I looked at him in total bewilderment, "Man, don't get weird on me, I have never been you and you certainly won't be me. Your dead and I'm alive. I'm young and you're old."

Looking at me with sympathetic eyes, he said, "Yes, you and I are all of those things, but I f you want to reveal the truth you must stop thinking like you and start acting like me."

"Okay, Okay, just what does that mean?"

"It means, why would I give you all of this information if there was not some form of logic that can assist you in getting to the truth?"

"I whole heartedly agree with what you just said. So if you can only help me with what I know then how do I get to know what I need to know?"

"That's a good question. But remember one significant point; things are not always what they appear to be. I will give you one clue and then must leave. After all it is getting very late. In the poem that you have probably memorized by now, what does the first line say?"

"It says, 'Seventeen sparrows went abroad.'"

"That's right. So what does abroad mean?"

I was actually getting quite tired and just wanted to get back to sleep, so I told him rather brusquely, "Look enough of your silly games, if you continue to speak in riddles, than I'm going to go to sleep."

He stood-up. "Just humor me. Tell me one last time, and keep it simple, what does abroad mean."

"It means that they went away, that they are no longer here, that they left."

"Yes, now you should know the rest of the poem."

He reached over, switched off the light and disappeared. I laid back down and glanced over at the clock. It was now four thirty-three. *What a waste of ten minutes. He couldn't tell me anything important.*

I took hold of my blankets to pull them up around me tight, as I did so; I heard the door to my room gently close. I had the impression that it was the strange man leaving, and I fell back asleep.

At eight thirty, Hammer came barging into my room. He jumped onto my bed and woke me up.

"Get up sleepy head, today's Friday and we're going to have a long day ahead of us."

I groaned and pulled the sheets up over my head. I just wanted him to leave me alone, but instead of going away, he grabbed one of my pillows and whacked me with it. He laughed out loud,

"Get up sleeping beauty."

I muttered, "Leave me be, I have had a tough night. I just want to sleep another ten hours."

"Nope, we have too much to do today. We have a sheriff to talk to, some planning to do, a trip to Idaho Falls, and much, much, more."

Whacking me again with my pillow, he said, "If you don't get up, I'm going to get a glass of water and pour it all over you."

"Alright already, I'm up. Cut me some slack."

I sat up. "You know, I had another strange dream last night."

"Yeah, what about? I didn't hear you screaming," he said, looking at me.

"It wasn't a scary dream like the first, but the same old man came and visited me."

"Really, maybe you ought to become some TV psychic or something, after all you keep talking to the dead."

This comment frustrated me so I threw my pillow at him. As I did so my wallet fell to the floor. I got out of bed, picked it up and began to speak.

"It's nothing like that. But I stayed up late last night trying to decipher the poem. Here, take a look."

I opened my wallet and took out two sheets of paper. I unfolded the one with the poem on it and the one with the numbers.

"Remember last night you said its twelve o'clock? And I said I got it."

He nodded his head, "Well, I came back to my room and looked at this poem. I thought that some how there must be a numerical code or system in play here. As you can see, I discovered the numbers 17, 4, 34, 3, 2, and 12. They correspond with the poem. At first when you said twelve o'clock I thought perhaps that is the time something Saturday is to take place. But the other numbers make little to no sense at all. So I tried and tried to uncover some pattern but, I must confess, I can't. What do you think? Is there something here or am I crazy?"

Hammer responded in a very serious tone of voice, "With the way you keep talking to the dead, I would say crazy; however, there has to be something here. So tell me, what did the dead man say this time around?"

I began by telling him how my dream seemed so real. That the stranger and I talked for exactly ten minutes. Hammer question this statement,

"How do you know it was ten minutes?"

"Well, you see, I looked at the clock by the side of the bed and it said four twenty-three a.m. When he finished talking to me, I rolled over and it was four thirty-three a.m. Hammer, the dream was so real, I even heard him shut the door as he left my room."

"That's interesting Billy, I got up last night to go to the bathroom. As I was about to hop back in bed I heard the faint sounds of a car starting up in the parking lot. I glanced at my alarm clock and it said four thirty-six a.m. I felt it might have been you so I glanced out the window and saw a car driving away. I remember saying aloud; someone is up kind of early."

He continued, "Can you show me the original envelope and book? I would like to look at it just in case you may have missed something."

"Of course!"

I went to my dresser drawer to retrieve both items. I opened the drawer and moved my clothes around, to my horror, they were not there. I turned to him and in a ghastly voice exclaimed, "They're not here."

He came over to where I was standing and looked into the drawer. He moved my clothes around, "Are you sure you left them here?"

"Definitely! Last night just before I went to bed I made sure they were still here, and now they are gone. Someone has taken them."

We stared at one another for a few seconds. We both felt like we had lost a significant piece of the riddle. I said sorrowfully,

"What are we to do?"

He thought for a moment, "Well fortunately you had the foresight to write down the information contained in the book and envelope. So, in a sense, we have not lost anything. But they on the other hand have gained a considerable advantage over us. They now know what we know and then some."

He continued, "They probably know the specific details such as when and where and perhaps even more importantly what. After all we have no idea still what we are trying to prevent."

While he was speaking an idea hit me, I confidently exclaimed, "Maybe you're right, but we still have two things they might desperately need."

He paused for a second, "And what might that be?"

"I still have the key that was in the envelope. Remember I told you that I had replaced it with an old apartment key."

"That's right," shouted Hammer, "And what is the second thing we have?"

"We still have the last words of a dying man. Somehow, 9, 3, 9, and 14 must play an important part in all of this."

"Oh this is great," exclaimed Hammer. "They don't appear to have what might be the most important clues after all."

Pacing back and forth for several moments, he finally said, "Let's return to your dream. You began to tell me about it when we got side tracked. I want you to take a moment and try to recall it to the best of your ability."

I told him about my dream in great detail, explaining how the strange man emphasized to me that he was now me and I was now him. That he could only help me with the things I already knew, that some things are not always what they appear to be. I then reached the part where I told him about how the strange man knew I had the poem memorized. How the strange man kept returning to the word abroad. How he said, "Just one last time, and keep things simple, what does abroad mean?"

Hammer listened to my entire dream without interrupting. When I had finished he asked, "So how did you finally answer him with regards to the word abroad?"

"I told him it meant that they went away, that they were no longer here, that they had left."

"Did this answer satisfy him?"

"Yes, I believe it did, because he told me that I now should know the rest of the poem and he left."

Hammer took the sheet of paper with the poem on it and carefully studied the first line. He read it aloud, "Seventeen sparrows went abroad. So, if we agree that the numbers have some importance then what I am hearing you say to me is that this line is saying 17 abroad. But this weird man asked you what abroad meant. You told him away, no longer here and that they had left. Let's look at trying to place them together. We have 17away, 17no longer here and 17 had left."

I added, "He said to keep things simple. So we should have 17 away, 17 longer or 17 left."

"Perfect, now the second line reads, Four seasons of struggle past without much time. We both agreed that it means four. If we place the two together we have seventeen away four; or 17 longer 4, or 17 left 4. Now he used the last word abroad with some meaning, does he want us to use the word time in a similar fashion? If so, we now have 17 away 4 time, or 17 longer 4 time; or 17 left 4 time."

Just then Hammer smiled. I looked at him, "Do you think you know what it is?"

"I may be wrong, but when I was in prison they gave me a padlock. Whenever I left my cell for work, to eat, to exercise, for whatever reason, I could lock up my stuff. Billy, this may be a combination to a padlock somewhere. Take a look at your numbers. You have 17, 4, 34, 3, 2, and 12. Let's now look at what we know. We have 17 left 4 times. We have 34 flight on the next line of the poem. Could flight mean right? We would now have 17 left 4 times, 34 right. But how many times? The next line down says, Because three fair maidens were nowhere in sight. Thus three fair maidens, or three times. If I place all of these numbers together we now have 17 left 4 times, 34 right 3 times. Now, let's study the next line of the poem. It reads, Twice the king he was in opposition but nothing did he possess. Now my lock in prison was basically left four times, right three times, left two times and then to the final number. I think when he says opposition he means opposite of right which would thus take us to the left. We now have 17 left 4 times, 34 right 3 times, and then to the left again."

"You're brilliant. So when the poems says nothing did he possess, nothing means zero."

Hammer grinned, "You got it, thus we have 17 left 4 times, 34 right 3 times, 0 left 2 times to the magical number that unlocks the lock, which in this case is the last line of the poem. Until the bells tolled out the midnight doom. You guessed that to be 12. At first you thought it was a time in which whatever was going to happen would happen, but according to your dream, the strange man said, 'You think the number 12 stands for the time of day something is going to happen when in reality it does not.' You see, your dream was right on. It does not stand for a time but for a number that will open up a padlock."

He continued. "Whatever is locked up behind this padlock is probably the answer to our case."

"You're a genius."

Blushing, Hammer said, "Maybe so, but you're not so bad yourself, after all you were the one who thought of the number 12. Matter of fact, you're the one who has the gift of talking to the dead."

"Enough of that, the sheriff will be here shortly. We must decide right now whether or not we will tell him what we know."

"I am in favor of talking to the sheriff, if he shares information with us. I'm still having too much fun trying to solve this riddle to just up and quit."

"Okay, sounds like we have a plan. Let's find out what he knows first. Whatever I tell the sheriff, I want you to play along with me."

"No sweat, I can do that."

"Good, now I wonder who was in my room last night."

"Ten to one odds, that it was one or both of the masked men. We know the one was following us and even checked out the car. Perhaps they decided to come back and check your room."

"Yeah, I feel you may be right, I look forward to finding out what Del has discovered. I really want to know what the strange man meant when he said, 'Lives might be spared.'"

CHAPTER SIXTEEN

I was about to continue when we heard a knock on my door. Lynn opened it up,

"Hey, boys, I've been calling for the two of you for the past several minutes. The sheriff is here a little early. He wants to ask you both some additional questions."

She then said in a very loving manner, "Don't mind him a bit. His bark is worse then his bite. He is a good man; I just think he has never really handled a murder case before. He is acting a little high and mighty."

"Thanks for your concern, we will be right down as soon as we have had a chance to shower and get dressed."

"Fine, I'll see if he wants some breakfast, but please hurry. I don't know if I can keep him entertained for very long."

She shut the door and went back downstairs to the kitchen. Hammer said, "I've already showered, but I'll wait in my room before I go down. That way the sheriff won't interview me alone. When you're done, knock on my door and we can go down together."

"Sounds good to me."

About twenty minutes later I was knocking on Hammer's door, he came out of his room and together we went to meet the sheriff. When he saw us he said, "Good morning boys. Did you have a good time last night?"

We both said that we did. He asked, "What did you end up doing?"

Hammer responded. "We ate at a pancake house and then took in a movie."

"Sounds like you had fun. As you both know, I am trying to get to the bottom of this murder. I'm hoping you have some more information to share with me."

I blurted out, "Oh do we ever. Last night after we came home from the movies, Hammer went off to bed, but I decided to wash my apron. It still had blood on it from the shooting two days earlier. I took the apron and reached into the pockets to remove any items that I didn't want to get ruined in the wash, such as my pens and ordering pad. As I did so, I found a manila envelope and an appointment book. I had never seen them before. I remembered that the strange man had bumped into me as he walked by. He must have dropped them into my apron at that time."

The sheriff shouted, "Eureka, boys! This just might be what we need to break this case wide open. Can you hand them to me?"

"We'll, sheriff, that's the problem, I don't have them anymore."

"What do you mean you don't have them anymore?"

"Just that! Last night I placed them in my dresser drawer so that I could give them to you this morning. I went to bed and now they are gone."

He looked very disturbed, his face was flush and he was trying to control his temper.

"I thought I told you to call me when you had any information."

"Sheriff, it was past midnight when I made the discovery. I knew you were coming this morning and had placed them in my drawer for safe keeping. I had no idea that someone would take them from me as I slept."

He mellowed somewhat, "You still should have called me. Do you know who might have them now?"

"No I don't."

Hammer jumped in, "We think who ever may have them now took them early this morning."

He looked over at Hammer, "Why do you think that?"

"Because I got up to go to the bathroom around four thirty a.m. or so and heard a car pulling out of the parking lot."

"Did you see the car?"

"No, it was too dark. I thought maybe someone had just stopped for a moment and then drove away."

"So tell me, did you see this book and envelope?"

"No I didn't. But this morning when I went to wake Billy he told me about his discovery and I asked to see them. We went to his dresser drawer and they were no longer there."

The sheriff returned his gaze to me, "Billy, did you open the envelope or the book?"

"I was going to open the envelope, but I felt I had better not, just in case there were some finger prints or something like that. I did however open the book."

"And what did the book have inside?"

I debated for a moment, whether or not to tell him that the book was empty. After a few seconds I decided to tell him about the characters.

"When I opened the book it appeared to be blank. I flipped through the pages and there really was nothing to see. However, when I was about to close the book I noticed some small characters on the bottom of each page."

The sheriff's eyes widened. "What did the characters say?"

"They didn't say anything. It was nothing but a bunch of letters and numbers. They made no sense what so ever. It was for this reason I was going to show them to Hammer. I wanted to see if he could make any sense out of it. But it was late at night and I knew you would want to see the book. So I placed it with the envelope in my drawer, and now they are gone."

The sheriff was still visibly angry about this, but made a great show at trying to be patient.

"Are you sure you don't remember anything more about this book and envelope?"

"I wish I did. It was there last night. I was waiting to give them to you when you came by this morning."

"I hope you won't take this the wrong way boys, but can I go and look for myself?"

"Certainly."

We all went upstairs to my room. He looked around,

"Where is the apron that you found them in?"

"Oh, I took it downstairs last night."

As I said this I saw Lynn slightly smile. I then looked back at the sheriff.

He went to the dresser drawer and looked under all of my clothes.

"Do you mind if I open the rest of the drawers?"

"No, please go ahead."

He opened each and every drawer. He moved what little items I had around while looking for the book and envelope.

"You told me you placed it in the top drawer. Did you sleep with the door to your room opened or closed?"

"I always sleep with it closed."

"Did you hear anyone come into your room?"

I was not going to tell him about my dream so I simply said, "I did not, but I do feel I heard someone shut the door."

"And what time was this?"

"It was around 4:30 in the morning. I had just rolled over in bed and glanced over at the clock when I heard the door shut."

"Did you see anything?"

"Nope, it was dark."

He left the room and went back downstairs. We followed him to the kitchen. He then went into the dining room area. He wrote a few notes down and turned to me.

"I wish you would have called me last night. I was close by and could have picked up these items. Now we may never know how important they are in solving this case."

"I'm sorry, I just didn't think someone would steal them during the course of the night."

For the first time in several minutes, he actually spoke in a friendlier tone.

"I understand."

I asked him, "Did you find out anymore about the man who died here Wednesday evening?"

"Yes I did. I made a few phone calls yesterday. It appears he was a reporter from Chicago. His name was Anthony Jackson. He worked for the Chicago Herald. He was working undercover on a very top secret assignment."

He continued, "I came by earlier then planned this morning because I have to leave town. I will be flying to Chicago this evening and will not be back until Monday or Tuesday of next week."

I was about to tell him not to go, that Hammer and I we're aware of something important happening this Saturday, but we did not know what or where. Before I opened my mouth to speak, I realized how silly it would sound, so I just said,

"Thanks for telling us about the man who died. If we remember anything else we will call you immediately."

The sheriff excused himself and went to his car and drove away.

As he drove away, Lynn broke the silence. "Billy, your apron was not in your room last night. I had washed it the morning after the shooting. The apron pocket was empty. So if you found a book and an envelope in your apron, you did so the night of the shooting. Is there anything you should be telling me?"

I looked at Hammer and he at me. "Maybe I stretched the truth just a little bit."

"Just a little bit, do you realize the trouble you can get yourself into by withholding evidence from the sheriff? And Hammer, do you realize that you could be sent back to prison for helping Billy in all of this?"

"I do, but Billy is like my brother and I would do anything for him."

She angrily said, "Anything, including breaking the law?"

"Yes, if that is what it takes to protect my best friend. I would do anything, including breaking the law."

She reproachfully looked over at him. "You're wrong, you should never take the law into your own hands. And shame on you Billy for bringing Hammer into this. Now I want the two of you to sit down and tell me everything you know. I will decide then how we should approach this with the sheriff when he returns."

Lynn went to a table and sat down. We followed and sat across from her. I began to speak when she interrupted.

"No, I want to hear Hammer's version first."

"It's quite simple. Billy found the book and envelope in his apron pocket, just like he said. The strange man must have bumped into him when he first came into the restaurant and secretly placed the items there. He told me about them the next morning after his nightmare. We thought we would keep them for a day or two just to see how important they were. We ended up spending all day fishing and relaxing in Idaho Falls that we completed forgot about them."

He continued, "This morning I went into his room to wake him up. I hit him with a pillow and threaten to drench him with a cup of water. He told me he was awake and proceeded to tell me he had the strangest dream. That someone came into his room last night. As he rolled over in bed, he thought he heard someone shut his bedroom door. I was up just about the same time and had heard a car drive away. He said, let's open the book and study it together. I agreed, up to this point I had not seen the book or the envelope and was quite excited to see them both. We went to the dresser drawer and they were gone."

During this entire time, Lynn was looking at and listening to him. When he had finished, she said, "And that's it?"

"That's all I know."

She turned to me, "Okay, your turn."

"Hammer has pretty much summed up the whole story for you."

Lynn shook her head sadly,

"Not so fast. I don't want to be calling the two of you liars, but something just isn't ringing true here."

"I know it sounds funny but we were just caught up in the moment and actually forgot that I had the information until this morning."

Lynn looked at me in disbelief. "Okay, tell me why you didn't give them to the sheriff the night you found them? He was still here because I moved your blood stained apron from off the floor where you had laid it and the pocket felt empty then."

I made the decision to tell her some of the truth.

"When the man bumped into me he must have dropped the items into my apron at that time. When the two masked men were beating him he could have easily told them that he gave the items to me. They would have left him and came at me. So when I went to clean up I noticed the envelope and book. I was going to immediately bring them to the sheriff's attention, but I did not."

"And why not?"

"It seemed to me that the strange man wanted only me to know about the items, so I determined to keep them a secret for just a little while."

"So you said there was a book and an envelope, what did they say?"

"Like I told the sheriff, the book had nothing but some weird characters on the bottom and I didn't even have time to open the envelope."

Lynn stood up and walked around the table. It was apparent that she was pondering what we had told her. She then went back to her chair and sat down. She placed both of her hands on the table and looked at me and then Hammer.

"Boys, I'm sorry, but I must confess that I just don't believe you. First off, you have not told the sheriff the truth and now you are not telling me the truth."

When she said the truth, my mind again raced to the strange man and his plea to me to reveal the truth. I thought, If I only knew what the truth was, I would be more than happy to tell you, the sheriff and anyone else who wanted to know."

She continued, "I don't believe for a minute that you didn't open the envelope. If it was I who had the envelope, and I had decided to keep it for awhile, I would have opened it without delay. Curiosity would have gotten the best of me. I would have wanted to see what was inside it. If there was a letter of some sort, I would have wanted to read it. I have been working with the two of you for nearly four months now and I know a little about both of you. You are like two kittens, curious about everything that is happening around you. Billy, there is not a day that goes by that you are not drilling one of my customers about where they had been that day on the river. You are a regular snoop, and I am willing to bet that you opened the envelope. I am also willing to bet that Hammer knows just as much as you do. So come clean with me. I have been your friend for nearly four months. I hope that I have earned a little of your trust by now. I hope you both realize that I could have told the sheriff that you lied about finding the book in your apron last night. After all, I already knew you had found it the night of the murder. But notice, I did not do so. I feel a responsibility to protect the two of you because you're both so young and because you are both employed by me. I do not want anything to happen that might jeopardize my business nor our reputations. So come clean, tell me more."

As she looked at me, I made a decision to share some more of the truth. I felt that if Hammer and I were going to get into any kind of difficulty with the two masked men, that I did not want her to be involved. I didn't want her to get hurt.

"All right Lynn, you win. I will tell you what I know. The strange man did not bump into me and in doing so give me the book. He told me to take them from him. I wasn't even going to do that but he grabbed my arm and placed them into my apron pocket. He then ordered me to get him some coffee. As I was doing so the masked men came in and demanded to know where the stuff was. I thought they were talking about the items he gave me and was about to tell them when he looked at me so forcefully and then turned back to his assailants and told them to go to hell. That he had thrown the items out his car window miles back. I watched the taller of the two point his gun at the strange man's chest and fired. They yelled at me to stay down or I would be next. As soon as they left I ran over to the dying man. I told him to hang in there. He told me to use the items he had given me to reveal the truth. Truth to what, I have no idea. He then died in my arms."

Frowning, she said, "I am sorry that you had to go through that, but are you sure he told you nothing else?"

"If he told me anything else, I do not remember."

I was not about to give away perhaps the most important clue we had. She saw me pause for a second,

"Continue on please."

"When I took my apron off, I grabbed the book and envelope and hid them in my room. I quickly washed the blood off of me and put on some clean clothes. I came back downstairs to talk to the sheriff. I guess I just didn't know what to do at that time. So I kept the items a secret until I had the opportunity to read them."

"Now this is more like it, I think you are finally telling me some of the truth. So tell me, what was in the envelope?"

I looked at Hammer and he nodded his head. I knew he wanted me to share some of this information.

"There was a letter and a key inside the envelope."

Lynn gasped, "A key to what?"

"I have no idea. I placed it back into the envelope just like I found it."

"Okay, and what about the letter, what did it say?"

"It said something about Saturday being an important day. It also had a strange poem that talked about a King and Knights. I couldn't make anything out of it."

"I know you well enough that you at least talked to Hammer about it."

"Yes, but believe what you will; he never saw the book or envelope. We were always busy or away from the house. I was going to show them to him this morning but they were gone before I had the chance."

"Tell me, what the two of you were going to do with this information?"

"I guess we thought we might be able to solve this case."

"Oh, I see. So the two of you thought that, did you. So that tells me that you are still not telling me everything, because a book that was basically blank and a poem that you could not understand gave the two of you the idea that you could solve this murder. You know, if the two of you aren't more careful, your going to end up in serious trouble."

I nodded my head in concurrence.

Lynn again got up from her chair and walked around the table. She was reasonably upset that we were placing ourselves in harm's way. She returned to her chair.

"I want to know one more thing. You told the sheriff that you basically didn't hear the conversation that went on between the stranger and the two masked men, but I feel you did. So come clean, what else took place?"

"I heard enough to know that the taller of the two men spoke with a strong accent."

This startled her. "Do you think you would remember that person by his accent?"

"Yes I do, it was so original. I know beyond a shadow of a doubt, if I should ever hear it again, I would know the man behind the mask."

She stared at me for about ten seconds. "Okay, at the present time, we will not say anything more about this. But I want the two of you to stop prying into things that you have no business getting involved in. Now, go get something to eat and please stay out of trouble."

CHAPTER SEVENTEEN

Lynn got up and went to her room upstairs. Hammer and I got up from the table, not really knowing if she believed us or not. We went to the kitchen and made ourselves some toast. When we were finished we yelled up the stairs to tell her we were off for the day and would not be back until late. She did not respond so we left her a note. We then grabbed two bottles of water from the fridge and were out the door. Hammer popped the cap on his bottle, took a sip and asked, "Where to?"

"Off to Idaho Falls to call Del and use the library to do some research."

As we were driving, Hammer stared out the window and finally said, "Boy, I thought you were going to tell Lynn about us seeing the killer."

"I was for just a second. But before I did, I thought to myself, you've already told her too much as it was about the man and his accent."

"Yes, you're right on there. The less she knows the safer she will be."

"I sure wish we still had the book and envelope."

"Yeah, it would be nice, but we just got to deal with it. You're lucky they didn't decide to hurt or kidnap you."

"You think so?"

"I do, they're obviously very desperate to enter your room like they did."

"So, they have the book, the poem and my old apartment key. I have been thinking.if something is supposed to happen this Saturday and they don't have all of the clues such as the right key or the mysterious numbers, how are they going to solve this puzzle?"

"You know, I have been thinking about that as well. I think that the writing in the book must also be a clue. The same way the poem is. We need to sit down and try to figure it out."

Handing Hammer my wallet, I said, "While I drive, I want you to study the characters I wrote down from the book. See if anything jumps out and grabs you."

He commenced to study the sheets of paper that were in my wallet. Meanwhile, I reflected about the man who had been shot in the restaurant. The sheriff said he was a reporter from Chicago, that he was on an assignment. What kind of assignment and for how long?

As we reached the city limits of Idaho Falls I noticed in the rearview mirror a car off in the distance. It pulled out of a side street and started our way. The only reason it caught my eye was the fact that it was green and looked like it might be a Ford. I chuckled to myself. *Am I now going to worry about all green Fords that I see? I must have passed at least twenty just driving here.*

I drove down Yellowstone Hi-way until I reached Broadway Ave. I took a right and went two blocks, hung a left onto Park St. and pulled into the library's parking lot. As I parked 'Old Red', I noticed the same green Ford drive by. I tried not to stare, but did manage to take a quick glance at the driver. It looked just like the man the sheriff had pulled over yesterday.

"Let's be careful today, I think we have our friend following us again."

Hammer took a quick glance, "Let's call Del and then start our research."

We entered the library and went over to the payphones. I dialed Del's cell. He answered on the first ring,

"Hello."

"Del it's us. Did you find out anything about the man who was murdered?"

"Yes, I found out quite a bit about him and am waiting to get some additional information that I requested as well."

"Well, what can you tell us?"

"First off, everything I am going to tell you is extremely confidential. I obtained this information through several key contacts. The man who died was a reporter."

I butted in, "Yes, we know that he is from Chicago."

"How do you know he was from Chicago?"

"Sheriff Thompson told us this morning, he also told us that he was on assignment for the Chicago Herald."

"That's correct. What more did the sheriff tell you?"

"Not much, except that he was going to fly out this afternoon to meet with the dead man's boss."

"Well I had the opportunity to talk with his boss by phone this morning. His name is Eric Anderson. I told him of my contacts and that I had no official capacity in the case, but was trying to assist some friends out who had some inside information that might assist the local authorities in apprehending the two culprits. Mr. Anderson knew my contacts and felt comfortable in sharing some key information with me but would not under any circumstance share it all. He told me that Mr. Anthony Jackson had been an excellent reporter with his paper for about twenty-five years. Mr. Jackson won several awards for his stories. He even had some experience working undercover in the past."

It was at this point that he stopped talking. I heard a sneeze. "Excuse me, I had to sneeze, now where was I?"

"You were telling me about Mr. Jackson winning several awards and that he even worked undercover in the past."

"That's right, Mr. Anderson told me that about six years ago Mr. Jackson's son moved to Eastern Idaho to work as a nuclear engineer at the INEL site. That Mr. Jackson's son was a good kid but got mixed up with the wrong crowd. He died of a drug overdose about five years ago. The local authorities did all they could, but never were able to make an arrest. It was at this time that many rumors started to surface that Eastern Idaho had become a warehouse for illegal drugs, such as heroine and cocaine. The drugs are not intended for use in Idaho, but they are stored in Idaho for later distribution thorough out the Northwest. The dealers keep the drugs off the market until they have successfully covered up their tracks. The true source of where the drugs are coming from is extremely difficult, if not impossible to figure out. It is even more difficult to prosecute those involved."

With great excitement I blurted out, "I knew it. I just knew it. The information that Mr. Jackson gave to me would be important."

"It appears you were right on, but let me finish. Mr. Jackson took an undercover assignment to infiltrate the various gangs involved. He reported to his boss as recently as last Tuesday that he had confiscated a truckload of pure heroin and that he successfully hid the truck. However, in stealing the truck, he knew that the drug cartel had made him a marked man."

"Del, that might explain why he was in such a hurry Wednesday evening to give me the book and envelope."

"That could be. You see, Mr. Anderson indicated that Mr. Jackson had obtained documented evidence that could possibly put over one hundred illegal distributors out of business throughout the entire Northwest. Furthermore, the information he has obtained will allow the federal government to prosecute three major drug rings located in Columbia and Mexico. Billy, what I am going to tell you right now is extremely important. You and Hammer have stepped into a hornets nest. If the two of you aren't careful, you may end up as Mr. Jackson, dead. So I am on my way right now to Idaho Falls. I expect both of you to meet me at the hotel. Do you remember the name of the hotel?"

"Yes, you will be staying at the Red Lion Hotel. It's located downtown by the falls."

"That's right. I should be there in about five hours. I want you to call me back on my cell phone then. Meanwhile, I strongly suggest that you and Hammer take your information and head straight to the police."

"Alright we will."

All of a sudden, Hammer tapped me on the shoulder. "We've got to go."

He pointed out the library window where the killer and three other men had gathered next to my car. They were pointing at the library and talking. They started to walk towards the main entrance.

"Del get here quickly. We will call you back this evening."

I slammed the phone down. Hammer took my arm. "Quick! Out the side door."

We took off running through the library. As we were about to exit the door, a patron carrying an armload of books stepped right in front of us. We slammed into him and sent him and the books flying. We didn't stop to help him out, causing the man to yell at us. As he was yelling, the killer and the other three men were walking into the library. They heard the commotion and looked our way. The killer pointed at us.

"Don't let them get away." he yelled.

All four of them began to chase us. We darted out the side door, as we ran out, I yelled, "Do you remember where we ate dinner last night?"

"Yes."

"I'll meet you there in about two hours. For now we must split up."

Hammer took off down Broadway towards the railroad tracks and I headed west towards the river.

Splitting up helped us out. It caused the four men to stop momentarily. They quickly divided into pairs, one pair started after Hammer and the other after me. I had always been a good runner and felt that I could lose them after a few minutes. As far as Hammer, he was on his own. I could only hope that he would be safe. Once I hit the river I crossed over the Broadway Bridge and turned right towards the falls. I ran for two minutes constantly glancing over my shoulder. The killer and one other man were close behind but I felt that I had gained some ground on them. As I scurried through the Best Western Driftwood parking lot, past the Outback Stake House and towards the Super 8 Motel. I noticed I was putting more distance between us. All along I had planned on doubling back to my car, where I could take off and hide out until I met up with Hammer.

Hammer on the other hand, headed east towards the railroad tracks and the Yellowstone Highway. He could not run as fast as me and the two who were chasing him were gaining ground. He crossed the highway and just barely avoided being hit by a semi truck carry sugar beets. He ran past the Jiffy Mart, into a remodeled office complex that used to be the old OE Bell Junior High School. He hid by the side of the entrance door. The two men chasing him were only a few seconds behind.

They burst through the main entrance door. Now these two men were strong and in great shape. They both were over six feet tall and easily weight two hundred pounds or more. They looked like bouncers at a bar, but ran as if they were wide receivers on the local football team. Now Hammer did what only he can do, instead of continuing to run he charged right into them. Both men saw him and prepared for the impact. But his intent wasn't to run them over and take off in a different direction. Instead, he lowered his shoulder and plowed into the first person knocking him to the ground. The second man swung at him, as he did so, Hammer step to the side and grabbed the man's arm. He then in a sweet, swift, sweeping motion flipped the man on top of the other man who was getting up from the ground.

The two collided and both tumbled to the ground. As they were attempting to stand up, Hammer ran up to the first and did a round house kick to the face. In the exact same motion he back kicked the second. The blow was accurate and powerful. Both men slammed their heads into the ground and were immediately knocked unconscious. He walked over to the two men and bent over them to make sure they weren't seriously hurt. The men were moaning, but he could tell that they would be alright. Now several people who were working in the building came out of adjacent office rooms when they heard the racket. They witnessed Hammer standing over the two.

One of them over heard him say, "That was fun. And remember guys, you don't mess with the Hammer."

One witness, who worked as a secretary for a small accounting firm, watched as he smiled at her, brushed off his clothes, and strolled confidently out of the building. Two other witnesses, employed by a printing company, went to the two injured men. As the two on the ground were beginning to regain consciousness, they asked them if they needed help. The two men slowly got up, shouted, *"Hell no!"* and staggered out the door.

CHAPTER EIGHTEEN

While Hammer was having fun, I made it safely back to 'Old Red'. I drove to Wal-Mart's parking lot because there were a lot of other cars and people present. I went down one of the parking lanes and parked my car between two large SUV's. Before getting out, I looked in all directions to assure I was not followed. Feeling somewhat safe, I entered the store to use a payphone. I called Del on his cell but his phone service politely told me that the cell subscriber I was trying to reach was not in service at this time. Taking advantage of Wal-Mart's huge selection I decided to buy a new t-shirt, sunglasses and a baseball cap in order to better disguise myself from those who had been chasing me. While I was shopping I picked up the same items for Hammer. I made my purchases and went into the restroom to change.

I knew I told Hammer to meet me in a couple of hours so I went into the sandwich shop inside of Wal-Mart to reread the clues that I had. I felt we had deciphered well enough the page with the poem on it. If it was a combination to a padlock we would be able to unlock it. So now the remaining part of the mystery is, what is the key for and why the numbers 9, 3, 9, 14?

As I was pondering the numbers, several customers came into the sandwich shop to order something to eat. One particular customer had a shopping cart full of groceries and three young children with her, around the ages of ten, six and maybe four. They each were carrying new books that their mother had just purchased for them. As they walked past me to sit down to eat their sandwiches, the ten year old dropped her book. I bent over to pick it up for her. As I did so I noticed it was a book of simple cross word puzzles, number games, diagrams, and other nifty games especially put together for younger children. One puzzle on the cover leaped out and captured my attention. It was a puzzle in which you eliminate letters by following certain clues given in the book. As you eliminate the letters it forms a sentence. I handed her the book and she thanked me.

I was returning my attention to study the sheet of paper with the various characters on it, when an idea hit me. Perhaps I too had a puzzle. The secret would be to remove certain numbers or letters from the page to reveal a message. Could this be what the stranger had in mind when he told me 9, 3, 9, 14? I looked at all the numbers, letters and characters written down on the sheet of paper. I started to decipher my own little conundrum. I looked at the ninth character on the list. It was the letter T. I then counted over three spaces and had the letter H. I then counted over nine more spaces and the letter E was there. I had T..H..E. So far I had successfully formed the word THE.

Was this just a fluke or was I on to something important? I counted over 14 more spaces to the letter S. I now had T.H.E.S. I was not certain if I had the word THE and the start of a second word with the letter S. Was I close to discovering some sort of a pattern? Or not? I made the decision to repeat the steps. Perhaps this is why Mr. Jackson repeated himself. He wanted me to do the same with the numbers and letters that I had written down from the book. So I repeated the process. I counted over nine and came up with the character >. I then counted over three and had the letter U. I counted nine again and reached the letter J. I finally counted over 14 more spaces and had the letter D. I had for the second go round the following information. >...U...J...D.

I put all of the characters together. (THES>UJD). Common sense told me that I was going nowhere with this, but, to be on the safe side, I repeated the procedure one more time. I came up with *, G, D, N.

I placed all of the characters together. (THES >UJD *GDN). I studied the characters for a few seconds. I knew this approach was useless. If 9, 3, 9, 14 was a code to decipher the characters, then I was out of luck. It only made the numbers, letters and characters even more confusing.

I glanced at the clock in the sandwich shop. It was approximately two hours since I last saw Hammer. I knew he would begin to worry about me if I didn't show up soon. Fortunately the Wal-Mart store was less than half a mile from where we ate dinner the night before. I chose to hastily walk to the restaurant. I did not want to run the risk of being seen driving 'Old Red', so I put on my new hat and sunglasses. As I left the store, I glanced over the parking lot. Nothing seemed to be out of the ordinary, so I took off at a quick pace.

Within a few minutes I was at the pancake house. I was about to enter when I heard someone call out my name. I promptly turned around to see who was yelling at me. When I did so, I saw Hammer sitting down on the curb behind some plants. I rushed over to him and gave him a pat on his back.

"Am I glad to see you, are you okay?"

He smiled. "Never been better."

We quickly shared our stories of escape when he asked, "Where's 'Old Red'?"

"I parked it at the Wal-Mart just west of here. We will get it later. Let's head to the hotel where Del said he would meet us. It's down the road about half a mile from here."

I pointed to the tallest building in Idaho Falls, "See that building?"

"Yup."

"That's the hotel. I will go first just in case they're still out here looking for us. Give me six minutes and then follow. I will meet you in the lobby of the hotel."

I handed him a bag that I was carrying.

"Here is a hat, shirt and sunglasses for you to put on."

He cackled, "I see, we're going incognito."

"That's right. I do not want to be chased again. I don't know about you, but I was pretty scared."

I took off towards the hotel. I made it there without any difficulty and waited in the lobby for Hammer to show up. About seven minutes later he came strolling into the lobby and walked up to me. We went to the front desk clerk and asked if a Mr. Montgomery had checked in yet. The clerk said no, so we decided to wait in the lobby. I told Hammer about my attempt to decipher the letters and numbers that we had. I explained how a young girl dropped her book and it gave me the idea to remove certain letters or numbers. With that said, I showed him the results and how it really led to nothing. Studying my notes, he said, "That sure was a great idea, too bad it didn't work out."

"Yeah, I felt I was onto something when I got the first word THE, but the rest was nothing but garbage. It's actually quite frustrating not knowing what all of this means. Sometimes I wonder if we are just wasting our time, or is there really something to all of this?"

"Time will tell, but I firmly believe we're doing some good here, give me a logical reason why four complete strangers would chase us today?"

We continued to discuss the pro's and con's of what we were up to while waiting for Del to show up.

It was around 9:45 p.m. when Del finally arrived. We were both very pleased to see him. He checked into his room and asked if we were hungry. We told him we were starving, so we walked across the street to Applebee's. We studied the menu for several minutes when the waiter came over and asked if we were ready. Del ordered the Santa Fe Chicken salad. It sounded so good that Hammer and I completely forgot what we were going to order and ask for the Santa Fe Chicken salad as well. As we were waiting for our food, we began to talk.

"Did you go to the police?"

Hammer responded, "We were going to but got sidetracked."

Del looked at him, "What do you mean by being sidetracked?"

Hammer told him about what happened at the library and how we split up. He further told him about his escape and then turned to me so that I might tell Del about my little adventure.

Once I finished with my story, Del remarked, "So you think you can ID the killer?"

"Sort of."

We walked back to the hotel and took the elevator to the sixth floor. We were about to enter his room when I noticed it was room number 614. I stopped at the door and looked for several moments at the number. Noticing my hesitation, he asked, "What are you thinking about?"

"I really don't know, but there is something about this number that has captured my attention. You know, it's kind of like when you feel you left the lights on just before your leave to go on vacation. You think you turned them off and yet you sit there and wonder."

"I know the feeling. Matter of fact, before I left to come here I had to pause for a moment to think about the water in the kitchen sink. I really can't remember if I turned it off or not, oh well, I guess I will find out when I get home."

Hammer stared at both of us, "I never had to worry about that when I was in prison."

We all broke out laughing and then entered the room.

Del pointed towards the table in his room. "Why don't the two of you take a seat there at the table? Now boys, fill me in, I want to know it all."

Unlike when the sheriff or Lynn asked this question, we told him everything. We informed him about how busy the restaurant had been that night. About the strange man who came in just around closing time and all he had to say including the numbers 9, 3, 9, 14. We told him about the appointment book and manila envelope. We enlightened him about the key that was in the envelope and how I had exchange it for an old apartment key that I had. We showed him the two sheets of paper that I had copied. We explained how we had deciphered the poem on the first sheet of paper but were still trying to figure out what the characters were on the second. We talked about my two dreams and the man with the accent. How we saw him when he was pulled over by the sheriff and then later how he followed us around Idaho Falls. Lastly, we conversed concerning our car being searched and informed him that someone had been in my room and took the book and envelope. When we had finished, we retold him the story about us being chased.

During this time, he listened without interrupting us. When we were finished, he thoughtfully said, "You boys have stumbled across something very big here. I am glad you have not gone to the police. You say they have the book and envelope, yet they still chased you this afternoon. They obviously don't have all of the answers and must feel that the two of you do. So tell me again about this first letter, how did the two of you come to the conclusion that it must be a combination to a padlock?"

We revisited the story on how we worked through the numbers and how Hammer linked it to a combination of some sort. We had pretty much finished when it was Del's turn to tell us what he had discovered.

"I've told you the name of the man who was shot. He was sent here on assignment by his newspaper company. But he was the one that requested the assignment. It turns out that his wife died about ten years ago and the only family member he had remaining was his son. When his son relocated to Idaho, Mr. Jackson was initially very happy for him. However, his son got caught up with the wrong crowd. Mr. Jackson tried several times to get his son to return to Chicago but did not succeed.

He had made up his mind to fly out to Idaho and personally drag him back but just before he could do so, he got word of his son's apparent overdose."

He continued. "Mr. Jackson took it very hard and was about to quit the newspaper but instead asked his boss for the opportunity to work on the story of drugs in small towns. His boss approved a one month assignment. Mr. Jackson came out here and never told anyone his real purpose, that he was working undercover for the paper. He obtained some very valuable information and his boss decided to keep him on the assignment. Five years had actually passed and they felt they had enough evidence to blow the lid off of the entire affair. But about three weeks ago Mr. Jackson emailed his boss with some major concerns. He indicated that someone had discovered who he was and for whom he was working. His boss directed him to return immediately but he refused. He informed his boss that he had come this far and was not about to quit. All he needed was a couple of more weeks to safely get all of the incriminating information out of the state."

Del opened up a notebook that he brought with him and showed us a picture of Mr. Anthony Jackson. The picture was about fifteen years old but I recognized him at once.

"That's Mr. Jackson. I will never forget what he looks like."

Del nodded and then continued with his story.

"Two weeks ago his boss lost complete contact with him and was about ready to inform the FBI when out of nowhere Mr. Jackson called him up. It was early Tuesday morning the day before he was murdered. He told his boss that he confiscated a truck load of illegal drugs worth millions of dollars. He explained that he had safely hid the drugs, but that he had to still obtain a few more names in order to break the entire cartel operating here in Eastern Idaho. He called his boss later that same day and informed him that he had obtained all of the details and was now ready to turn over the evidence. But he feared for his life. He explained to his boss that if he did not make it back that he had made a code and was in the process of sending it to him by way of FedEx. Mr. Anderson never heard from him again."

I jumped in, "This would explain everything we have. He gave me a book and an envelope. He was probably on his way to mail them to his boss when he felt trapped and stopped at the restaurant. He gave them to me hoping somehow I would be able to, as he put it,"

Pausing for a moment, I finally said, "Reveal the Truth."

I was about to continue on again when an idea hit me. I shut my eyes and began to reflect on what the strange man had told me. He said 9…3…9 and then he paused. Was it because he was weak and needed a moment to continue or was it intentional. I had thought about this several times and came to the conclusion that he was just weak, but what would happen if I took the pause to be another number totally separate from the first three numbers. Just like Del's room number, it was 614. The 6 represented the floor but the 14 represented the room on the floor. Together they made the whole, but what if the numbers 9, 3, 9 represented the code and 14 was yet another clue, and together they represent the whole picture.

Just then Hammer shook me and Del said, "Hey Billy, wakeup, are you daydreaming on us?"

I shouted out in excitement, "I hope not. I think I may have solved another part of the riddle."

"Oh no, not another one of his dreams," Hammer jokingly remarked, looking at Del.

I looked at Hammer in reproach, but continued on with what I was going to do. I took the sheet of paper that had the numbers, letters and characters written on it and placed it in the middle of the table for all to see. I walked over to the dresser and snatched the hotel stationery and pen. I then returned to the table. During this time they both looked at me as if I had lost my mind.

"Remember how I explained to you how I used the numbers 9...3...9...14 to try and decipher these characters and all I came up with was garbage."

"Yes, I remember, you said it made no sense at all," Hammer said.

"That's right. It made no sense, so I stopped trying to use the numbers as sort of a decoder. Del, do you remember how I stopped at the door to stare at your room number?"

"Yes, it was obvious to me that you were thinking about something."

"Remember I said it was like a feeling of forgetting to do something?"

He nodded his head in agreement.

"Well my mind was looking at the number 14. I felt that the strange man was telling me about all four numbers at the same time, but I forgot how he paused after the first three numbers. At first, I felt he was struggling to get the entire sentence out when in reality he wanted me to know that 9, 3, 9 was to be used separately from the 14. He was so concerned that someone else was listening in that he believed he could not fully explain it to me. He even told me to hush because he sensed someone was watching us. Therefore, he must have used the pause as a way of telling me that the numbers are separate. I hope I'm not crazy, but let's give it a try."

I handed the stationery and pen to Del.

"I'm going to use the code 9, 3, 9 to decipher what is here. I will repeat the code each time. When I get to the characters I will say them aloud and you will write them down. Hammer, I want you to look over my shoulder to make sure that I do not miss anything. Are you both ready?"

They both responded in the affirmative. I began with T...H...E... just like the first time, but instead of going out 14 characters and getting S, I returned to the pattern of 9, 3, 9... and we had all together:

T...H...E..T...R...U...C...K..A...T...O..L...D...S...N...O...W...B...
A...L..L...C...A..F...E..,...U...S..E...K..E..Y..I..F...W..I...T
...H..O..L..D..G..R..A..Y...D...O...G

The three of us looked at the letters that were on the hotel stationery. It read, *"The truck at old snowball cafe, use key if with old gray dog."*

Del looked over at me. "I think you may have solved the code, but it still makes little sense to me. What does he mean by Snowball Cafe?"

Hammer answered the question. "The Snowball Cafe is an old dilapidated building that is right off of the highway. It is actually not far from the Log House. Mr. Jackson must have hidden the truck inside the building. What has me confused is the second part of the message. What does he mean by saying, use key if with old gray dog?"

"We will figure that out later, we still have to figure out where the number 14 comes into play." I said,

"Boys, I have requested some additional information that should arrive here at the hotel sometime early tomorrow morning."

When he said this he looked at his watch. "Oops, sometime early this morning, it's already 12:30."

I let out a groan. "Oh boy, we have got to call Lynn. She will be worried sick about us. Can we use your phone to call her?"

He pointed at the hotel phone. I hurriedly called the Log House. Lynn answered on the third ring.

"Hello?"

I heard concern in her voice and swiftly said, "Lynn, it's me Billy."

She immediately interrupted me. "Are you boys alright? It's so late. I was just about ready to call the police to see if there was an accident or something."

"We're okay, were in Idaho Falls."

She sighed a breath of relief. "When will you boys be home?"

Placing my hand over the receiver, I said, "Would it be okay for us to sleep on the floor?"

"No problem, I'll even rent you a room."

I smiled at him and removed my hand from the receiver.

"Lynn, it's so late, we thought we would just spend the night in Idaho Falls."

She let out another deep sigh. "Billy, if you don't mind, I would like for you and Hammer to come back to the restaurant. There were several men who came by earlier this afternoon. They wouldn't tell me what they were looking for but they scared me. I just don't think I could sleep here at the restaurant tonight by myself."

"Okay, well be there, but give us about an hour or so to return home safely."

Lynn was elated. "Oh thanks, Billy. I owe you one."

"Oh no you don't. Think nothing of it, we will see you soon," I said as I hung up the phone.

Del said, "I thought you wanted to stay here tonight?"

"Well I did, but it appears that Lynn was visited by some men this afternoon. They might be the same ones who chased us earlier. She is somewhat scared and would like us to come back to the restaurant."

Hammer stated, "I understand where she is coming from. For the first three months I was in the juvenile detention center I was scared. I had no friends and didn't know what to do. I guess I just became angrier with each day."

Del and I looked at Hammer. We both saw a side of him that we had never seen before. This was the rough and tough, take no sass Hammer, and he just shared with us that he was scared.

Del broke the silence. "You boys take my car. Leave yours in the parking lot at Wal-Mart. This way, if anyone is out there looking for you tonight, they won't suspect the two of you to be driving a Beamer."

I let out a yell, "You're kidding me! You're going to let us take your car?"

"I know, I know, it's against my better judgment, but I don't think we have a choice in this. Let's hook up, first thing in the morning. We know where the stolen drugs are located. The two of you know who the killer is. Whatever is to take place tomorrow," Del paused. "I mean today, must have some bearing on all of this as well. We just need to figure out what 14 stands for."

I butted in, "And what gray dog stands for."

"That's right," said Hammer.

Del pushed us towards the hotel door and handed me his keys. "No speeding. I want the two of you to call me no later than ten this morning on my cell."

We agreed, and he gave each of us a pat on the back.

"Take care boys. I don't want anything to happen to the two of you."

"Don't worry, Hammer is with me and I will make sure he stays out of trouble."

As we left the hotel, we both glanced around. It appeared we were alone. I unlocked Del's car with his remote and we hopped in. I put the key into the ignition and gently turned. The car started promptly and the engine purred like a kitten. I looked over at Hammer and said with a slight cowboy accent, "Buckle up buster, it's the law and where we're going, you going to need all the protection you can get."

He smiled. "You're not going to obey the speed limit, are you?"

"Who me, are you kidding? With this puppy we have to at least hit a hundred or so once or twice don't you think?"

He nodded, than we squealed out of the parking lot and headed home. The clock on the dashboard read 1:30 and at this time of night there were only a few cars on the road. Nothing

was going to stop us from having a little fun on the way back to
the restaurant.

Chapter Nineteen

It was a clear late August night and the moon was just about full. It made for the perfect drive home. The wind was blowing faintly out of the west and the usual noise of the day had died down. We turned on the radio and found some traveling music. I punched the accelerator and with a burst of energy we were doing 105 mph. We raced along the road for a few minutes at this speed when up ahead I detected movement on the freeway. I began to break when all of a sudden several male deer tore across the road right in front of us. I swerved first to the left to miss the lead buck and then to the right to avoid the two that were following him. The beamer's suspension handled the sudden movement as gracefully as a professional skater handles a figure eight. We were back on the road and the three bucks were unharmed.

I turned to Hammer, "That was a close one." I then whistled and continued, "And boy oh boy this car is a beauty."

Hammer, with great excitement in his voice, replied, "Man that was awesome, I'm so glad you missed those deer back there."

"So am I, guess I'll have to slow up for now just in case there are more animals out tonight. I would hate to hit one wouldn't you?"

"Definitely!"

So I slowed down to 70 mph. It felt like we were crawling after going 105 mph, but this way the deer were safe, we were safe, and even more importantly, Del's Beamer was safe.

We drove for another fifteen minutes listening to some tunes on the radio. We had just crossed the Swan Valle Bridge when Hammer blurted out, "Hey lets swing by the Snowball Café to check it out. You know, kind of detective work to see if our hunches are right or not. It will only take a few extra minutes to do so."

"Awesome idea, and while were doing so, let's check around the area to assure that there is no strange cars parked anywhere."

"Sounds like a plan to me."

We covered the remaining four miles or so listening to 'Dust in the Wind' by Kansas. As we approached the Log House, we slowed up enough to peek into the dining room windows without drawing any attention to ourselves. The kitchen light was on but all looked okay. We sped up and continued down the road a little further to the Snowball Café. Again, we slowed as we passed the café. We saw no other cars in the area and felt confident that we were alone, so we turned around and pulled behind the old café. After we parked the car and leapt out, we looked around in every direction. Not seeing anything, we headed to the back entrance. As we approached the back of the building, we could see that the rear part of the building was built like a garage door. However, the door did not open up like most garage doors, instead it slid open like a closet door.

It was plain to see that the door could open wide enough for one to easily drive a pickup truck through it. We both spotted the lock on the sliding door at the same time. It was a combination padlock. I turned to Hammer, "Do you remember the combination?"

"Yes sir-ree, its 17 left 4 times."

As he said this he took the padlock into his hand and began to turn the wheel. He continued, "34 to the right three times, then turn to the left twice to zero and finally back to the right to the number 12."

He looked at me, "Cross your fingers, here we go."

He pulled down on the lock and it clicked open. We were in. I whistled out loud, "This couldn't be cooler. We really are on to something significant here."

Hammer said, "I wonder what three hundred and fifty million dollars worth of drugs looks like?"

"We'll soon see," I retorted.

We then slid the door open and walked into the café. It was dark inside, but with the help of the moon light we immediately saw the shape of a truck. It was actually a dark black Ford F-150. It had a large tarp wrapped around the cargo area. The cargo area was loaded and the tarp extended around the back of the truck and above the cab. We walked cautiously to the rear of the truck and moved part of the tarp back. It was hard to see but we could make out the shape of many boxes about three feet long, two feet high and two feet thick. Hammer reached out and touched one of the boxes. It was covered with a very thick coat of saran wrap to keep air and water out.

He turned to me, "It looks like we have hit pay dirt."

"We sure have, I wonder if the key that was in the envelope. is for this truck."

"Let's find out."

I removed the keys from my pocket and went to the driver's side of the truck. I tried the door, it was unlocked. So I opened it up and climbed into the cab. I took the key and tried to place it into the ignition. It did not fit.

"Well it looks like this key if for something else."

"Yes," he said intuitively. "The old gray dog. Let's go back to the Log House to see how Lynn is doing.

We turned and exited the backdoor of the café. We slid the door shut and fastened the lock. We again looked all around to see if we could detect anyone watching. We didn't see anything so we reentered Del's Silver Beamer and drove back to the Log House Restaurant. Seconds before we got there I said, "You know the old church building which is down the road from the Log House by about two hundred or so yards?"

He nodded. "Let's drive by the Log House one more time really slow to make sure all is right and then park Del's car behind the church. We will then walk back, this way no one will suspect that we have returned."

Again he nodded his head in approval, and we drove slowly by the restaurant. All appeared to be normal so we continued on to the rear parking lot of the church. We slid out of the car and I locked the doors with the automatic key. I turned to Hammer and showed him Del's keys.

"I'm going to place them on top of the left rear tire for safe keeping."

He looked puzzled. "I have never driven a car in my entire life. Why leave them there?"

"We'll both have access, just in case we have an emergency of some sort."

He remarked still somewhat baffled, "Its okay with me partner. You know what you're doing."

We promptly returned to the Log House, keeping an eye out for any unusual activity. We made it back without any cars passing us or without seeing anything. We went around to the back of the restaurant and entered through the kitchen door. As we entered, Lynn was just coming down the stairs. She heard us unlock the door and cried out, "Boy am I glad to see you two." She continued, "Go sit down at the kitchen table, I baked you a chocolate cake and I bought some fresh milk."

We went and sat at the table while she cut the cake and poured the milk. She brought us each a large piece and a tall glass of cold milk. She placed them before us and then sat down to talk. As she began to speak Hammer and I ripped into the cake. It was our favorite and she normally made it only on special occasions.

"Where were you two today?"

Hammer said with a mouth full of cake, "We went fishing for an hour or two and then into town to party for a bit."

"Where did you go fishing?"

"Oh the usual spots, but we didn't catch anything."

She looked at him and then me, "So what happened in town today? How come you're home so late?"

I joined into the conversation, "Nothing much, we took in another movie and had a bite to eat at Applebee's."

Lynn stood up. "Boys, do you have anything else to tell me about the man who was shot? For example, have you remembered anything or discovered any additional clues?"

"No, we haven't given it much thought," Hammer said.

"Boys, do you remember this morning when I told the two of you to quit prying into things that you have no business being in?'

We both said, "Yes."

"Remember when I told you two to be careful, that this is no silly game you're messing around with?"

Again we said, "Yes."

She then said in an angry voice, "Remember when I told you that I didn't believe you?"

We were about to say yes for the third time but she waved her hand and told us to be quiet.

"I didn't want this to happen but the two of you just don't know how to tell the truth. The last two that worked here didn't either. "

Hammer open his mouth to speak, but she irritably stared at him, "How could you have gone fishing today when your fishing poles are still by the side of the house? No boys, you've been up to no good, so now were going to have to do this the hard way."

She shouted out, "Gregorio, come here."

Hammer and I looked at Lynn and then heard the swinging doors to the dining area open and in walked the masked man, the man with the accent, the man who the sheriff had pulled over, the man who chased us at the library, the man whom we knew to be the killer. Hammer was about to spring up and tackle the killer. However, Gregorio must have sensed his intention before hand because he pulled out his revolver and aimed it not at Hammer but me. He said in his thick Spanish accent, "Go ahead hero and make your move, and if you do, your little amigo here dies."

I recognized the gun It was the same one that had killed Mr. Jackson. I looked at Hammer and watched him slowly ease back into his chair. Lynn shouted for a second time, "Carlos, Miguel, Ruben! Come here at once."

Down the stairs came the other three men who had chased us this afternoon. She directed them to tie us up.

"That way they won't do anything foolish."

Gregorio kept his gun aimed at me while the one called Carlos took a hold of me and placed my hands behind my back. He wrapped some black duct tape around my wrists and arms and secured them tightly to the chair I was sitting on. When he had finished with me he went to Hammer to tie him up. Hammer place his hands behind his back, but I noticed that he was flexing his muscles as he did so. Carlos wrapped the tape around his wrists and secured him to his chair.

Lynn shouted, "Enough fooling around, you have both wasted valuable time and we need answers now."

"We don't know what you are talking about." I said,

She turned and glared at me. I had always thought she was an unattractive woman, but if you mixed her glare in with her looks you had one very ugly woman. She then walked up to me and bent over. She placed her face about ten inches from mine and screeched ,"*You know damn well what i am talking about!* I want to know right *now* what you were told Wednesday night by that old bastard."

Up to this point, I had never heard her swear before. She had always been a very caring and uncomplaining person. I looked her in the eyes.

"I already told you what he said."

When I said this, she reared back, raised her hand behind her head and slapped me violently across the left side of my face. She hit me so hard that that it shook the chair. I would have fallen over if it weren't for my hands being tied so firmly to the back of it.

She continued, "I have been patient long enough. I have given you both, several times, the opportunity to tell me the truth, but you and muscle boy over here have done nothing but treat me like some dumb piece of shit. Well, *what did he say?*"

I was still smarting from the slap to my face. But I had no intention of telling her or her four cohorts anything, thus I boldly replied, "He told me nothing."

Lynn went berserk. She took hold of my right ear with her left hand. She raised her right hand as high as she could reach and again brought it down with such velocity that my head jerked. As my head jerked to the right she continued to hold my right ear tightly. This made the sound of her slap twice as loud and caused unbearable pain not only to the left side of my face but to my ear as well.

She released her grip. "Perhaps I can help your memory. Do you remember when the dying man said, 'Hush, someone is listening?' You looked around and saw no one, but I was there. I was watching and listening through the portal where we slide the dirty dishes. He saw me and I saw him. I even heard him say the number 9, *but that was it!*"

She raised her hand high above her head to slap me again when Hammer yelled out, "Stop! Billy told me what he said. He told him 9, 3, 9. The old man then repeated the same numbers for a second time. So enough with the violence, what do you want from us?"

She chuckled and brought her hand down slowly. "Oh, so mistertough-as-nails is the first to crack, and all along I thought it would be you Billy."

Lynn returned to the table and sat down.

"Let me tell you boys something. Do you think this restaurant idea came because I love to talk about fishing? *Hell* with fishing, it's a waste of time, grown men splashing around in the water, spending countless hours trying to catch a slimy, stinky, little fish. No, the idea for a restaurant was conceived so that a more sophisticated plan could take place."

Gregorio interrupted, "You shouldn't be telling them all of this?"

Lynn, still speaking in a hostile voice, bellowed out, *"What does it matter? They'll find these two boys downstream in a week or two anyways? It will be a simple case of two enthusiastic young fishermen trying to wade across the river to get to the other side."*

With much sarcasm, she continued, "To find that perfect little fishing hole. But instead, the current was too strong and they both slipped and accidentally hit their heads on the rocks."

Then clasping her hands together as if she was a saint and with a tone that denoted great pleasure exclaimed, "They must have been knocked unconscious."

Her voice skipped. "Their poor little bodies must have drifted downriver for miles before they surfaced. Boo hoo hoo."

When she finished, Gregorio and the other three broke out laughing. Carlos declared, "Perhaps their bodies will never be found."

Lynn gave a sinister grin to Carlos and began to speak again in her normal voice.

"I want the two of you to know the truth before your last little fishing trip. You think all of those letters were of past fishermen sharing their prize photos with me? Well you're wrong, it was our way of safely communicating. They were telling me how much goods could be delivered securely at any given time."

I boldly proclaimed, "You mean drugs, not goods."

"Oh, yes, little great one, I do mean drugs. When I got a letter from someone saying, you should have seen that four pound trout that I caught last summer. You boys pictured a fish if I left the letter innocently lying around, but instead they were telling me they wanted four kilos of pure cocaine. Yes, yes,

yes, when you read about the salmon up north that was caught, they were telling us to send them heroine. Oh, and a lot of my repeat customers from out of town, what do you think they were up to?"

Hammer spoke up, "To buy your filthy drugs, you witch."

She looked at him. *"Witch?"*

"You heard me right. I saw many people in prison hooked on the stuff you sell."

"Yes," she said sinisterly. Business does boom everywhere, doesn't it?"

Hammer still quite angrily inquired of her, "Tell us about the man last Wednesday, why did you kill him?"

Gregorio again protested, "Don't tell these two dogs anymore."

She didn't listen to his complaint, but instead barked out an order, "Go and get the book and envelope from my room. Let's see if these two are still lying about the things they know."

Gregorio shouted at Carlos and he ran upstairs to fetch the items. As Carlos ran up the stairs I noticed that the other three men were all about the same size as Gregorio. This meant that the second masked man was not among those here tonight.

Lynn continued her story. "We run a smooth ship here boys. We have been making successful deliveries for the past seven years and the two of you are not going to screw it up for us. No one would ever suspect a group of innocent fishermen traveling up and down the river on a daily basis of being drug runners, now would they? After all, this area has been touted as one of the best areas in the west to fish. So easy for customers to come into the restaurant and place their innocent orders. Kind of gives a new meaning to take out doesn't it?"

Hammer glanced over at me to see how I was doing after having been brutally slapped twice across the face. He could see that my lip was bleeding and the left side of my face was extremely swollen and turning a dark purple color. He felt if he could keep her talking that it would perhaps strengthen the odds of us getting out of this situation alive.

He was about to say something when Carlos came back down the stairs with the book and envelope. Gregorio handing his weapon to Miguel, said, "If they move shoot them."

Lynn jumped in, "Shoot them in the leg first. We may still need some valuable information from them."

While Miguel kept us covered with the .45, Lynn and the other three studied the book and the information written in it. Gregorio exclaimed, "All of the stuff in here is a bunch of shit. That ass hole had to tell them more than three lousy numbers."

They then opened the envelope and studied the letter that was inside. Carlos said, "What is this, a stupid poem, it makes no sense."

I thought to myself, Use your imaginations you morons. The answer is right there if you have any brains.

Lynn shouted, "Enough of this shit! We have to be at The Great Feeder Canal by 10:00 this morning to make this delivery or we'll all end up swimming face down in the Snake by evening time."

She stood up and took the gun from Miguel. She turned to Hammer and then to me. She was frowning when all of a sudden a silly smirk crossed her mouth. She walked up to me.

"I know the two of you have some valuable information that we need. Unless you give it to me in the next fifteen seconds, I'm going to blow your left knee cap to smithereens."

She started counting. "One…Two…Three."

"We know no more than you do." I cried out.

She kept counting. "Four…Five…Six.

Again I screamed out, "What is it you want from us?"

Calmly she said, "I want to know where the drugs are, and I want to know now? I also know that son of a bitch reporter has a boat load of incriminating evidence hidden somewhere and I want that as well."

I stuttered, "We don't know what you're talking about."

"Seven…Eight…Nine."

"Look, Lynn, we've told you all we know."

"Ten…Eleven…Twelve."

Hammer blurted out, "Okay, you win, I will tell you what we know, but first, how did you ever come to suspect this Mr. Jackson fellow?"

Lynn looked at her watch, it was a quarter after four. She placed the revolver next to my left kneecap. "Thirteen…Fourteen."

During this entire count down, my mind was racing. Somehow we had to buy some time. I'm not certain how, but if we don't, we'll both end up dead and a little fighting chance is better than no chance at all. It was my hope that if I could get the five of them to split up somehow, perhaps then Hammer might be able to escape. As these thoughts raced through my mind I heard Lynn begin to pull back on the trigger. I shouted out, *"Stop! Stop!* I know where the drugs are hidden."

CHAPTER TWENTY

Lynn gently lowered the trigger on the .45 and removed it from my kneecap. She proudly exclaimed to Gregorio, "You see, all we needed to do was some persuasive talking."

She turned back to me. "How do you know were missing drugs are?"

"Because, I've seen them and touched them!"

Hammer yelled, "Don't tell them anything."

I looked over at him, "We have no choice. They have us right where they want us."

"That's right," Lynn retorted, "So where is it?"

"I will show you where it is only after you tell us why you killed that poor man last Wednesday evening."

"You are in *no* position to tell us what to do!" she barked.

"Perhaps not," I gallantly exclaimed. "But it sounds like you have less than six hours to make your rendezvous. And what the heck, you're going to kill us either way. So kill us now. But if you do kill us now, you'll never find out where the drugs are. Besides I don't believe you are as stupid as you are ugly."

Lynn smiled, she bent over and kissed my swollen cheek, she then turned her back for a moment and suddenly whirled around, and with even greater force than before, slapped me so hard that this time the chair and I tumbled to the ground.

I was on the ground moaning when Carlos and Miguel came over and started to laugh at me. Carlos knelt down by my side, "Who's the stupid one now?"

Lynn shouted out, *Enough!* Help him up, time is wasting. I will tell you why we killed Mr. Jackson and then you will show me where the drugs are."

Carlos and Miguel hefted me and the chair up and she began to speak.

"We called him Anthony. He came into our lives about five years ago. He was supposedly a business man living in Shelley, Idaho. He made some minor purchases from one of our associate's. Over time, he became a regular customer. It took him several years to gain our misguided associate's trust, a mistake the associate won't make again. Remember the fishing accident about a week ago? The poor fisherman whose boat capsized on Palisades Lake?"

I was in great pain, the entire left side of my face was swollen, but I still responded to her question, "I remember a Mr. Keith Smith."

"That's right, Keith. Now let me see, if I recall right, they still haven't found his body. I guess wearing a jacket full of lead isn't conducive for swimming, now is it? But let me continued on with the story. Anthony wormed his way into the business. He slowly became one of our runners, or should I say boaters. But the only contact that he was aware of was still our poor associate. So Anthony made up a story that he had some significant contacts in Chicago that would be willing to make a major purchase. Our associate offered to be the go between us and them. Nevertheless, Anthony insisted that his contacts in Chicago would only trust him. He produced a brief case full of money, $200,000 dollars to be exact and gave it to the associate. He told him that if he made the arrangements the money would be his to keep. However, our associate forgot one important principal, and that is, in this business, if you want to stay in business, you don't make side deals. It's just not good for your health. But our ignorant associate was tempted and over the next year continued to pave the way for contact between Gregorio and Anthony. Finally, the meeting took place and Anthony actually became a trusted associate. He provided us with several key contacts in the Midwest and our business grew. Anthony obtained our complete confidence and we like fools started to open up. He was probably a week away from being introduced to me. Up to this time he worked directly with Gregorio and one other key person whom will remain anonymous. Unknown to us, this little bastard was busy taking notes. He discovered who our contacts were, where we obtained our shipments, how we slowly filtered it into the Northwest after it was deemed clean, who are runners were and who they distribute it to."

While telling her story, Lynn looked pale. The stress of the situation was wearing on her. She coughed once and then continued.

"His scheme would have worked had it not been for a fortunate accident. You see, about three weeks ago I was shopping in Idaho Falls when I spotted Anthony. I knew who he was but he did not know who I was. I noticed him make a couple of phone calls from a payphone. He looked suspicious, so I decided to trail him. He went into the post office to deliver some packages. I followed him into the post office and stood behind him in line. When it was his turn, he told the person behind the counter he had to send some packages overnight with top priority. I listened, but could only make out the word 'Chicago.'

He left and I walked up to the person behind the counter and nonchalantly said, 'Did he say Chicago? My daughter lives in Chicago'.

The person behind the counter responded, 'He sure did'.

I quickly made up a street name, 'By chance was he sending them to Baker St?'. The person behind the counter said, 'No, to the Chicago Herald'.

I bought some stamps just to make it seem like I was there for a reason and was out the door. I quickly returned home and did some research."

She glared over at Gregorio and turned back to me.

"Yes, research, something that should have been done along time ago. But, oh no, no one ever takes time anymore to do research. I discovered while surfing the net that our little friend was a reporter. I obtained this information from an old newspaper clipping. I contacted the newspaper and they said they never had an employee by that name. I knew they were lying because the article I had read showed a picture of him receiving their prestigious Herald award ten years earlier. The award is given every year to their top employee. I knew immediately that it was a cover up. That he must be doing an assignment undercover and that we had been setup."

She took a moment and crossed her arms.

"So we set a trap, we invited the associate who got us into this mess, to arrange a meeting between Anthony, Gregorio and the mysterious partner. Anthony was more than delighted at the chance to meet one of the two key figures in this entire operation. It was agreed upon that he would go fishing with Keith. While they were fishing the mysterious partner would meet them in the middle of the lake. There they would exchange key information. Keith was informed that if all did not go according to plan he would become fish bait, therefore he did as he was told. But poor, stupid, Keith decided to pull a fast one over on us. When Anthony showed up that morning as planned, Keith told him it was a setup and that he must leave town immediately. He told him about our next shipment and where it was stored."

She paused here and went to the kitchen sink and poured herself a glass of water. She took a few sips and then put the glass down in the sink. She sighed audibly and walked back over to where we were sitting and pulled her chair closer to me.

"I still do not know why Keith decided to tell Anthony it was a trap. We told Keith if he followed-up on this we would not hurt him. Our goal was to eliminate Anthony. I think Keith must have felt we were going to do away with the two of them and determined that his last act would be one of trying to right the ship, even if he was the ass hole that caused it to go astray in the first place. He took the boat out to the middle of the lake and awaited his fate. We thought that Anthony was aboard the boat with him and went to meet them both in the middle of the lake. When we got alongside his boat we discovered the double cross. So we did what we were going to do all along, we eliminated him. But this unfortunately event cost us dearly, because it provided Anthony with the time he needed to escape, not only with his life but with our shipment of drugs which are scheduled to leave this morning at 10:00."

Again she got up and went to the kitchen sink for some water, taking the glass she had previously placed into the sink and refilled it. This time she drank the entire glass and then placed in on the kitchen counter. She looked at her watch and then us. She was in obvious pain, not physical but more mental. She was extremely stressed over the loss of her merchandise and it was apparent to all in the room that she wanted to get this shipment of drugs off on time. She walked back to her chair and proceeded with her story.

"We knew Anthony did not have time to go very far with our shipment, because when we discovered the double cross, we radioed ahead to several of our other associates to be on the lookout. They established key positions within a ten mile radius of where we had the drugs originally stored. Not a single associate saw him that day and we knew that he must have stashed our shipment somewhere close by. Gregorio and one other key player saw him Wednesday night and pursued him to the restaurant."

"So boys, as Paul Harvey would say, now you know the rest of the story." Hammer said.

"Paul who?"

Lynn smiled, "Never mind, I've kept to my part of the bargain and now Billy, you will keep to yours."

While she was telling her story, I had noticed that Hammer had been working ever so tactfully on the duct tape that kept him bound. By flexing his muscles when he was originally strapped to the chair he had obtained enough wiggle room to

potentially free himself. I knew with his strength it would be
fairly simple for him to break free. But with five of them and at
least one of them with a gun it would be futile for him to try
right now. His only hope, and mine for that matter, was for
Lynn and her four henchmen to somehow split up, hence I was
ready to lead some of them away.

"Okay, you win. Untie me and I will show you where the
truck is hidden."

Lynn beamed. She rose from her chair and bent over me
and pinched my swollen cheek. As she did so, I let out a small
moan. She heard me and reverted back to her old loving self.

"Oh Billy, I'm sorry I had to slap you."

She then turned to Gregorio and handed him back his .45.

"You and Miguel come with me. Carlos and Ruben keep an
eye on Hammer. We will return once we have the goods."

Gregorio came over to where I was sitting and ripped the
duct tape from off of my wrists. I screamed in agony, "You
dumb shit! That hurt."

Lynn looked over at Gregorio, "Be nice to Billy, he's taking
us to papa."

He mumbled under his breath, "Be nice to Billy."

He removed the rest of the tape that secured me to the
chair. I stood and began to walk when he forcefully shoved me
towards the kitchen door. I maintained my balance and
shouted over my shoulder to Hammer, "I'll be okay."

Before Hammer could say anything, Gregorio shoved me
again out the kitchen door. Lynn, Gregorio, Miguel and I
walked towards her truck. She took the drivers seat and Miguel
jumped in the front next to her. Gregorio opened the cab door
and yelled at me to get in. I climbed into the cab and he
followed.

Lynn immediately locked the doors, "In case you try to do
something stupid."

She started her truck. As she did so the clock on the dashboard read 6:58 a.m. She then looked over her right shoulder.

"Where to, Billy?"

"Take a left at the road and go about three miles."

She pulled out of the parking lot and turned left onto Highway-26. She stepped briskly on the gas pedal and within a few seconds was going sixty miles per hour. As she did so, I could only hope that Hammer would somehow escape. We traveled for about four minutes when I said.

"Pull in behind the old Snowball Cafe."

She slowed when she saw the cafe. She hit her blinkers and pulled in behind the café. She parked the truck and turned off the engine.

"Miguel, make sure he doesn't try to escape."

She unlocked the doors. Miguel jumped out and opened my door. He took me by the arm and forcefully dragged me out. Lynn and Gregorio exited the truck and the four of us walked towards the backdoor.

We approached the sliding door. As we did so she saw the padlock and turned to me.

"I hope you didn't lie to us, this door is locked."

"No problem, the combination was in the envelope that you opened."

Gregorio blurted out, "I don't remember any combination."

I turned to him and then back to her. "Do you remember the poem?"

"No, refresh my memory."

"It said, 'Seventeen sparrows went abroad…'"

I continued from memory the rest of the poem. When I had finished Gregorio rather impatiently shouted.

"What about it?"

"Well, you see, we figured the poem was a code of some sort. We came to the conclusion that it was to a combination lock."

I took the padlock in my left hand and while repeating part of the poem, turned the wheel on the padlock with my right hand.

"Seventeen sparrows left four times, Thirty-four knights to the right three times, zero or nothing twice to the left and finally to the midnight doom or the number 12."

The three of them watched in amazement as I turned to the last number 12 and the lock opened.

Lynn, with a schoolgirl squeal, said, "You and Hammer are quite the clever ones. So tell me, is 9...3...9 really part of what Anthony told you?"

"Yes it was. Do you remember the characters at the bottom of the book?"

"The stupid ones that makes no sense?"

"Yes those, if you chose the ninth character, then the third, and then the ninth again you form three letters. If you repeat the process over and over, you will get a message."

Gregorio was dumbfounded. "What was the message?"

"The message was, 'The truck at the Snowball cafe'."

I was not about to tell them the rest of it because I still had no idea what it meant and I surely did not want to assist these crooks any further than I had too.

She looked at me with great admiration, "Really, the two of you are very bright, it's too bad you didn't work for us. We could use more runners who think on their feet like the two of you do."

I said boldly. "But we would have never stooped to selling drugs."

She sighed. "Yes, this I knew."

I removed the padlock from the door and placed it back on the frame. Miguel slid the garage door open. It was around 7:00 a.m. and the sun was beginning to rise, providing us ample light to clearly see inside the old cafe.

Gregorio declared, "That Anthony was a sly one, who would have ever thought of looking inside an old café?"

Miguel went to look behind the tarp. As he did so, I realized that this was perhaps my one and only chance to escape. I turned to Gregorio and held my hand out as if I had something in it.

"You will need a key to start the engine."

As he reached for my hand, I suddenly took a hold of his arm and took one step back, pulling him towards me, exactly as Hammer taught me in the past. He lost his balance and staggered forward. As he stumbled, I stepped back towards him and planted my right knee squarely in his groin. He immediately fell to his knees screaming in agony. Miguel was still behind the tarp, so I sprung on him and with my two hands tightly clinched together as if they were a sledge hammer struck him below his right ear in the neck area. The blow sent him reeling into the truck and then to the ground.

Lynn reached out to seize me, but as she did so I lowered my head and ran her over. As she fell, she tried to clutch my shirt and pull me down with her. It almost worked but I managed to keep my balance and she only succeeded in ripping my shirt. I darted through the backdoor as fast as I could and stopped for just a moment to slide the door shut. I took hold of the padlock and refastened the lock. They could have easily escaped through any other door, but I hoped it would buy me some extra time. All I could think of was how am I going save Hammer as I sprinted towards the street.

CHAPTER TWENTY-ONE

It was still early and there were few cars in sight. I began running back to the Log House. Within seconds, I saw a car in the distance approaching me at a very rapid speed. I felt I could flag it down so I continued to sprint towards the Log House. The car speeding towards me began to take shape and I recognized it as Del's car. The driver jammed on the breaks to avoid hitting me. It was Hammer.

While I was masterminding my escape, Hammer had already begun his. When we had driven off in Lynn's truck the remaining two thugs walked up to him.

"Do you remember us?"

"Yes. The two of you are the wimps that I kicked ass on yesterday afternoon."

This comment infuriated Ruben so he turned to Carlos, "Let's kill him now."

Ruben reached into his pocket to pull out a switchblade. As he did, Hammer let out a loud yell and ripped through the duct tape.

He went straight for Ruben, who was still fumbling around in his pocket for his knife. He threw two quick left jabs to Ruben's face and then followed up with an uppercut to the jaw. Ruben began to fall but before he hit the floor Hammer took a hold of his shirt and spun him into Carlos. Carlos, who was still dazed at Hammer's miraculous escape, lost his balance when Ruben tumbled into him. Carlos spun around and fell to his knees. Once on the ground he immediately reached for his gun.

Carlos was taking aim at Hammer when Hammer took a rapid side step to the left and grabbed Carlos' wrist. He forcefully pushed it away from his body. As he was making his move Carlos squeezed the trigger, but because of Hammer's quick move the shot went harmlessly into the wall. Before he could get off a second shot, Hammer followed his initial side step move with the heel of his right palm directly into Carlos' nose. His nose broke instantly. Hammer didn't stop there; he jerked Carlos's hand violently to the right causing the gun to tumble from his hand. He picked up the gun but noticed that both Carlos and Ruben were incapacitated. Hammer smiled and as calm as calm could be exclaimed, "I am not certain if you two will ever learn, but never, ever mess with the Hammer."

He picked up the appointment book and manila envelope from the table and tucked them into his shirt, taking one last glance at Rueben and Carlos. They were both still laying unconscious on the ground so he dashed out of the restaurant to Del's car. On his way to the Beamer, he took Carlos' gun and emptied out the bullets onto the ground and threw the gun into the dumpster at the church. Finally making it back to the car, he reached up under the fender and removed the keys off the top of the rear tire. With the keys in hand, he fumbled around with the automatic door lock for a second or two, but finally figured it out.

Hammer had never driven a car before but he had seen several TV shows on how to drive. He had also watched me over the past several months. He took the key and placed it in the ignition and gave it a turn. The car started without any problems so he pressed the gas pedal and the engine roared, but the car did not move. Studying the situation, he took hold of the emergency brake and released it. Again he pressed the gas pedal and the engine roared, but the car did not budge. This time, he looked at the other lever and noticed several capital letters; they were P, R, D D1 and D2. The little arrow was currently pointing at P. Hammer fumbled around for a second but finally found a side button on the lever and moved the little

arrow to R. He pushed his foot down on the gas and the
Beamer took off. However, it did not go forward. Instead, it
raced backwards. Hammer, freaking out, jammed his foot
down on the other pedal and the car screeched to a stop.

He studied the letters for a second time and decided that R
must mean reverse and P must mean park. He thought for an
instant about the D, D1 and D2 and pushed the button for the
second time and moved the lever to the letter D. Crossing his
fingers, he pushed down on the gas pedal and the car lunged
forward. He removed his foot from the gas pedal and jammed
the other pedal to the floor. The car again screeched to a
sudden halt.

Okay, I think I have it, Hammer thought to himself.

Placing his foot on the gas pedal, the car shot forward. This
time, he eased off of the gas and the car gently slowed up. He
removed his foot off of the accelerator and realized that was
how he could control his speed. Essentially to speed up or
slowdown for the next four miles, he would have to use his foot
to control the gas pedal. He turned on to the highway towards
the Snowball Café and pushed the gas pedal to the floor. Again,
the engine roared and the Beamer took off.

All of a sudden, he saw something moving in the road. As
he got closer he noticed a person running towards him. He
took his foot off of the gas pedal and jammed the other pedal to
the floor. The car squealed to a stop and the tires left a large
skid mark on the road.

Running up to the car, I grabbed the door handle and tried
to open the door, but it was locked. I screamed, *"Unlock the
door!"*

He shouted back, *"How?"*

"Push the buttons by your side of the door."

Hammer hit every button and finally one of them unlocked
the door. I was just about ready to open the door when he hit
the same button again and locked the door again. Hammer,
seeing what he did to unlock the door, hit the button again and

the door unlocked again. Proudly smiling for figuring out the door, he forgot about everything else and took his foot off of the break pedal and the car began to roll forward.

"Hit the brakes!" I shrieked,

But instead of hitting the brakes, he hit the gas pedal and the car quickly lurched forward. He took his foot off of the gas pedal and jammed the break pedal to the floor and once again the car screeched to a stop. I ran up to the car, but because of the movement the door had relocked itself. For a third time I squealed at him, *"Unlock the door!"*

Hammer seemed to forget what he learned in the last ten seconds and hit several buttons this time before finding the right one. The lock clicked and I quickly opened the door and jumped in before he accidentally locked me out again.

Back at the Snowball Café, Lynn began to shout at Gregorio and Miguel.

"Get up, you two bums, !e's getting away."

Gregorio, still moaning, got to his feet and halfheartedly ran to the door. Miguel was just as slow in getting up. He had a big lump on the side of his head from where it had hit the truck during his fall. Gregorio shouted back at Lynn "The damn door is locked."

She pointed at the side door which was made out of glass, "Go through the side door."

He and Miguel both made it to the door with Lynn right behind them. It was locked from the inside so they fumbled for a moment with the latch. After unlocking the door, they pushed it open. Gregorio pushed so hard that when it opened, it slammed against the side of the café and the glass shattered. They took a quick second to see exactly where they were and then hurried to the front of the café.

Hammer appeared to be somewhat nervous as he drove. The car was slowing down and speeding up with violent jerks as Hammer alternated between the gas and the brakes. I kept hitting my head on the headrest and finally shouted out, "Stop the car. I'll drive. You can practice later!"

As I glanced out in front of us, I saw Gregorio running out onto the highway.

"No time! Give it gas!"

Hammer removed his foot from the brake pedal and slammed it down on the gas pedal. The tires spun for a second before they got enough traction to zoom ahead and my head to hit the headrest once again. Maybe I should have switched with Hammer!

By this time, Miguel had made it to the side of Gregorio. They both reached for their guns. Hammer was heading straight for them and before they could get off a shot, Gregorio dove to the left side of the car onto the hard asphalt while Miguel dove to the right side. Hammer drove right between them without hitting either one. Taking his foot off the gas pedal to look out the back window, he accidentally hit the brake pedal. The car jerked to a sudden halt and my head smashed into the dashboard.

It was at this time that Lynn reached the highway and screamed, *"Get back here, you little bastards!"*

Gregorio and Miguel were starting to get to their feet when I turned to Hammer, "What are you waiting for? Let's get out of here."

Again, he pushed the gas pedal to the floor and the engine raced, but the car didn't move. I looked down and saw that Hammer had his feet on both the pedals.

I screamed, *"Take your foot of the brake pedal and give it gas!"* As he let off of the brake, the Beamer took off.

Gregorio was ready to fire a shot at us when Lynn reached over and lowered his arm, "Too late for that. Get to my truck and phone our associates to intercept a Silver BMW heading east on Highway 26 towards Alpine."

She continued, "We have associates up there waiting for further instruction. Its part of the plan we had discussed last night before the boys showed up."

She turned to Gregorio, "How stupid of you to think that he had the key to the truck! I have a copy of it right here."

He was furious and shouted back, "How stupid of me, when you're the damn one that told them everything!"

He pointed his finger at her face and continued to scream, *"Never have I seen such ignorance in all of my life."* He took his pistol and waved it carelessly in the air.

Miguel jumped in "Not now. We have things to do. We can only hope our other associates are in place to stop those two."

Gregorio continued to glare at Lynn and she glared right back at him. He finally put his pistol back into his holster and returned to her truck to make the call. Lynn spit on the ground, "We've got to get this truck out of here. We only have a few hours to prepare for our drop-off."

In the meantime, Hammer and I were racing down the road towards the dam. I kept glancing out the back window and noticed they were not following us. I reached over and put on my seatbelt and told him to do the same.

"We need to head to Alpine. There's a state police station up there and we can notify the authorities."

"Great. I have a surprise for you."

"What is it?"

"When I left the restaurant, I picked up the book and envelope that Anthony gave to you."

"You're kidding me? What a stroke of genius that was. Where is it?"

"It's tucked into the back of my shirt."

He took his hands off of the steering wheel and began to reach for the book. The car slowly drifted to the left.

I yelled, "Keep your eyes on the road and your hands on the steering wheel!"

Hammer's driving was pretty erratic as he kept punching the gas and then taking his foot off of the pedal. He also had a hard time staying in the right lane as the car swerved back and forth. To any casual observer, it would look like he was drunk as a skunk driving down the road. But overall, he did a good job of driving for his first time. We were at the base of the dam and started heading up the hill to the top when I looked back one last time to see if we were being followed. As I did so Hammer also turned around and the car quickly drifted into the left lane.

Coming in the opposite direction was a large bus carrying tourists from Jackson Hole, Wyoming. The bus driver had noticed us drifting and jammed on his brakes causing the bus to lose control and skid down the highway. I was in the process of turning back around when I noticed that Hammer was in the wrong lane and that a bus was now heading sideways straight for us, I yelled, *"Hit the brakes!"*

He turned back around and saw the bus coming towards us and slammed the brake pedal down. The Beamer began screeching to a halt, but it was too late. As we crashed into the side of the bus, all four airbags instantaneously deploying as we rocketed forward. My already bruised face sunk deep into the airbag as the bus and car grounded to a halt.

It must have been several seconds before I regained consciousness. Hammer had already exited the Beamer. He had several cuts and bruises to his forehead, chin and arms. As he was running over to my side of the car to checkup on me, I opened my eyes. I thought we had died and gone to hell because he was standing over me with blood dripping off of the cuts he had sustained. He smiled when he saw me open my eyes.

"Are you okay?"

It took me a moment to remember what had just happened. "How's Del's car?" I asked.

"Well big buddy, it looks better than your face does right now."

My bruised left cheek actually did not sustain any worse damage than what Lynn had afflicted on it a short time ago. But the right side of my face was now severely bruised with several scratches from the top of my forehead to the bottom of my jaw from where my face scraped against the air bag when it deployed. Between the crash, Lynn's beating, and Hammer's driving, I was a mess. However, we both could not complain. We were alive, thanks to the superior workmanship of Del's car. Had this accident taken place in 'Old Red' which had no airbags, we would probably be dead by now. I gently removed my self from the wreckage and looked at Del's car. It was totaled.

"He's going to kill us!" I screamed in agony,

"Naw. He has insurance. Besides, I noticed the car already had 9,000 miles on it."

"Hammer, 9,000 miles is nothing. It's still brand new."

Just then the bus driver came up to us. "Are you two okay?" he asked.

Hammer answered for the two of us. "Yes"

The driver, somewhat flustered said, "What in the hell were you doing driving on the wrong side of the road?"

"Sorry, just learning how to drive for the first time. Is everyone okay on the bus?"

"Yes. Fortunately, I saw you coming and had time enough to slow the bus down."

I looked at the bus and noticed that it was one of the Greyhound buses that make daily trips between Idaho Falls and Jackson Hole. The front end of the Beamer had hit the bus right in the middle, directly below the logo of a greyhound.

The driver looked at me and back at Hammer, "I need to get some help out here immediately. The two of you both look like you may need some medical attention, especially your friend there. Look at the way his face is swollen."

He looked at me and agreed with the driver. The driver took his cell phone from his shirt pocket and was in the process of punching in some numbers when I said, "I need to make a call."

I walked right up to him and snatched the cell phone from his hand.

"I'm sorry, but this call can't wait."

I hit the stop button on his cell phone and pressed the numbers to Del's cell phone and hit the send button. The phone rang twice, and on the third ring he picked up.

"Del, it's me Billy."

He could tell by the way I was talking that something was not right.

"What's wrong?"

Because my face was so swollen I could hardly hear a word he was saying.

"Your car is totaled, but there is a good explanation."

"I don't care about the car, how are you and Hammer doing?"

"We're okay, but we need your help immediately. Something important is going to happen this morning."

"No problem, but before you go any further, I have some very important news to share with you."

It was just then that I noticed the sheriff's police truck driving down the hill side with his lights flashing.

"Del, the sheriff is here. He'll be able to help. Do you remember The Great Feeder canal?"

"What?"

"Del, I'm having a hard time hearing you. The sheriff has just pulled up and I'll get him to explain everything to you."

As I removed the phone from my ear he screamed into the phone.

"Billy, Billy, wait. You need to know that there were twins."

I did not hear a word he said and raced over to the sheriff.

CHAPTER TWENTY-TWO

Hammer saw the sheriff coming as well and went straight towards him. We both got to his side at the same time. The sheriff asked, "Boys, what's going on?"

"Man, are we glad to see you. We have found a truck full of drugs and we need your help to stop Lynn and her friends," Hammer said.

"Wait a minute, one thing at a time. Are you boys okay?"

"I am. Not certain about Billy though. He looks like he could use a doctor"

"Alright, we'll get to that in a moment. What about the people on the bus?"

"The driver says that they are all fine."

"Good, I want the two of you to come with me to my truck."

We followed him to his truck. Opening the back cab area, he said, "Wait here for just a moment until I have talked with the bus driver."

He pushed the lock down on his door and went over to talk to the bus driver. We thought it was funny that he had locked us in but felt he knew what he was doing. It was a few seconds later that we noticed several other deputies pull up to the scene of the accident. The sheriff pointed at the wreck and the bus driver. He motioned to the other two deputies to the back of his truck. He made some other gestures and the two deputies began to assist in the cleanup of the wreck.

While the sheriff was giving directions I looked at Hammer, "You know; we're lucky the sheriff was so close by, we should be able to stop Lynn now that he's here."

He looked at me, "Billy, something doesn't seem right here. I thought the sheriff said he was going to fly to Chicago last night. What is he doing here?"

"Perhaps his flight was canceled."

"Maybe, but I'm not feeling good about the situation were in. Why did he lock the door?"

"I don't know, but I'll ask him."

The sheriff returned to the truck and opened the sliding window that separated us from him.

"The deputies should be able to get this mess under control."

I was going to ask him why he was not in Chicago when he said, "Just a moment Billy."

He phoned the sheriff's station and reported the accident. When he had finished he looked back at me, "Now what did you want to ask me?"

"Well, we thought you were going to be in Chicago, what happened?"

"Oh, I was going to go, but to be downright honest with you, I had more important business to attend to here in the valley."

"What kind of business?"

The sheriff's radio blared, "Just a moment."

He picked up the set. It was dispatch informing him that a wrecker had been contacted and would be out there in an hour or so.

"Good, when he gets here have him work directly with deputy Larson. Oh by the way, I will be out of radio contact for the next several hours."

Dispatch responded, "Rodger that, lets us know when you're back on line."

He adjusted his radio receiver to a different frequency, "Black Cobra, package has been picked up, no damage done."

Another voice came on the radio, "Copy that, deliver package to drop off site, great job."

The sheriff started his truck, "Fasten your seatbelt boys, I'm in a hurry."

He fastened his belt and began to drive towards Swan Valley. As he cautiously pulled by the bus, I looked out the back window at Del's BMW. It was crushed and we were lucky to be alive. I glanced up one more time at the bus and saw the Greyhound logo. It was then that I had another one of those strange feelings come over me.

The sheriff placed his radio back on the receiver, "Well, boys, what is this about Lynn and a truck full of drugs?"

I was going to tell him what we had just discovered but Hammer tapped me on my knee.

"Sheriff, before we tell you what we know, tell us what was more important than going to Chicago? It seems to me that a murder in these parts would take precedence over any other event?"

The sheriff shut the sliding glass window and secured it in place. He pressed an intercom switch on the dashboard that allowed him to communicate with us and said, "Well, I see you have figured it out. What about you, Billy? Where are you in all of this?"

I thought for a moment, "You were the other masked man Wednesday night. You helped murder Anthony. That would explain why you were the first to arrive on the scene. You really didn't go that far away after the shooting."

He grinned, "Lynn was right. The two of you are very clever."

"Clever enough to know that you must be the anonymous associate," Hammer snapped.

He made a quick move and tried to break the glass window to get at the sheriff. The window wasn't even phased by his effort.

"Hammer, I know you're one tough cookie. What you did to Carlos and Ruben not only once, but twice, is very impressive, but that window is made to withstand the force of ten people. So, my advice to you would be to settle down and save your energy."

The sheriff drove for several minutes until he reached the Snowball Café. He hit his blinkers and pulled behind the building. The sliding door was open and Lynn came strolling out. Peering through the window at us, she opened the front side door and climbed in.

"Great job, Sheriff. You sure have saved the day."

"Oh it was nothing. They ran into a bus up the road and made my job very easy."

She turned and gazed at us. "Boys, it's going to be tough to lose the two of you. You've made our lives very interesting these past few days. But I'll tell you this, you deserve a chance to she how we distribute our merchandize before we stage your little fishing accident."

She turned back to the sheriff, "Do you think they told anyone?"

"No, they didn't have enough time. I asked the bus driver if they said anything to him about why they were driving like idiots. He said, 'No the only thing they said to me was they were learning how to drive'."

"Good."

She rolled down her window and shouted, "Okay Gregorio, follow us to the restaurant."

As Gregorio drove their truck full of contraband cargo out of the Snowball Café, Miguel jumped into Lynn's truck. The sheriff pulled out onto the highway and Gregorio and Miguel followed. We drove down the highway a few miles and stopped at the Log House. According to the dashboard clock, it was now 9:00 a.m. Lynn hopped out and ran inside. She was gone for ten minutes when she reappeared with a couple of duffle bags, followed by Carlos and Ruben who were also carrying several duffle bags each. The bags appeared to be empty by the way they were carrying them. Carlos had placed several bandages on his broken nose to stop the bleeding and Ruben had an apparent limp from the beating he took at Hammer's hand.

Lynn signaled for Carlos and Ruben to ride with Miguel in her truck. She yelled at Miguel and Gregorio, who was still driving the truck full of drugs, "Follow us to the drop-off site."

She hopped back in the truck with the sheriff and off we went. We drove for about thirty minutes until we got to a turnoff in the road which indicated that there was a boat ramp two miles to our right. The convoy continued down the road and went by the turn off to the boat ramp and headed towards the Great Feeder canal.

CHAPTER TWENTY-THREE

In this particular location, three main feeder canals (and a smaller one that is rarely used) funnel water off of the Snake River for local farmers to water their crops. We passed the first feeder canal called 'Eagle Rock,' then the second by the name of 'Farmers Friend' and finally the smaller one with no name that is seldom used before arriving at the 'Great Feeder Canal'. The Great Feeder got its name from being the largest canal in the area. With eight spillways, it channels about thirty percent of the river's flow to the local farmers. The Great Feeder was originally built in 1916 and updated in 1967. Strategically placed where the river bends, it is here at this bend that about seventy percent of the water flows west past 'The Great Feeder' canal. Years ago, there use to be a boat ramp where the river bends, but it is no longer used as such.

Thousands of people fish this particular place. The Snake River is known for its fabulous cutthroats and throughout this area fly fishing is superb. An interesting event also takes place at 'The Great Feeder'. As the river bends west, one can continue floating the Snake River, but where this thirty percent of extra water flow enters the feeder canal, several thousand fish each year fail to continue with the main flow of the river and end up trapped within the canal system. Most fish like to swim upstream, so once entering the canal by mistake, they have a tendency to congregate at the mouth of the canal. In early spring and throughout most of the summer, the head gates of 'The Great Feeder' are turned wide open to allow the maximum flow of water through the canal. Towards the end of August or beginning of September, the farmers need for water is not as demanding and so 'The Great Feeder' will operate with anywhere from three to five head gates opened. When this happens, the fish have the opportunity to head back upstream more easily.

When a few of the gates are shut, an ideal pool of water is formed right at the base of the canal in which thousands of rainbow trout, browns and cutthroat gather. As they assemble in these pools, the fish will attempt to hurdle the rapids and get back to the main body of the Snake. You can sit for hours watching them dart out of the quieter pools and hit the main flow of the canal. It's much like a fish ladder, except the water roaring through these head gates is not conducive for the fish to successfully make it back upstream. Hundreds of fishermen fish these pools each year hoping to catch a nice size trout. Those who have been successful in landing the fish have caught some beautiful cutthroats well over seven pounds.

It has always been a struggle to catch the big fish here because once they're hooked, they have a tendency to head towards the faster water and downstream. If you try to force the fish back upstream, you more than likely will lose it. If you go downstream with the fish, you again run the risk of losing it because you have given it too much line or slack and more than likely, the fish will come unhooked. Once in the fast water, the fish has more than a sporting chance to escape. It takes patience and skill to land the big ones here. Indeed, in all of my time fishing this part of the river, I have only known two people to successfully catch the really big ones here. One of these individuals was my father. He enjoyed the quick trip form Idaho Falls to the feeders and always told me that you can catch just as many fish here than any other spot on the river.

Whenever we came this way to fish, we would first stop to check out 'The Great Feeder 'canal. It was like a sign. If the head gates were wide open, we knew the fishing that day may not be as good as when two or three of the head gates were turned down. No matter what the flow of water was through the canal, my father would always take a moment and at least cast his fly out once or twice. If there was no action, off we went.

I had often tried to catch the big fish here, but lacked the patience and skills to ever be too successful. I had brought Hammer here several times and he, like me, found it a difficult place to fly fish. The only other person that I was aware of who could fish this spot with consistent success was Del. When he visited us in June and July we brought him here and he did rather well, but I still have never seen a better fisherman at this spot than my father.

This area is also an ideal spot to enjoy the beauty of nature. Several bald eagles nest in the trees along the river and there is hardly a day that would go by that you wouldn't spot them overhead. Now, on this late August morning there was several people already fishing the canal and the river near the canal. There were also several boats that were anchored upstream, as well as one boat that was anchored right next to the old dilapidated boat ramp. According to the clock on the dashboard of the sheriff's truck it was exactly 9:58 a.m. when we pulled up.

The sheriff parked his truck next to a shed which housed an electric pump for the head gates. Gregorio, who was behind us, drove his truck past us and across 'The Great Feeder' bridge, slightly past the old boat ramp and then backed down the embankment to the cement platform below. Miguel, Carlos and Ruben also crossed the bridge in Lynn's truck and positioned it directly in front of the boat ramp, basically obscuring the view of anyone driving up the gravel road from the Hi-C area.

Lynn looked over her shoulder and proudly exclaimed, "Everyone you see here today works for me. Each person has an assignment. They may look like they're all fishing, but they're not."

She looked at her watch, "Perfect timing, its ten o'clock and we can prepare to unload the goods."

She turned to us, "Now if you boys promise to behave, I'll let you join us."

The sheriff immediately protested, "I don't think that is such a good idea. These two have been very difficult and have eluded us several times. If it wasn't for pure luck they may still be on the loose."

She smiled, "With all of our boys here, I doubt they will try anything too foolish, but if it makes you feel any better you can personally escort them at gunpoint across the bridge. After all, you are the sheriff. We will all vouch that they were causing a ruckus and you had to come and arrest them."

The sheriff reluctantly gave in. "Okay guys, get on out of the truck, but if you try to do anything stupid, I will shoot to kill."

We exited the truck and followed Lynn across the canal bridge. The sheriff was right behind us and he had his .45 out and ready to use it. We went down the boat ramp to the truck full of drugs. As we did so, the crew on the first boat that was anchored to the boat ramp waved at Lynn and began to drift downstream. She yelled, "See you guys later."

Then see barked at Gregorio and pointed at us.

"Put them to work. They can help unload the truck." Gregorio looked at us and then he said to me, "I can't wait until we're finished. You thought you kicked me in the balls hard, wait until I get my hands on you."

As he was removing the tarp from off the truck, we noticed that each box was labeled 'fishing supplies.' If anyone happened to pass by, they wouldn't suspect a thing. If they wanted to fish the canal, they would also see that it was extremely crowded and more than likely keep on driving, looking for a less crowded spot.

We started to unload some of the boxes and noticed that the first boat, which was anchored upstream, began to drift towards the ramp. The boat had three people aboard, two who looked like they were fishing, and a third who acted as their

8

guide. The boat drifted downstream until it came alongside the ramp. At the ramp, the guide threw out a line to Miguel. He took the line and brought the bow of the boat around and tied the line to a small metal bar alongside the ramp, the guide anchoring the stern of his boat to the ramp. Carlos and Ruben quickly took three boxes labeled fishing supplies down to the boat. The two fishermen took the boxes and carefully stowed them in their boat. Miguel grabbed one of the many duffle bags that were brought from the restaurant and handed it to the guide.

The guide opened his large tackle box and place several smaller items into the duffle bag. The smaller items looked like they could be stacks of hundred dollar bills. Miguel retrieved the duffle bag and placed it on the boat ramp. He and the guide had a few parting words and then he helped them untie the lines from the ramp. The guide pulled up anchor and the boat began to slowly drift downstream. The two fishermen picked up their poles and commenced to fish. It looked like any other boat on the river enjoying a beautiful summer day on the Snake.

Hammer and I could do nothing but helplessly watch while hundreds of thousands of dollars of drugs would float downstream to eventually end up in the mainstream of society. We felt that all of our hard fought effort and sacrifice was for nothing. We would be unable to follow-up on Anthony's dying request, "To Reveal the Truth." Lynn, the sheriff and the rest of their bunch of hooligans would be future millionaires while we would more than likely end up fish food.

Suddenly, one of the boats that had previously drifted downstream made a hasty retreat. The guide started the boat's engine and raced quickly back upstream towards us, while the two fishermen threw their poles into the boat and sat down for dear life. Everyone on the ramp stopped what they were doing to watch. The boat took about twenty seconds to reach us and when it did the guide cut the engine and yelled, "It's a trap! Every man for himself!"

Miguel yelled back, "What do you mean?"

"Downstream are about ten boats loaded with cops of all sorts. They're stopping all of us." He then started the boats engine and took back off upstream.

At the precise moment that the guide started back upstream, six state police cars came roaring up the gravel road from the main road and another four Jefferson County officers came racing down from the road that the sheriff had taken no more than thirty minutes earlier. Everyone who was innocently fishing moments ago began to flee in all directions. Some ran down the feeder canal while others took off into the woods.

Lynn began to scream and took off towards the truck still half full of boxes labeled fishing supplies. Carlos and Ruben both jumped into the river and began to swim to the other side. Miguel had three duffle bags full of money near him. He took two bags and ran up the boat ramp and threw them into the back of Lynn's truck. He jumped in, started the engine and gave it his best effort to dodge the six state patrol cars that were rapidly approaching. He made it by the first two, but the third forced him to swerve to the left causing him to dart up the small embankment and into one of the many trees by the edge of the road. He hit the first tree head on and his truck halted. The fourth state police car stopped and two officers jumped out, immediately running up to Miguel and ordering him out of the truck. Defeated, he opened the cab door and raised his hands up slowly.

During all of this upheaval, many events happened at the same time. Hammer and I were in the middle of the boat ramp near the truck with the drugs when Lynn rushed by us and jumped into the driver's seat of the truck. She started the engine and was in the process of putting the truck in gear.

Gregorio, who was standing a few feet away from me roared, "You bastard! I don't know how you did it, but somehow you did!"

He drew his gun and aimed it at me. He squeezed the trigger but Hammer, who had been watching all of this, slammed into me at the exact same time. The handgun fired, missing me but hitting him. Gregorio was prepared to shoot for a second time, but Hammer, who never stopped moving after knocking me down, was on top of him. He hit Gregorio at the precise moment that he was firing a second shot. The shock of the collision caused the shot to go astray. The wild shot went over me but hit Lynn while she was getting the truck into gear.

Hammer began to wrestle with Gregorio and a third shot was fired before he was able to wrestle the gun away. I was running up to help him when the pistol was jerked out of Gregorio's hand and fell towards me. Picking it up, I aimed it at him and yelled, *"Freeze!"*

Gregorio had blood on him and I wasn't sure if he'd been shot. "Lie on your stomach and don't move a muscle," I commanded him.

"Move away from Gregorio," I shouted to Hammer.

Hammer's shirt was covered with blood. He attempted to stand up and made it to one knee when he his legs buckled and he fell face down on the boat ramp and stopped moving.

"Hammer!" I screamed.

I went to help my friend when Gregorio leapt to his feet and tackled me. We both tumbled to the ground and the gun was jarred out of my hand. He reached for the weapon and as he did so I pulled him back towards me. I was now wrestling for my life with Gregorio.

He took both of his hands and slapped my already sore face. The pain was excruciating and I lost my grip on him. I remained on the ground while he crawled over to the pistol and picked it up. I forced myself to sit up just in time to see him turn around and look me in the eye.

"Now you'll finally get what you deserve."

He raised the revolver and a loud shot rang out. I flinched, but I didn't feel anything, it must have missed me. As I continued to look at him, his eyes glazed over and he dropped his gun. His body slumped over and he fell lifeless to the ground. Just then, I heard a familiar voice. It was Del's. He had shot him seconds before he would have shot me.

Lynn, trying to take advantage of the chaos to get away, put the truck in reverse instead of drive. Weak from being accidentally shot, she slumped over the steering wheel as the truck slowly backed towards the river. Sheriff Thompson, who was observing all of this, raced towards her. "Lynn, hang in there I'm coming."

He took hold of her arm as the truck entered the water and struggled to pull her out. Caught in the seatbelt and in a frantic panic, she was fighting harder than a freshly caught fish.

"Help me, Rick!"

He shrieked in agony and went in after her. For a short while the truck floated downstream, but the current was strong and the truck soon sank. The sheriff went under with the truck trying to release her but was soon tangled up with her and the seatbelt, both disappearing under the fast flowing water.

Del ran up to me. "Are you okay?"

I could hardly speak. My entire body was throbbing from all of the beatings that I had suffered through, during the morning hours. I looked at him and cried, "What about Hammer?"

Del raced over to him and felt his pulse. It was weak. He yelled at one of the state police officers to call in the ambulances. Several of them had been dispatched with the rest of the party, but were instructed to wait at a safe distance until they were summoned.

"Is he alive?"

Del responded, "Yes, but he's lost a lot of blood. We've got to get him and you to the hospital immediately."

Again he yelled at the state trooper, "We need to get a medical airlift out here on the double."

The trooper nodded and made the call. Several other officers came down and assisted us. We laid on the boat ramp for several minutes before the first ambulance arrived. The two paramedics raced over to Hammer and began to assist with his injuries. Hooking up an IV to his arm, they worked quickly at stopping the bleeding. It appeared that he had taken a shot directly in the chest area above his heart when he knocked me over. Even though he was seriously injured, he still managed to stop Gregorio from shooting me. He fought valiantly, but now he lay critically injured on a boat ramp twenty-seven miles from the nearest medical facility. I owed my life to him.

As I was watching them help him, I found myself extremely faint. I heard one of the state troopers shout out, "Over here—he's passing out…"

Chapter Twenty-Four

I awoke and found myself in a hospital bed. I was in the Eastern Idaho Medical Facility. As I looked around my room I saw Del, who was sitting in a chair reading a book. He noticed me stirring and put the book down. He stood up, "My God, you had us worried. You've been unconscious for the past two days."

I wanted to ask him how Hammer was but could not find the strength to even open my mouth. He knew, however, what I wanted to ask him.

"Brace yourself, Hammer is…," but before he could say another word I mustered the strength to say, "Dead."

"No, what made you think that? I was going to tell you that he is doing better than you are. The bullet wound was clean and went right on through him without inflicting much damage. He passed out on the boat ramp due to the loss of blood. Once we airlifted the two of you to the hospital, the doctors gave him three and a half pints of blood and he was up and about the next day. However, you are not so lucky. It appears that during the car crash you sustained some internal injuries and had some serious bleeding. The doctors have miraculously fixed you up, but it will be another week or so before they even consider letting you out of the hospital."

Del continued, "Hammer told me everything that happened to the two of you since you left my hotel room early Saturday morning. He let me know about the beating that you took from Lynn, but that both of you were very brave, kept your cool, and said nothing. He also told me about how she put a gun to your kneecap and was going to shoot you. Furthermore, he described his escape from Carlos and Ruben and how he re-obtained the book and envelope. It sounds like the two of you went through a great deal of pain to bring the sheriff and Lynn to justice."

I nodded my head.

"I know you are probably wondering what happened to the rest of the gang at the river, so lay back and listen to what I have to say. First off, when you called me you asked me if I remembered 'The Great Feeder'. I answered you by saying what? I thought you had something more to say but instead you told me that the sheriff was pulling up and that he would explain the rest of it to me. I shouted at you that there were twins, but you apparently didn't hear me. You see Billy, I told you that I was waiting on some additional information and that I expected to receive it sometime early Saturday morning."

Del took the chair he was previously sitting in and slid it next to my bed.

"Around 7:00 a.m. the hotel contacted me and told me that I had received several faxes. I went down to the front desk and grabbed them, curious to find out more information about Lynn. It appears that she told you boys some of the truth but not all of it. She told you that she was an only child but she lied. She was actually the second child. The first was a baby boy born about fifteen minutes before she was. All went well in delivering the first child but there were some complications on the second. The doctors struggled with her delivery and it left permanent scars. This would explain some of her deformities."

I held my hand up for him to stop and with great effort, I tried to sit up. Del, seeing my predicament, reached over and adjusted the bed until it was in an upright position. Once I was more comfortable, he carried on with the story.

"Let's see, where was I? Oh yeah, Lynn's birth. The delivery was also very costly on her mother's health and she passed away a week after that. Her father, being unable to cope with the loss of his wife and with two babies barely a week old decided to place both kids up for adoption. Because of Lynn's deformities, he knew it would be difficult for her to be adopted, so he stipulated that whoever was to adopt his children would have to adopt both of them. Well, a wonderful couple came along that could not have kids of their own and they adopted both her and her brother.

"Her adopted parents did die in a tragic accident, but it wasn't a mining accident. They were driving home late one evening when her adopted father fell asleep at the wheel. This terrible accident took place a month after Lynn and her brother had graduated from high school. They had always been very close and throughout their younger years, he protected her. He was very popular in school and played on the football and basketball team. But Lynn, because of her deformities, was not so well liked."

"Once their adopted parents died, they grew even closer to one another. Together they traveled the country in search of work. It didn't matter what they did or how good they were at it, they kept getting laid off, mainly because of Lynn's appearance. They finally knew something had to change so they went their separate ways. Her brother moved to Eastern Idaho and got into law enforcement. Within a very short period of time he became the local sheriff. You and Hammer knew him as Sheriff Thompson. When I asked you to go to the police, I meant it. But if you recall, I told you that I was glad you didn't because of a growing concern that several officers here in Eastern Idaho may be operating above the law. No one has been able to identify them until now but there was an underlying feeling that they are involved in some serious drug dealings. You may have inadvertently told one of these crooked officers what you knew and that would have stopped everything you and Hammer had accomplished."

"Do you remember when I was going to tell you about Mr. Jackson, the reporter who was killed?

I nodded my head.

"You said you knew he was a reporter. I asked how you knew this. You said the sheriff told you. Well, when I had talked to Mr. Anderson, the manager at the Chicago Herald, he specifically told me that he had not shared any of this information with anyone else. I thought it was strange that the sheriff told you he was going to Chicago. I found it even more bizarre when you told me on the phone that the sheriff was there and he would explain everything to me. To make matters worse, he never called me to explain anything. There were just too many coincidences involving the sheriff. I had a very strong feeling that Sheriff Thompson must be up to his neck in this whole affair."

"You see, after the sheriff came here, he got involved immediately with the wrong elements. They assisted him in becoming a sheriff quickly and he in return assisted them in filtering their drugs into the local communities. The sheriff invited Lynn to come to Eastern Idaho. He convinced her to assist him in running the entire operation. Together, they came up with the restaurant idea. It was brilliant and everything was going according to plan until Mr. Jackson, or Anthony, as he is better known around these parts, came along."

"They had a rather ingenious plan and it all looked just like innocent people fishing the river. The first boat would drift downstream for several hours to its designated drop off point. From there they would funnel their boxes of fishing supplies to an assortment of runners who would then transport their shipment throughout the Northwest. In essence, the drugs had been successfully seasoned. Any contact with its original source would all but be impossible to prove. Who would ever suspect that these innocent fishermen were a key part of the successful drug smuggling ring that hand now been operating in Eastern Idaho for several years?"

"As soon as the first boat drifted downstream, the second boat would begin the journey. Even further upstream were other boats that would begin the same process. They would leave their spot on the river and drift down to where the boat in front of them had just left. After a very short period of time, they would begin drifting again until they finally reached the boat ramp. At the boat ramp they would follow the very same procedures as the first boat did. This was orchestrated to perfection and there were a total of twenty-one boats involved in the entire process. Again, to the casual observer, it would appear that they were just fishing various spots along the river."

"Some boats would take only two boxes and others would take as many as six. This way, if anyone got caught, only a small part of each shipment would be lost. Each time, the duffle bags would also exchange hands with the guide of each boat paying for their part of the shipment when they received it. What they did after that was their business. Lynn and Sheriff Thompson were just the suppliers and the guides were their distributors. It was a well oiled machine and hundreds of people made this yearly pilgrimage. Lynn and the sheriff were making a fortune until Anthony and the two of you came along.

"Anthony was able to disrupt the entire operation. He successfully made off with their merchandise and was about ready to reveal the entire plot, but before he could do so, he was discovered and went into hiding. That's where you and Hammer came into the picture. The two of you did a fantastic job in decoding Anthony's message. Like I said, when you told me 'The Greet Feeder', I at first was stumped. But I remembered you taking me there to fish. It was a beautiful and somewhat secluded spot. I immediately contacted some friends of mine with the local FBI and Idaho State Police. I explained what I felt was happening and where it would happen. We formed a group of about forty trusted officers in a short period of time along with the Jefferson County deputies. As you may remember, we showed up just in the nick of time."

I looked at Del and managed to ask him, "What about Lynn and the others?"

"When she saw us coming, she must have decided to try to escape with the remaining drugs. She went for the truck and was about ready to flee the scene. However, from the reports that I have gathered, she was shot by Gregorio when he was wrestling with Hammer. The shot must have seriously injured her because, instead of driving up the boat ramp to escape, the truck slowly drifted backwards towards the river. When the sheriff saw that his sister was hurt, he went to rescue her. Together they were pulled under by the weight of the truck. The truck was towed out of the river about two hours later. We thought that they would be found with the truck, but were not. They are presumed drowned and a search is currently underway to locate their bodies. Up to this point, they have not yet been found. The drugs aboard the truck floated downstream and were seized by officers stationed in several boats down river."

"As far as the others, Ruben tried to make off with several duffle bags of cash. He made it past the first two officers but once he wrecked his vehicle, it was over for him. Carlos and Miguel made it safely across the river and took off through the trees. They went north for several miles and might have made it if it wasn't for two Fish and Game officers who were inspecting licenses and heard through the radio dispatch that several armed and dangerous men were on the loose. They had just finished giving a citation to a guy from Utah who was fishing without a non-resident fishing license when Carlos and Miguel ran across the road in front of them. Appearing out of place, the two Fish and Game officers immediately went after them."

"Gregorio, as you may remember, was trying to shoot you. I got him first. I only wanted to wound him, but felt if I had done so, he might still be able to get a shot off at you. We caught several other people who were serving as lookouts as well as ten boats full of illegal drugs and their passengers. Unfortunately, we think that potentially thirty to forty other suspects may have escaped. The local authorities are hoping that some of the others who have been captured will come clean, but so far they have all kept quiet. It appears that this particular drug ring is backed by three major international dealers. Past experience with these dealers indicate that anyone caught talking would be killed, including their families. Thankfully, Anthony's detailed notebook would deal a severe blow to these organizations…if we could find it. Some believe it may not exist; but according to Anthony's boss, it does. I guess time will tell."

Just then, the doctor came into the room. His name badge read Dr. Ted Epperson, a local physician who was well respected by his peers and throughout the community.

"Glad to see you're awake. You had us all pretty scared, especially your two friends. I almost had to hog tie the one down. Even though he was shot and lost a lot of blood, all he could talk about was you and insisted on visiting you. I told him that as soon as you're awake, I would allow him to make a short visit. That is, if it is alright with you."

I liked this doctor immediately. He had a good bedside manner and I could tell he really cared for his clients'. I whispered, "Please let him know that I'm awake."

"I will as soon as I am done here."

He turned to Del, "Now that he's awake, I strongly recommend that you get some sleep."

The doctor smiled at me, "He's been like a little puppy. Over the past two days, he hasn't left this hospital. Between you and your friend, he hasn't had five minutes to himself."

Del grinned, "They both mean so much to me."

"The power of friendship," Doctor Epperson said.

He took my blood pressure, reviewed the bruises on my face, and examined the stitches in my belly from where they had to do an emergency operation to stop the internal bleeding. After he pressed the call button for the nurse, he wrote a few notes on the chart. Dr. Epperson was checking my pulse when a beautiful brunette nurse walked into the room. She must have been about twenty-four and could have easily passed as a movie star. I quickly glanced and noticed she had no wedding ring on.

The doctor smiled when he saw the nurse, "You literally made his heart skip a beat when you walked into the room."

The nurse blushed. "What can I do for you, doctor?"

"Would you please bring some Jell-O and crackers for our patient here and while you're at it, ask his friend what he would like to have."

The nurse replied she would be happy to do so. As she walked around to the other side of the bed to check my water bottle, I noticed her name was Gladys, an appropriate name for someone so beautiful. She smiled at me and turned to Del to see what he would like to have.

Gladys turned to Del, "What can I get for you?"

"I would like a large turkey sandwich."

As she was talking to Del, the doctor said "There you go again, you made his heart skip yet another beat."

This time I must have blushed, because the doctor continued, "And look at those cheeks. I've never seen them so red."

Doctor Epperson, still grinning, finished checking all of my vital signs and turned to write some notes on my chart.

"I'm going to Hammer's room next. I expect he will be in here as soon as I tell him you're okay."

Doctor Epperson shook Del's hand and left the room. Just as the doctor predicted, Hammer came bursting through the door with a giant smile and ran up to my bed.

"You don't know how worried I have been about you. I thought you were going to die."

With great difficulty, I replied, "And I thought you had died."

Del joined us, "Well guys, I think the two of you have something special between you. You both have just solved a giant mystery, visited death, and have returned to talk about it.

But more importantly, you have established a friendship that will last forever."

Hammer reached over and gave Del a big hug. "And you have just inherited our loyalty forever. We wouldn't be alive today if it wasn't for your fast thinking."

Del and Hammer continued to talk while I basically nodded my head and occasionally let out a groan or two. Gladys came back with some Jell-O and crackers for me and a large turkey sandwich for Del.

"I hope strawberry Jell-O is your favorite?" she said.

Then turning to Del, "I made sure the chef in the kitchen made you a fresh sandwich. I brought some chips as well."

Finally, turning to Hammer, she asked, "Is there anything you would like?"

"No, I ate already, but thanks for asking. The sandwich does look better than what I had though! Matter of fact, I'm not even sure what it really was!"

Laughing, she said, "I can't argue that point. And by the way, you're welcome."

She walked over to my bed and picked up the water jug and poured some water into the glass by the side of my bed.

"If you need anymore crackers or Jell-O, just press the yellow button."

She took hold of the plastic cord that was attached to the wall and placed it near me, gave me a little wink and left the room. I am more than certain that my heart skipped two beats and was pleased that the doctor wasn't there to tell the whole world.

As the door shut, Hammer said, "Wow I think she likes you."

Del chipped in, "I think so, too. I could tell by the way she said 'If you need anymore crackers just page her'."

I mustered up enough strength to say, "Oh knock it off you two."

They both broke out laughing.

Hammer could not keep quiet the whole time we were eating. He kept chatting about how we had discovered the drugs and all we went through. Then in a very serious tone, "I have never done something like this in my entire life. It feels good to have done something worthwhile. This is definitely something I will never forget."

As he continued rambling, Doctor Epperson returned to the room.

"Okay guys, enough for now. I want Billy to get some rest. Hammer, I also want you to get back to your room. Just because you think you're okay doesn't mean you are. After all, you were shot no more than two days ago."

"Can't I stay just a little longer?" he complained.

"No, say goodnight to your friends. You can have breakfast together tomorrow morning."

He gave in. "See you tomorrow buddy."

Grabbing the nurse's call button, and in a scratchy, high pitched voice, he mockingly said, "Just hit that if you need me."

Smiling, he turned around and gave Del another hug.

He turned towards the doctor. "See you later gator." And off he went.

Doctor Epperson remarked, "That's some kind of special friend. Most people who have been shot like he was would take at least a month to recover, yet he looks like he stubbed his toe."

The Doctor turned to Del. "Okay, enough is enough. We have allowed you to stay here for two days. If you stay any longer we will have to bill your insurance. I called my wife and told her we were going to have company tonight, so grab your stuff and come with me."

He finally turned to me, "Now if you really do need something, don't be afraid to call the nurse."

He then lowered his voice, "By the way, I think she must like you. I've never seen her blush before. Now get some sleep."

The doctor put his arm around Del's shoulder and escorted him to the door. He was about ready to turn the lights out when he stopped and looked at me. "Seriously, if you really do need anything, be sure to page the nurse."

I reached over and took hold of my water glass and slowly drank the cool liquid. It felt good to have a little food in my stomach. I began to think about all of the things that had transpired over the past six days. I was grateful for my friends. Slowly, I shut my eyes and soon fell asleep. It seemed liked I was only asleep for a few minutes when I heard the door to my room open and the lights come on. I glanced toward the door and saw Anthony. He walked over to my bed and took one of the crackers that I had not eaten.

"You boys did a great job. You have succeeded where I could not."

I could tell by his voice and expression that he was genuinely proud of us.

While eating the cracker, he reached for the water jug, filling my glass full of water and then one for himself. He pulled one of the chairs close to my bed and sat down.

He took a long sip of water and began to speak.

"You know Billy, it's been a pleasure working with you and Hammer. I'm afraid this will be the last time that I ever come to visit you. I just had to remind you that you're not quite done yet. Yes, you have stopped Lynn and her gang from delivering their goods, but there will be others that take their place if you don't reveal the entire truth. Tomorrow morning when you wake up, take a moment and finish what I started. You have all of the clues you need. So, my friend, thanks for helping me."

He took one more cracker and popped it in his mouth. "Not bad for hospital food." He turned and walked towards the door. As he reached the door, he paused for a moment. "Oh, one last thing. Be careful."

He opened the door, reached over, and flipped off the lights. The door slowly shut as Anthony faded away forever.

I found myself sitting up in bed. I was sweating and swore that Anthony had been in my room. I reached over and pressed the yellow button, hoping that Gladys would come in and tell me she saw Anthony. She opened the door and turned on the light. She came up to me and asked, "What can I do for you young man?"

As my eyes grew accustomed to the sudden change in light, I noticed that the nurse was not Gladys, but instead an elderly lady by the name of Lois. She was polite but not who I had hoped to see. I still asked her, "Who was the man that just left my room?"

She glanced around, "You must have been dreaming. I have been the only person on the floor for the past two hours. No one has come or gone."

She placed her left hand on my forehead. "You appear to be sweating."

She took a thermometer from her vest and checked my temperature.

"You're running a slight fever."

She opened the closet door and brought over two extra blankets, wrapping them tightly around me.

"Now get some rest."

She turned the lights out and shut the door. I knew I had talked to Anthony even though it was just a dream. I must admit I was quite relieved by his comment that he would not be back. I knew we had not revealed all of the truth yet because he had enough information hidden somewhere to do serious damage to several major drug rings. Perhaps Hammer, Del and I could figure out what that last clue meant which would help bring those who did manage to escape to justice. I also had to admit that I wondered what he meant by 'Be careful'. It sure appeared to me that we had removed most of the key players, at least here locally. As I was mulling over all of these thoughts, my eyes got heavy and again I was asleep.

CHAPTER TWENTY-FIVE

I awoke around 9:00 a.m. to both Del and Hammer, who were waiting patiently for me to stir. Once they saw me moving, they stood up, and walked over to the bed. When I finally opened my eyes they both greeted me with a smile. Del spoke first. "I'll bet you're hungry."

I found it much easier to talk since the swelling in my face was nearly gone.

"I'm starving. I would love to have some bacon and eggs, maybe a couple of pieces of toast as well."

Hammer jumped in, "Well, press the little yellow button, we're all hungry! We've been waiting for over an hour for you to wake up."

I pressed the button and in came yet another nurse. Her name badge said, Sandy. Walking up to my bed, she asked, "What can I do for you three?"

Del ordered for us. "We would like to place an order for breakfast. We would like to have eggs, toast, bacon, pancakes, juice, sweet rolls, the works."

Sandy chuckled. "Sounds like we have some hungry people here. Give me about ten minutes or so and I'll be back with some food."

She took the water jug, refilled my glass, and left the room carrying the jug.

About fifteen minutes later, an orderly came into the room pushing a cart loaded with food. There was everything imaginable; bacon, ham, eggs, toast, juice, pancakes, fruit and even some sweet rolls. The orderly adjusted my bed and placed me in a sitting position. Del and Hammer slid the table in the room over to the bed and the three of us began to eat. For about four minutes no one said anything. We were all too busy eating. While I was eating, I thought to myself, *Not bad for hospital food.*

I took a moment and thought about where I had heard those words before? Then it hit me last night. Anthony, in my dream, had used those exact words. It caused me to snigger. Del and Hammer both looked at me. Del put down his glass of orange juice.

"Okay, are you going to tell us what you're laughing about, or is it some secret?"

I finished chewing the piece of bacon that I had in my mouth.

"The two of you won't believe who visited me last night?"

Now this comment peaked their curiosity and they both put their forks down in almost perfect unison.

"Anthony visited me last night."

Hammer let out a slow whistle, he then turned to Del.

"Do you realize, this makes the third time that Anthony has visited Billy? I'm starting to think we have a psychic amongst us."

I took a piece of toast from off my plate and threw it at him. He looked at me with big puppy dog eyes, "What did I say?"

"You know very well what you said, I'm not crazy."

"I never said you were crazy. Maybe a little wacko, but not crazy."

Del interrupted. "Okay, boys. So what did he have to say this time?"

"He told me that he was proud of us. He also told me to finish the job, to reveal the rest of the truth."

"So tell us, what do you think he meant by that."

"Well, I think we must already have the final clue. We just need to take sometime and work through it."

Del finished his glass of juice. "Okay, so what clues do we have?"

"Well, we have the scrambled message. It told us that the truck was at the Snowball Café. It also told us about using the key you found '*if with the old gray dog.*' The old gray dog must have some serious meaning. If we focus in on the last clues, we should be able to decipher what he meant."

Just then, there was a knock at the door. Before anyone could say 'come in', the door swung open and three men entered the room. The first two, wearing every day clothes, had their badges out and identified themselves as detectives. The third was wearing a dark blue suit and identified himself as the county prosecutor.

The prosecutor said, "I hope we're not interrupting, but we have quite a few people in the county jail. They are all claiming to be innocent victims of a sting operation. We will need to get some kind of testimony form the three of you if we have any hope of keeping them locked up. If not, we may have to let a lot of them go."

The detectives, continuing on, were saying that they had been working undercover on this case for the past three years.

Del, knowing that this might take awhile, spotted an orderly walk by and asked him if he would be kind enough to bring in some extra chairs. The orderly nodded his head and within minutes had procured three extra chairs for our guests. We spent the next hour filling them in on most of the pertinent details, making sure that we did not tell them about the book and envelope that Anthony had given me. We also did not tell them about the hidden message *Use key if with the old gray dog* and the number 14. Those were still two clues that we had to discover first before we would tell anyone the whole story. They asked us several questions with regards to where Anthony's alleged book may be, implying that without this book, the case against most of them was very weak. The prosecutor emphasized that most of them would probably go free.

When they were finished, the prosecutor proudly proclaimed, "Oh, by the way, you three are officially considered heroes. A big article is coming out in the paper tomorrow highlighting your efforts in halting this large shipment of illegal drugs. Furthermore, it appears that Governor Stevens is coming out here tomorrow afternoon as well to officially award the three of you with the State Citation of Valor and a substantial reward for your efforts in foiling the cartel's attempt at transporting illegal drugs through the state. Indeed, all the major networks have paid special mention to what took place here in the last couple of days. They are planning on interviewing the three of you. Perhaps that is the real reason the governor cut short his vacation. You know, it never hurts to have a little free publicity, especially during an election year."

The county prosecutor stood up and motioned to the other two to do likewise.

"We have a lot of work to do. We'll stay in touch."

After the three of them left the room, Hammer stood up.

"Wow, can you believe that we're heroes? I wonder how much the reward is for. If it's a lot, I would like to buy a boat."

Del joined in, "I'm not certain if it will be much, but if it is, I would like to buy another Beamer."

Hammer quickly sat back down. "We're sorry about your car. I guess I shouldn't have been driving, or at the very least, I should have paid better attention to what I was doing."

I too felt guilty for the mess we made out of Del's car.

"Yes, it is a shame about your car. You should have seen it smashed into that great big bus. I still remember driving away in the sheriff's truck. I made sure I took one last look at it."

As I said this, I stopped talking. I had a strong feeling that went through my body. My mind began to piece together the final clue.

When they saw my expression change, they knew something was up. Hammer whispered, "That's the way he looked when he figured out the poem."

Del nodded. "And that's the way he looked when he stared at my room number and figured out the code, so Billy what gives? What great thing did you discover this time?"

With immense pleasure I smirked, "I think I know the final clue."

"Because you looked out the sheriff's truck at Del's Beamer one last time, you figured it out?" Hammer asked,

"Yes, I think I did. What kind of vehicle did you hit?"

"I hit a bus."

"Correct, and where was that bus heading?"

"I think the sign in the front window said Idaho Falls."

"Yes, you're right again. And what abbreviation do the local people use for Idaho Falls?"

"They call it I.F."

"Now think really hard, do you remember the animal that was painted on the side of the bus?"

"Yes it was a dog. I think you call them greyhounds?"

"That's exactly right. So my point is that Del's car ended up hitting the bus directly below the logo of the greyhound. The bus company is called Greyhound and they use the logo of a gray dog to signify that they get you across the country quickly. In addition, the bus company has been around for along time."

Del interrupted, "So you mean, 'If with old gray dog' represents the city of Idaho Falls and the Greyhound bus company is somehow involved?"

"Yes, you're both right. I feel that Anthony's hidden information will be at the Idaho Falls bus station."

Hammer pondered this idea for a moment. "But where at the bus station?"

"I'll give you another clue. Do you both remember the numbers that Anthony repeated to me just before he died?"

Del said, "Yes you said he said 9, 3, 9, 14."

"Exactly, but he paused at the end of the second 9. This was his way of telling us that 14 had nothing to do with 9, 3, 9. He knew that Lynn was listening in. He didn't know who she was, but he still had to do his best to tell as few people as possible. When I saw your hotel room number it triggered my subconscious mind and we deciphered the code. Talking about the car wreck has done the same thing. "If with old gray dog" stands for the Idaho Falls bus station. I'm willing to bet that there are lockers inside the terminal. Number 14 will be the locker number and the key that I found will unlock it."

"Wow," said Hammer.

"You really do have some off-the-wall visions. Perhaps this is a special talent or something. You know, the kind that helps you see into the future."

"Hammer, you make me out to be some freak or something."

"Not at all. While I was in prison, I've read about people that have had special gifts given to them after they have had some strange occurrence in their lives. Like you, you had your father die in your arms and then Anthony. How often does that happen? Perhaps it took Anthony's death for you to realize you have this gift."

"I don't feel like I have any gift, I just get strange feelings at times."

"Strange is right," said Del. "Strange enough for you to see dead people, not just once, but three times."

"Come on guys, you make me out to be some sort of wizard."

"Not at all, Billy. We undeniably think this is something special. Something so unusual that you should be able to use it to do good, isn't that right Hammer?"

"Yes, exactly that. Don't take this wrong, Billy. This is a good thing."

I took a moment to study their facial features. I wanted to assure myself that they were not placating me. Once I established their sincerity in words and appearance, I proceeded to enlighten them on my point of view.

"Good thing or not, we still need to finish what Anthony started. It sounds like the governor is coming to town to make us heroes. What do you say to us personally delivering to him Anthony's hidden information? Wouldn't that make for a great ending? Here is the governor of Idaho, revealing to the press that we have been instrumental in shutting down several cartels. Let's go and get the hidden information right now!"

Hammer leapt to his feet. "I'm in. Let's go!"

Del looked at the two of us.

"I don't think the two of you are going to be up to doing that today. The doctor said it might still be another four to five days before he would even consider letting you leave the hospital."

"A team of wild horses couldn't keep me away. With you being with us, what could go wrong?" I shouted.

Del frowned. "Hopefully nothing."

He paused for a few moments to collect his thoughts. "I'll go by myself today and check out the bus station. The two of you will stay here and rest. If all goes well, then I will take the both of you tomorrow morning with me to get the information. After reviewing it, and if it looks promising, we will give it to the governor."

Hammer added, "Sounds like a terrific plan."

I deliberated for a split second, "Let's keep this between the three of us until we have Anthony's information in hand."

Del nodded his head. "Look, it sounds like a lot of people will be in town for the rest of the week to interview the two of you. Don't talk with the press until after I get back. I'm going to go and run some errands and check the bus station out. I'll be back sometime this afternoon."

He was headed towards the door when Hammer shouted out, "Be careful, partner."

Del stopped at the door for a second and was about to say something to Hammer when he looked my way. "What's wrong, Billy? You're giving me that look again."

"There is one thing I forgot to tell the two of you. The very last thing Anthony told me in my dream before he walked out the door."

"And what might that be?"

"He said what Hammer just said, 'To be careful'."

Del took his hand and rubbed his chin several times. "Hmm, I wonder what he meant by that. I will be careful, and the two of you do the same."

Chapter Twenty-Six

Hammer and I spent the remainder of the day resting in the hospital. We had several visitors from the press who wanted to interview us, but as previously agreed upon, we were waiting for the last bit of information before we talked to anyone. We asked the doctor on duty to tell the press that we were still recuperating from our injuries and that hopefully tomorrow afternoon we would be available to answer any questions they may have.

Around two-thirty in the afternoon, we did have one visitor that we warmly welcomed. It was Gladys. She was scheduled to work at three p.m., but came in early to give us a gift. She had purchased a jig saw puzzle.

"When I was out shopping I couldn't help but feel that the two of you needed something more to do then watch TV all day long. I saw this interesting puzzle and knew that it would help relax you and make the time pass more quickly," she explained, handing the box to me.

"Thanks Gladys. This is really nice. We'll start piecing it together right now."

She slightly blushed and looked at her watch.

"I've got to run. Otherwise I will be late for my shift."

She headed straight for the door and down the hallway to check in. Hammer took the puzzle from out of my hands and began to gently open the box.

"I told you, she really does like you."

It was now my turn to blush.

Meanwhile, Del was busy all day long. Visiting several of his friends who worked with the FBI and the state police, he was trying to discover more about the local law enforcement and their potential involvement with Lynn and the sheriff. He also made various visits to the local authorities. Finally, after obtaining as much information as possible, he went to the Idaho Falls bus station. Examining the layout of the facility, it appeared like most small town bus stations. On the outside, it had two bays for the buses to park and the inside had a small ticket counter and several benches for people to sit on while waiting for their buses. A number of vending machines full of soda, candy bars and fast food snacks lined the walls. As Del kept looking around, he noticed a sign that read 'Restrooms' off to the right and to the left was another similar hallway in which a sign read 'Lockers'.

Del laughed quietly to himself, "*That Billy is very sharp.*"

He walked down the corridor on the left to a glass door with 'Employees Only' written in big letters on the door. He tried looking through the glass door but could not see anything, so he just opened the door and entered the room. *I'm a cop. What are they going to do? Throw me in jail for trespassing?*

The room was dark and he fumbled for a light switch. After a second or two, he found the switch and flipped on the lights. He immediately saw several boxes that were stacked against the far wall. Just to the left of the boxes, he saw eight lockers and to the right of the boxes he saw another eight lockers, sixteen in all. They stood about seven feet tall and were at least two feet wide. The lockers on the left were numbered one to eight and the ones on the right were numbered nine to sixteen. He was about ready to walk up to locker fourteen when he heard the door open behind him. He rapidly wheeled around and saw a very large man wearing a Greyhound bus station shirt. This man seemed to be out of place. He looked more like a professional body guard and his demeanor was hostile.

"What are you doing here?" he growled.

Not wanting to cause a scene, Del apologized. "I'm sorry I must be lost. I thought the bathrooms were down here."

The huge man glared at him. "Can't you read? This room is for employees only. The toilets are down the other hallway."

Del again apologized and attempted to get by the man who was now blocking the door. He sheepishly looked up, "Excuse me sir, I really do need to use the men's room and if you don't move, I'm afraid I might have an accident."

The giant man continued to glare angrily at him and then stepped aside. Del straightaway left the room and began walking down the hallway with the man following closely behind him. Del did not want to give this person any reason to doubt him so he went down the corridor on the right and entered the bathroom. Even as he entered the bathroom, he noticed that this oversized man was paying close attention to his every move.

Once in the bathroom, he decided to take advantage of an opportunity to relieve himself. When he had finished, he washed and dried his hands and headed for the door. As he left the bathroom, he noticed the huge man was talking to two suspicious looking individuals. One of them noticed Del leave the bathroom. As Del returned to the main waiting area of the station, the two quit talking to the large man and left through the front door. He was not certain if they were talking about him but it sure appeared that they may have been, so he decided to continue the allusion that he was there as a normal patron wanting to purchase a ticket for an upcoming trip.

He walked up to the big man and asked, "How much is a ticket to Pocatello?"

This beast of a man snarled and pointed towards the counter.

"How would I know? The ticket counter is over there," he said rudely before storming off.

Del went to the counter where a very pleasant bus station attendant asked, "What can I do for you, sir?"

Del thought to himself, Quite the contrast of service!

"How much is a ticket to Pocatello?"

She smiled. "One way or roundtrip?"

"One way."

"One way is eighteen dollars, but the next bus won't be leaving for another three hours."

He took out a twenty and handed it to her. "Please make the ticket for tomorrow."

"No problem."

She typed a few things into the computer and a ticket printed out. She handed the ticket and two dollars back to Del. He kept the ticket but slid the two dollars back to the attendant, "Keep the money as a tip, you're so much nicer than the other guy working here."

"Oh he means no harm. He just thinks he owns the place," she said giggling.

"Well with that attitude he won't be here very long."

"You'll be surprised. He's been here just about five years. He's normally a nice enough person, but for the past week he's been a bear."

At that moment another customer came up to the counter.

"How much is a ticket to Malad, Idaho."

"Excuse me sir," she said to Del. "I need to help this customer.

He nodded his head, looked one last time at the two hallways and then left the station.

As he was exiting the front door of the station, he felt as if he was being watched. It was hard to detect anyone person or thing, but he decided to still play it safe. He thought to himself, "*If I'm being watched, I want to mislead them as much as possible.*"

He drove his rental car to the nearest post office and parked. After glancing in the mirror twice, he went inside to see if they had any mailboxes. In a loud voice he asked a clerk, "Where are the mail boxes?"

The clerk waved his hand to the right, "Down the hallway and to your left."

Del deliberately walked slowly down the passageway, hoping to see if anyone else would follow him. He looked at all of the boxes. After taking about three minutes he returned down the hall and exited the post office door. He next went to a UPS store that had in their window a sign that said, P.O. Boxes for rent. When he opened the door he saw the boxes off to his left. Again he purposely took his time to study each box while occasionally glancing over his shoulder to scrutinize anyone that might be observing him.

Del spent the next two hours visiting several other places. At each location he would exit his car and act as if he had something important to do all the while doing his best to survey any unusual behavior or spot any vehicle that might look familiar. Even then, he never could hone in on one particular person, car or thing.

"I might be over doing this a bit. Billy and his dreams have me a little edgy. I have begun to suspect almost anybody or anything," he thought to himself.

He looked at his watch and realized that he was hungry and it was getting rather late. While driving down 17th Street to return to the hospital, he spotted a Subway sandwich shop off to his left. He said aloud, "I bet Hammer and Billy would like a little extra to eat."

Del went in and ordered three twelve inch long turkey subs, all on wheat bread, with extra turkey, cheese, lettuce, tomatoes, olives and mayonnaise. Along with the sandwiches he also picked up three bags of chips and six cookies. As he drove back to the hospital, he started to plan out the next day's activities.

Hammer and I were in the process of building the jigsaw puzzle that Gladys had given us earlier in the day when Del came into the room carrying the sandwiches, chips and cookies. He took a look at the puzzle and then at the puzzle box. The puzzle was a picture of a painting depicting a small lake with a moose at the water's edge with a cabin off in the distance. The various colors of the painting blended in so well that it made it extremely difficult to piece together. To make matters worse, at least a hundred pieces were duplicated in such a way that they could virtually fit anywhere. You could only tell the subtle differences in their color. It was only after much exertion that we had pieced together some of the border.

"Do you boys want to take a break from that puzzle for a bite to eat?" Del asked.

I stood up, "Yes, it's driving us crazy."

Hammer agreed. "This is the coolest puzzle I have ever seen, but it's so hard to build."

Del spread the sandwiches on the table, "Where did you get the puzzle?"

Hammer jubilantly exclaimed, "Oh his girlfriend bought it for him."

I smiled shyly, "She's not my girlfriend. She just feels sorry for us."

"That's not what I think," said Hammer, "I think she really likes you."

I was about to protest when Del said, "I think you're right Hammer, but I want to tell you about today."

We took our sandwiches and began to eat. Between bites Del informed us of his activities of the day.

"I went and visited several of my friends here locally who are involved in law enforcement. They're of the opinion that what the two of you did this past week will severely cripple the cartel's actions here in Idaho. In fact, this might set them back several years. The bad news is that they will probably start all over again in the near future, unless Anthony's information is revealed. I got the impression that there is an uneasy feeling amongst quite a few of the local officers. With so many people sitting in the county jail who were involved with Lynn and the sheriff's unlawful activities, they are hoping that someone will spill their guts. Or make a deal that would assist the officials locally in apprehending the rest of the culprits. These same officials are also concerned that if they don't find Anthony's information, they may never fully remove the blemish placed upon the entire police department. I would personally say that about seventy-five percent of the local law enforcement officials in Eastern Idaho believe that there is no such book. The other twenty-five percent are hopeful that such a book exists."

I put my sandwich down and looked at him.

"What do you think?"

He took a chip and popped it in his mouth, "Well I think it exists we have more clues than the rest of the police force has. I also had a strange thing happen to me today."

Hammer, finished the last bite of his sandwich, "What happened?"

"Well I went to the bus station and discovered that there are sixteen lockers."

I yelled, "Yes! I knew it! I told you guys that it would be there."

Hammer gave an approving nod of his head, "You're the man Billy."

Del continued. "You appear to be right. The lockers are located behind a door that says 'Employees Only'. I went into the room and was about to check out locker 14 when a very large man yelled at me. He wanted to know what I was doing. I made up a quick story that I was looking for the bathroom. When I tried to leave, he blocked the doorway. At first I thought he was going to hit me or something, but I told him that I was in a hurry so he followed me to the bathroom. When I came out, he was talking to two shady looking characters. They saw me coming down the hallway and left. I asked the clerk behind the counter about the large man and she said he had been there almost five years and that he is normally okay, but has been quite testy this past week. His appearance and attitude make me somehow feel he was involved with Lynn and the sheriff. To top things off, when I left the station I had this strange feeling that I was being followed."

Hammer interrupted, "Did you see anyone?"

"No, I really didn't but I decided to visit several other places just to be on the safe side. I was hoping to throw them off our trail and potentially get a glimpse of them, but I never did see anyone."

It was my turn to butt in. "So if you never saw anyone, what made you feel you were being followed?"

"Nothing specific, but nonetheless, I still had this uncomfortable feeling. Maybe it's because of your dream, you said Anthony told you to be careful."

"That's right he did, so there must be somebody else out there."

"Yes and that somebody is in a position of authority."

Hammer added, "Not only authority but they also represent several actual cartels."

"Yes, that's right. We must remember this key point, they want to keep this information a secret just as much as we want to reveal it."

"Probably more so, and they are willing to kill to keep it that way," I said.

Del nodded his head. "For this reason we must be alert tomorrow. If the information is at the bus station, we must act fast once we obtain it. You know Hammer, I am so glad that you took the book and the envelope with you when you left the restaurant. It will serve as valuable evidence."

"I told you, Hammer. That was a stroke of genius when you had the foresight to retrieve the book and envelope," I piped in.

"Oh, it was nothing. I felt it may come in handy."

"Well," said Del, "It will come in handy. You know, at first I felt we should have given this information to the local authorities, but the more I think about it, I'm glad we didn't. Still not sure who we can really trust. I now feel that it will be more significant if we turn in all of the evidence at the same time. By the way who has it now?"

Hammer pointed at his back. "I still have it! I decided to keep it with me at all times."

He reached behind his back with both hands and un-tucked his shirt. As he did, the book and envelope slipped down his back and into his hands.

"Good. Keep it with you until were ready to turn it in. Alright boys, this will be our plan of attack tomorrow. We will leave the hospital after breakfast. I'll pick you up downstairs at the receptionist desk at exactly 8:30. When you leave, tell the nurse that you are going for a walk. If she protests, tell her you'll just be a minute or so and the exercise will do you good. The first stop will be to the post office."

"Why the post office?" Hammer asked.

"I want the two of you to be on the lookout. If the coast is clear, we will go to the bus station and retrieve the information and give it to the governor at the press conference scheduled for tomorrow afternoon. This way, it will be in the open and no one can stop us."

I nodded my head in agreement. "I like your plan, but what about making a copy of the information first, just in case something bad happens?"

Hammer added, "Yeah, just in case the governor is involved in this whole affair. If we were to hand him the evidence he could easily destroy it later."

Del grinned, "I don't think the governor is involved in all of this, but if it will make the two of you feel better, there is a copy shop about a mile away from the bus station. We can go there and make a copy."

"It sounds like we have a plan. Hammer and I will be more than happy to meet you at the receptionist desk tomorrow morning, but we will need your help with the press conference. Since we have no experience talking to the media, you may need to do all of the talking."

Del chuckled, "Don't worry boys, I have all the confidence in the world that you two will do very well. You've had no problems explaining to me what you both have done over the past week. And last night, Hammer, when Billy was eating his crackers and I my sandwich, you couldn't stop talking."

I broke out laughing as Hammer whined, "No fair, I was just excited."

"Well that's all the two of you need to do, remain excited. The world loves enthusiasm."

We all started to laugh with Del's last remark when there was a knock on the door. It opened up and Doctor Epperson came into the room.

"Am I interrupting anything important?"

Del replied, "No we were just having a good time."

"I'm glad to see that you're having a good time, but I want you, Hammer, to return to your room and get some rest. It's getting late and I've heard from the nurses that you have been in here all day. As for you, Billy, I am glad to see that you are doing better, but you need to get some rest as well."

Hammer started to protest when the Doctor held up his hand, "No complaining, you have had all day to play, its time now to rest."

Del barged in. "I'll help you out doctor."

He placed his arm on Hammer's shoulders and escorted him to the door. At the door they both turned around and said, "Goodnight, Billy."

The doctor was checking my chart when he looked up at Del.

"My wife baked an apple pie for us tonight. So as soon as I finish here, I'm heading home."

Del smacked his lips. "Apple pie is my favorite, how did she know?"

"She knows because you told us that last night."

I inquired, "What about us, do we get any pie?"

Doctor Epperson looked at me, turned to Hammer and then back to me.

"Yes, I will bring you each a large piece, but only if you both get some rest."

Hammer slyly said, "I'm out of here." as they both then left the room.

The Doctor finished checking my chart and took my blood pressure.

"114 over 66, not bad."

He looked at the incision where they operated and then examined my face which was still bruised. He finished up by checking my pulse and my breathing with his stethoscope.

"Billy, you look like you're doing just fine. Your pulse is a healthy fifty-nine beats per minute. Your bruises are healing well and the incision seems to be fine. Another couple of days and you will be as good as new."

"Thanks doctor for all you have done for me and my friends. You are the best doctor I have ever met."

Doctor Epperson smiled. "You probably haven't met very many."

"No, Doctor, I really have, and you have been awesome."

"Well Billy, I'll say thank you. Now I want you to rest well tonight, so here are two sleeping pills."

He reached over and filled my glass with water and handed it to me. I swallowed the pills and drank the entire glass. I handed the glass back to the Doctor who refilled it and put it by the side of my bed. He bent over and whispered to me.

"Be sure to press the nurse's button as soon as I leave. I think Gladys wants to tell you goodnight."

He paused for a moment, "You're not blushing are you?"

"Well what do you think?"

"I think she likes you, that's what I think. Now goodnight."

He turned and walked towards the door. At the door he stopped and looked back at me. "I'll let her turn out the lights," he said as he opened the door and left.

I adjusted the bed so that I was sitting upright and following doctor's orders, pressed the yellow button. It seemed like an eternity, but in reality it was only a few minutes before the door opened and Gladys walked in. She came up to the bed and with a beautiful smile

"What can I get you Billy?" she asked.

"Oh, I just wanted to say thanks for the puzzle."

She blushed. "I'm glad you liked it. I was shopping this morning for some clothes and saw it. I heard you and Hammer talking about the wildlife around Swan Valley and I felt it would keep you busy. It's tough being cooped up all day without being able to do anything fun."

I was about to ask her if she wanted to go to a movie with me once I got out of the hospital, but the sleeping pills started to kick in, and I found myself yawning.

"I need to let you get some sleep," she said.

She took the spare blanket that was sitting by my feet and covered me up.

"Goodnight, Billy, see you tomorrow."

She walked to the door, turned off the lights and was gone.

I watched her shut the door and thought to myself, "She sure is a wonderful nurse. I look forward to asking her to a movie or dinner."

My mind than began to wander. I thought about the day and how relaxing it was. I also thought back to what Del had to say about the bus station and his feeling of being followed. I knew we would be busy tomorrow and hoped and prayed that all would go well with all that we had to do. My mind began to envision us shaking the governor's hand. All the cameras would be on us and perhaps we would become national heroes. Before I knew it, I was asleep. As Anthony had promised, I did not dream about him, but I did dream about Gladys.

CHAPTER TWENTY-SEVEN

It was a long night and I slept very well. The only noise I heard was when Hammer came into my room.

"Wake up sleepy head, we have to go. It's almost 8:30."

"Why didn't you wake me sooner?" I said as I quickly hopped out of bed and started getting dressed.

"Oh you were sleeping so soundly, I thought it best that I let you rest as long as possible."

"Yeah, the doctor gave me some sleeping pills last night. Boy, did they ever knock me out."

I finished dressing and we headed towards the elevator. The nurse on duty was nowhere to be found so we pressed the button to head down. The elevator doors opened and we climbed aboard hitting the first floor button. The elevator took us to the main floor where Del was waiting for us at the receptionist area.

"Just on time. Let's go." Del said, looking at his watch.

We left the hospital and went straight to Del's car. Since we had completely totaled his BMW, Del had to rent a car until he was able to settle with his insurance company and buy a new one. His rental car, a dark green sedan was not nearly as nice as his BMW, but suitable to get us where we needed to go and wouldn't stand out as much. I still felt bad about his car as he unlocked the doors and we hopped in.

As he indicated the day before, we went to the post office first. A couple of times I saw a few cars that were trailing to close but after a short while it was apparent that we weren't being followed. We spent about five minutes inside the post office, seeing several people come in after us to drop off their mail. One person in particular appeared to be very suspicious. He was carrying a large package that was obviously not very heavy. He walked over to where we were standing and fumbled for a key in his right vest pocket. Pulling out his key, he opened one of the many mail boxes along the wall finding nothing inside. While he was supposedly checking his mail, he glanced over his shoulder, particularly at me, which made me feel that he was spying on us. He took an extraordinary amount of time to place his key back into his pocket and then, unhurriedly, walked back down the corridor to the main entrance. After about thirty seconds, he looked back down the corridor at us and then left. I watched him climb into a dark green minivan and drive away. Once he left, we didn't see any other people who seemed out of place.

"Okay, looks like the coast is clear. Let's head to the bus station," Del said as he motioned for me to follow him.

We drove to straight to the bus station. All the way there, Hammer and I kept looking behind us to assure we weren't being followed. Again, I saw a couple of cars driving somewhat erratic, but not one of them stayed behind us for very long. Within ten minutes, we arrived at the station. Del looked all around and then cautioned us, "Okay guys, we must be careful. We can't afford to be seen by anyone."

We climbed out of the rental car and walked into the station. Fortunately for us, there were only a few customers standing at the ticket counter. The clerk, too busy paying attention to them, did not even notice us even though the station was nearly empty.

Del pointed at the sign that read 'Lockers'.

"Good, it looks like no one has seen us. Follow me to the lockers."

He led the way down the passageway to the door marked 'Employees Only'. We paused for a second and looked around. With no one in sight, we entered the locker room. Del went straight to the light switch and flipped it on so we could see all sixteen lockers.

He pointed at locker number 14.

"There it is, use your key."

I marched over to locker 14 and removed my keys from my pocket, shuffling the keys around until I found the one I had removed from the manila envelope. Taking a deep breath, I placed the key into the lock and unlocked the locker door. Del and Hammer joined me and all three of us gazed into the locker. The only thing inside was a large black manuscript about the size of a phonebook. I wanted to scream out, but instead, trying to be careful and not get caught.

"It's here," I excitedly whispered as I reached in and pulled out the document.

I turned to them and showed them the book. I carefully opened it and flipped through the pages. On the first forty sheets, we saw hundreds and hundreds of notes written by Anthony. As I turned a few more pages, we saw only one name; it was the governor's.

"I told you Del. He was in on this!" Hammer said. It seemed that he was gritting his teeth while he was speaking. I could tell he was getting upset.

Del had a sinister grin and said, "Turn the page and see who else is in the book."

I again turned the page. There was only one name written down on the next page. When Hammer and I saw it, we both gasped.

"No, this can't be!" Hammer shouted.

The name we saw on the page read 'Del Montgomery'.

We turned and gazed at Del. He had taken several steps away from the locker. "Well boys, Anthony did tell you to trust no one."

"How can this be, you rescued us just the other day? You could have left us out there to die?" I cried out.

"Yes, I could have, but I couldn't run the risk of not knowing where the rest of the information was located. You two were right on just about everything. I got my marching orders to let one shipment of drugs go so that we might obtain this book. Plus, who will ever suspect me now, remember I'm a hero." "Besides, how do you think I could afford my car or for that matter, knew who Lynn was?"

"Okay Billy, give me the book."

"No way, I will never give you this book."

With a threatening snigger Del took one more step back. "Oh I think you will."

Reaching into his pockets, he pulled out a gun out of one and a silencer out of another. All we could do was watch. This was our friend who had played such an important part in both of our lives and now it appeared he was going to kill us.

Del fastened the silencer to his weapon and aimed it at Hammer.

"I hate to do this Hammer."

"No, Del, take the manuscript!" I screamed.

"I will, but I have to clean up the mess made by Lynn and the sheriff."

He fired twice, hitting Hammer squarely in the heart. Hammer, still with a look of surprise on his face, crumpled to the ground dead.

"Take your damn book! I hope you rot in hell!" I cried out, throwing the book to the ground.

I fell to my knees. Slowly I reached over to my friend and began to cry. Del bent over and picked up the manuscript.

"Billy, I'm really sorry it had to end this way. I really did like the two of you, but business is business."

As he aimed the gun at me, I made a desperate attempt to stop him from shooting me, springing to my feet and immediately beginning to kick, hit and scream. As I was screaming and throwing my hands wildly in the air, a light came on and I heard a female voice, the voice of the morning nurse. She heard me screaming and darted into my room. She came over to my bed but had to stop short. Since I was kicking and waving my arms in such a wild fashion, she was afraid of accidentally getting hurt trying to wake me up.

"Billy, Billy, wake up! You're dreaming!" she shouted in a stern voice

"Hammer is dead!"

Still startled by my behavior she responded, "No, he's not dead. I just left his room moments ago. He is sound asleep and all is well. You've just had a bad dream. Perhaps it was the sleeping pills?"

I was drenched in sweat and my heart was racing. I pleadingly looked at her.

"Are you sure I'm dreaming?" I wasn't sure if I was awake or still sleeping. Maybe the nurse was a dream and Hammer was dead. Maybe I was dead, too.

"More than sure," she calmly said. "Sometimes sleeping pills cause people to dream more than normal. You've been kicking and waving your arms about for the past few minutes, but all is okay now. Calm down and let me get you some water?"

"Yes please, I could use some water."

She poured me a glass of water as I sat up. I drank it all in one gulp and handed the glass back to her, asking for another.

"I must get out of bed for a moment to make sure this was only a dream. Can I please walk down the hallway to look in on Hammer?"

"Ordinarily I would say no, but you seem quite distraught, so as long as you are quiet, I'll let you."

I jumped out of bed and swiftly walked down the hallway to Hammer's room, gently opening the door and peering in. He was asleep and it really had been a dream.

I slowly returned to my room where the nurse was patiently waiting for me.

"It's still very early," she said as she peeked at her watch. "Why don't you try and get some more sleep."

My head felt light and sleep sounded good.

"What time is it?"

"It's about 2:30 in the morning. If you're lucky you still can get another five to six hours of sleep."

With great effort I returned to my bed

"Sleep sounds nice," I mumbled. "It's just all of these dreams that I've had lately. Did you know, I used to hardly ever dream. Now it seems like every other night I'm having one."

She listened to me ramble on and waited politely until I had finished before saying anything.

"Sometimes people have dreams when their under stress. God knows, you and your friend have been through a lot the past couple of days. I'm sure you're going to be okay."

"Now get some rest," she said, taking a hold of my blanket and tucking me in.

She went to the door, turned off the lights and left the room. As the door shut behind her, I said aloud, "What a dream."

CHAPTER TWENTY-EIGHT

The next time I awoke was to the noise of the morning shift nurse. She was talking to someone out in the corridor. I listened intently and swore I recognized the other person's voice. I made out a word or two here and there. "How are they doing…?, big day…, heroes…, lots of press…, governor…" I also heard, "Let us know if they leave."

When this statement was made, I was determined to see who she was chatting with. Carefully, I slipped out of bed and quietly walked over to the door. As I neared the door, the talking suddenly stopped. I could hear the footsteps of the person the nurse was talking to head towards the elevator. Quickly, I opened the door and glanced out but whoever it was had already stepped into the elevator. I hurried my pace towards the elevator to try to see who it was. The distance closed rapidly and I was within six feet of the elevator when the door began to shut. I was too late. All I saw was the person's right shoe, what looked like a new pair of Asics Gel running shoes.

Having missed the person who climbed aboard the elevator, I decided to chat with the nurse to find out who it was. . When she saw me, she placed her right hand into her pocket and pulled out a pen.

"And how are you today, young man?"

"I'm doing much better, but I was wondering who you were talking to just a moment ago?"

Pausing for a second, she said, "I really don't know. I think he might be with the police or a reporter with one of the major networks."

"Have you seen him here before?"

She placed the palm of her left hand on her chin and thought for a moment.

"I do believe he was here yesterday, but there have been so many people asking about you and your friend that I really didn't pay much attention to him. Why do you ask?"

"Oh, no reason. Just thought I recognized his voice. Well, I better get back to my room. Thanks for your time."

She smiled. "No problem."

I still wanted to find out who was coming by to see me and why, but knew I had to return to my room to prepare for the day,

Shortly thereafter, Hammer came to my room to join me for breakfast. The nurse had brought us each a bowl of oatmeal and a couple of doughnuts. I was wishing for the spread that Del had arranged for us the other day. Bacon and eggs sounded better than oatmeal.

"Are you ready for the day?" he asked.

"You bet. Today should be very exciting. How about you?"

"I can hardly wait to see if you're right about Anthony's information being kept at the bus station."

"Can I tell you something that happened last night?"

"Sure."

"Last night I had another dream."

Hammer slowly put his spoon down. "Not with Anthony, I hope?"

"No it wasn't with Anthony, I dreamt about Del."

"What about Del?"

"Well, you and I met him as planned. He took us to the post office and then the bus station. At the bus station we discovered Anthony's hidden information."

Hammer, in the process of eating his second doughnut said, "Sounds like a good dream so far, why the sad face?"

"In my dream the missing associate was Del."

"You're kidding me!" Hammer said.

"No, I'm not. You see, once we found the information, Del pulled out a gun."

I paused for a second.

"Yes go on."

"Well, he shot you and was in the process of shooting me when I woke up. I know it was just a dream, but it felt so real. What should I do about it?"

Hammer dropped his doughnut and looked at me nervously.

"First off, I can't belief Del is involved. He has been a true friend to both you and me. In fact, he even saved us the other day. If it wasn't for him, we'd be dead."

"I know, and this bothers me somewhat. You see, in my dream I asked him, 'Why did you save us?'"

"What did he say?"

"He basically said it was worth losing one shipment of drugs to get Anthony's information."

Hammer took a long moment to let what I had just said sink in. He stood up and walked around the room and then came back to the table and sat down.

"It doesn't make sense. If he was involved, he could have contacted Lynn. Together they could have made a plan to ship the drugs while he pretended to rescue us. Instead, they lost hundreds of thousands of dollars. I just don't see them throwing away so much money. Plus Lynn and the sheriff, two key players, are now dead. I just don't think that would be a wise move."

What Hammer said made a lot of sense. I had never thought about it that way before. Del and Lynn could have easily made a plan that would accomplish both of their goals. After all, we kept him informed on everything.

"I think you are right. I might have overreacted."

"I don't know if you have overreacted. You have had several strange dreams this past week, and they have been helpful. I just feel that Del is trustworthy."

"I agree, I feel terrible for even having had this dream."

"Not at all, you have been under a lot of stress. I tell you what I would do if I were you."

"What?"

"When we see Del this morning, tell him about your dream. Let's see how he reacts."

"Okay, but I hope he won't be mad at me."

"I wouldn't worry about him. If he's a true friend, and I trust he is, he will understand your concerns."

"You're right, Hammer. However, just keep in mind that the events in my dreams seem to have a way of happening and they never did find their bodies…"

Hammer looked at the clock on the wall. "Its 8:25, time to go."

We both leapt up from the table and headed out the door.

"We're going to go for a walk around the hospital," we said to the nurse on duty.

"Are you sure that you feel up to it?" she asked as she studied us very carefully.

"Oh yes, we need the exercise."

"I notice you both have gotten dressed," she replied, still not completely believing us.

"We didn't want to walk around the building in our night gowns."

The nurse chuckled. "Yes that makes sense. We would hate to have you arrested for streaking. After all, those gowns do reveal a lot don't they?"

Hammer timidly said, "Yeah they do. I feel that everyone is staring at me when I have it on."

"They may just be. The two of you are extremely handsome. Well it's obvious to me that you have made up your minds to go for a walk, so be careful. It hasn't been that long ago that you were both unable to even sit up."

"We'll walk slowly. If we get tired, we will find a chair to sit and rest awhile," I confidently said. This seemed to pacify her.

"Good. If you promise me that you will do that, then I won't worry about you."

We took the elevator to the main floor and quickly strolled to the reception desk where Del was waiting for us. When he saw us, he motioned for us to follow him as he headed towards the main entrance and exited the building. It was the first time in several days that Hammer and I had been outside. It was a beautiful September morning, rather typical for this time of year. There was a little haze around Taylor Mountain where some of the farmers had begun to burn their fields, but other then that, the weather was ideal.

We caught up with Del just outside the main entrance.

"The two of you wait right here, I will go and get the rental car." He began to leave when I tugged on his arm.

"Del wait just a moment. I have something to ask you." He stopped and turned back around towards me.

"I had another dream last night."

"With Anthony?" he asked with his eyes widening?

Hammer chimed in, "That's what I asked him."

"No, not with Anthony, I dreamt about you."

"Me, wow, what happened?"

"Well…" I told him my entire dream. When I finished, I waited for him to say something. He looked at Hammer and then back at me.

"I can see why you would be concerned. If you want, I'll wait here while the two of you go and check out the station. I would ask only one thing and that is that you be extremely careful. I still feel uneasy about yesterday."

I smiled. "Now that's the answer I was hoping for. Your willingness to step aside is all I needed to reassure me about you. I hope you're not mad at me?"

"Why should I be mad? The two of you have been through enough this past week and your dreams, as stressful as they have been on you, have been very helpful.

Hammer beamed. "That's exactly what I told him. I knew you would understand."

Del, placing his left hand on my right shoulder, said "So, what do you want to do?" The way he acted brought me great relief. I placed my left hand on top of his.

"We're going to do what you had planned all along."

"Fantastic! I'll get the car."

"See Billy, I told you he was a trusted friend."

"You're right, I feel bad for having even brought it up."

"Don't feel bad. Feel glad you have such awesome friends."

Hammer wrapped his arm around me and gave me a hug, squeezing me a bit too tight.

"Okay, Okay, enough. I've learned my lesson," I choked out, trying to catch my breath.

Del reached his car and drove around to the main entrance. As he did so, I noticed that the car was a dark green sedan, identical to the car in my dream. I thought to myself,

"Now that's not a good sign, but he is willing to let us go alone."

I was nervous from the coincidence so I said nothing to Hammer.

He pulled the car up to the curb and we both hopped in. I jumped into the back seat and Hammer took the front.

"Okay boys, I want you to be on the lookout for anything which might look suspicious. If you see a car following us, tell me the color and for how long it has been behind us. First, we'll drive to the main post office, taking several side streets. I'll drive fast and then slow. Whoever seems to stay behind us will probably be the one following us. Do you have any questions?"

"Nope" said Hammer. "We have seen our fair share of detective shows. We know what to look for."

Hammer turned to me. "I will look out the right side of the car, you take the left."

Del kept to his word, turning several times onto different side streets and at times, speeding up and then slowing down.

At one point in time I observed a tan SUV that appeared to make several turns with us.

"Del, check you're rearview mirror. Do you see that tan SUV?" I asked.

"Yes I do," he said, nodding his head.

"Well it has been behind us for several turns."

"Okay, got it."

Del hit his blinkers and turned left. The SUV kept going straight. "Looks like a false alarm Billy."

"Yeah I guess so."

He made several other quick turns, but we did not see anybody else who appeared to be following us.

Del eventually arrived at the post office, finding a parking spot next to the mail drop.

"Alright, I want the two of you to come in with me. After we enter the building, I want Hammer to stand at the entrance and check the parking lot for anything that seems unusual. Look carefully at all the cars that pull into the lot. When we leave, if you so much as think you see a familiar car, let me know."

Hammer nodded.

"Billy, you will come with me. We're going to go to where they keep the mail boxes. I'll look like I am interested in a particular box. If you see anyone watching us, I want you to loudly ask me, 'What time does the game start this afternoon?' Any questions?"

"Nope, I got it."

"Good, let's go."

We slipped out of the car and briskly walked to the main entrance of the post office. As we entered the building, Hammer took his position by the door and I followed Del to the mail boxes. He acted as if he had a key to open one of the boxes. While I was observing the comings and goings of the main entrance, one particular man stood out. He was carrying a large package that appeared to be very light. He walked the

short corridor to the mail boxes, laid his parcel down and
fumbled for his key. When he noticed me staring at him he
politely bowed his head and said "Hi".

This made me extremely uneasy and I halfheartedly
responded, "How are you today?"

"Not bad. Looking forward to Governor Stevens' visit this
afternoon. Should be a lot of fun don't you think?"

"I guess so."

He opened his mail box and there was nothing inside. "Oh
well, maybe next time. Have a nice day now."

"You too," I muttered.

He nodded his head, bent over and picked up his package,
and wandered to the front counter.

Del softly chuckled. "Looks like you made a new friend."

"New friend, after the way I treated him, it's amazing he
doesn't file a complaint to the Postmaster General." I was
somewhat flustered by his comment.

We waited for a few more minutes, but no one else came
down to the mail boxes. Del motioned towards the main
entrance. "Let's go."

We quickly walked down the passageway to where
Hammer was standing. Del waved at Hammer to follow and we
returned to the rental car. Once in the car he asked Hammer,
"Did you see anything?"

"No, not really. There were several cars that used the
outside mail drop and four customers who came in to use the
inside counter. But nothing looked out of the ordinary."

"What about the man carrying the large parcel? Didn't it
seem strange to you that the item was so light?" I asked.

"No, because he got out of a van marked 'Lampshades-R-
Us'. I figured he was in the process of mailing one somewhere."

Hammer's observation set my mind at ease. So, looking
over at Del, I said, "Let's go to the bus station!"

He started the car and we drove off to the station. On the
way there, Del gave us more directions.

"Okay, when we get to the station, I want the two of you to follow me. I'll head straight towards the room where the lockers are kept. Once we're inside the room, I want you, Billy, to quickly unlock locker 14. You do have the key?"

I reached into my left front pocket and pulled out my keys. "It's right here."

"Good, you will open the locker and look inside. If there is a lot of stuff inside, you will relock the locker and all three of us will quickly leave the station and head back to the car to discuss how to remove this stuff safely. If there are only a few items, we will decide how to remove them at that time."

Just then Hammer squirmed in his seat. Del looked at him. "What's the problem, are you nervous?"

"Not at all, I still have Anthony's book and envelope stuffed up my back shirt. I must have just sat down funny and it kind of hurt."

"Alright, so you're not nervous? How about you, Billy?"

"No, I'm too excited to be nervous. I just want to hurry and get this information out of the bus station."

"Me too. We're almost there."

Del made a few more turns and we saw the station in front of us. We were all paying such close attention to the station and to the plan that Del laid out for us that we had forgotten to check to see if we were being followed. The tan SUV that was behind us earlier had unexpectedly reappeared and we didn't notice it. Del pulled into the parking lot and we quickly exited the vehicle. He motioned to us to follow him and we hurriedly walked into the station and looked around. All we saw was the pleasant young attendant helping a few customers.   .

"Good, it appears that the coast is clear. Follow me."

He walked straight down the hallway to the 'Employees Only' room. Once inside, he fumbled for the light switch for a second or two. Finding it, he promptly switched on the lights and pointed to the right hand side of the room.

"There is number 14. Let's open it quickly."

I walked up to the locker and placed the key into the lock, it fit perfectly. As I turned the key to the left, we could hear the lock unlatch. Cautiously I took hold of the small handle and opened the door. My emotions were running high as I peered into the locker. I paused for an instant and let out a painful groan. "There's nothing here, it's empty."

Del rushed over and examined the locker. He anxiously said, "Try rubbing your hand along the side of the locker and along the top shelf in case he hid it."

I did so and at first felt nothing, but when I got to the shelf, I felt something towards the back. A deep sensation surged through my body and I became very excited.

"There's something in here."

I grabbed a hold of what appeared to be a small black appointment book. It was identical to the one that Anthony gave me at the restaurant.

I opened the book and flipped through the pages. On each page was a list of names and their connections to the drug cartels. I raised the book high into the air and waved it at them. "Look, there are hundreds of names and places written within this book. This is the truth that Anthony told me to reveal."

Looking at it together, we rapidly flipped through the rest of the pages. One page caught my attention. I held it open and saw the name of Sheriff Thompson.

"Del, this page has Sheriff Thompson's name written in it. That means if Anthony knew the sheriff was involved, there still must be an anonymous person out there. He said that there were two people he knew nothing about. One we discovered was Lynn. I guess I thought the other person was the sheriff, especially after you revealed to us that he was Lynn's brother. But if he has the sheriff's name written down here that means there is still someone else out there."

Del took two small steps back, just like in my dream. He said, "Well boys, Anthony told you to trust no one."

I began to panic. I thought, *"No, this can't be happening."*

Del slowly reached into both pockets at the same time. He slowly pulled something out of his pocket and looked over at us. He then gave us an enormous smile and started dialing his cell phone.

"Got you, didn't I. You thought I was reaching for a gun, just like in your dream."

Hammer broke out laughing as I angrily retorted, "Very funny, Del, very, very funny."

He looked surreptitiously towards me. "Okay now we're even! You thought I was a bad guy and I got you back."

"I admit you did, but it's still not funny."

Hammer was still bent over laughing. "I thought it was funny, you should have seen the look on your face."

Del turned to Hammer. "I don't know, I thought you were about to tackle me."

"Yeah, you too thought for a moment he was reaching for a gun," I gleefully retorted.

"Maybe I did, but it sure was funny," Hammer very coolly replied. The way he so calmly said what he did caused all of us to laugh.

"Okay boys, now let's be serious. There still is someone out there so we best be going before it's too late."

Hammer glanced over at me. "Quick, hide the book."

"Where? It's too big to fit into my pocket."

"Do what I did with the other book, tuck it up your shirt. This way when we leave, if anyone is watching us, they will see that we have all left empty handed."

Del nodded in agreement. "That's a great idea."

"Yeah, I thought so. I learned that in prison. Whenever I wanted something special, I always found a way to hide it."

Del momentary looking at Hammer, said, "Those days are over, aren't they?"

He nodded. "Yes, but if I have to rely on some old tricks to save us, I will."

"Now quickly Billy, we have to leave."

I un-tucked my shirt and slid the book under my shirt and tucked it back in.

"I'm ready, let's go."

CHAPTER TWENTY-NINE

We were moving towards the door when it unexpectedly opened. Standing there were the two detectives that met with us yesterday and the county prosecutor. They looked like they did yesterday except the prosecutor was not dressed in a fancy suit this time but instead had on a plain shirt and a pair of Levis.

The prosecutor was the first to speak.

"Gentlemen, I hope you don't get angry with me, but I have had you followed since we talked yesterday morning. I must admit Del, you had us going on some wild goose chases. I could tell by the way you acted that you knew you were being followed, but tell me, did you ever see us?"

"No, I really didn't. But you are right. I felt I was being watched. So tell me, how did you do it?"

"It was actually quite easy. We had your car bugged. When the three of us left you guys in the hospital, we felt something wasn't right. We came to the conclusion that you were withholding information from us so we promptly wired your car. Now if you guys don't mind, I really need to get this information before a judge so that we can successfully prosecute these people sitting in our jail."

As the prosecutor was talking, I recognized his voice. It was the same voice I heard talking to the nurse this morning. I looked down at his shoes. Sure enough, he still had on the Asics running shoes. I was about to say we discovered nothing in the locker when Hammer turned to me and then Del.

"Gosh, I'm glad to see you guys. We can now share all this information with you."

He reached behind his back and un-tucked his shirt, removing the book and envelope he was carrying. He walked up to the prosecutor and handed them to him.

"We found this stuff in the locker and we were going to turn them over to the governor this afternoon. But now that you're here, we'll let you give them to him instead."

"Thanks, this will make our life so much easier."

He opened the book and noticed that the pages were blank. He took a quick look towards the bottom of each page and saw the characters. He looked back at Hammer, "What is this? This must be some kind of joke."

Hammer, appearing very innocent replied, "What are you talking about?"

The prosecutor took the book and showed it to us. "There's nothing here but a bunch of garbage."

"I want to know where the other book is and I want to know now!" he yelled.

Realizing what Hammer was trying to accomplish, I joined in. "What other book are you talking about?"

He glared at me. "You know damn well what I'm talking about. I want the other book."

I persisted. "There is no other book."

I pointed at the book he was holding. "We just found that one in the locker. We were going to turn it…"

The prosecutor rudely interrupted me. "*Shut up!* I'm no fool."

He took the book and waived it in the air. "Lynn told me about this book already."

He motioned to the two detectives who were with him to pull out their weapons.

"I didn't want this to happen. All you had to do was tell us what you knew. But oh no, you three have to continue to play heroes, don't you?"

"So you're the other anonymous partner?" I blurted out.

He looked at me and smiled. "Lynn told me to keep an eye on the two of you. Now you definitely leave me with no options."

He turned to one of the detectives. "Search them."

The smaller of the two detectives stepped towards me. As he did so, the 'Employees Only' door swung open and n stepped the large man that had intimidated Del the day before.

"What in the hell is going on here?" he bellowed.

The prosecutor turned to the other detective. "Show him your badge."

"You're interfering with official police business," the prosecutor said as he turned toward the large man. "So I'm *telling* you to leave now."

The large man, not sure of what he should do, started to turn and leave.

Del observed this exchange of words and the body language of the large man, recognizing immediately that he had nothing to do with Lynn or the sheriff, but instead was somehow connected to Anthony. That would explain why the clerk at the desk said he had been here five years. He must have been assigned by the Chicago Herald to assist Anthony. Furthermore, the clerk said that he was unusually temperamental this past week. He had obviously heard about Anthony's death.

Del took a chance and shouted at the man,

"Don't Leave! These people are connected to the ones that killed Anthony."

This caused him to stop.

"That man's a liar!" The prosecutor shouted. "Now get going, this is none of your damn business."

"Remember Anthony!" Del shouted again.

This did the trick. He whirled around and charged the three men, his sudden movement catching them off guard. He slammed into them causing all three of them to lose their balance. *"Run!"* he yelled at us.

Del, Hammer, and I darted towards the door. The prosecutor reached out and tried to tackle us but we all made it by him without any problems. We dashed out the door and ran towards the main exit of the bus station. The prosecutor and two detectives tried to follow, but the large man continued to block their way. This gave us the time we needed to make it out of the station and to Del's car. We quickly piled in and he started the engine. He put the car into drive just as one of the detectives raced out of the station. With no delay, he punched the accelerator and we sped towards the parking lot exit.

He didn't even think of stopping as he turned onto the street and barely avoided hitting another car coming from the opposite direction. The detective, seeing us leave, aimed his gun and fired three times. One shot hit the rear window causing the glass to shatter. The other two shots hit the trunk of the car. Del roared down the street towards the intersection. The light was red, but that didn't stop him as he hung a sharp right into the busy intersection causing two cars to jam on their brakes and crashed into one another. Del's sharp right forced him into the wrong land and straight into the path of an oncoming car. The driver of the other car quickly swerved to his right and crashed into the sidewalk. Del didn't let the wreck stop him as he quickly regained control of the car and continued down the street until he got to another light. It was also red and had a car waiting for the light to change. Del switched over to the left lane in order to go around the car, slowing just enough to avoid hitting two cars in the middle of the intersection. The two cars in the middle of the intersection both jammed on their brakes and lost control, crashing into a couple of parked cars. *Hopefully no one was hurt,* Del thought.

Once he felt we were somewhat safe he slowed the vehicle down.

"Is everyone okay?"

Both Hammer and I told him we were fine.

"I have several friends in town who work for the FBI. I'm heading to their office. I know we will be safe there."

He continued to drive aggressively until we reached their office. He found a parking spot and promptly parked. He yelled, "Okay, jump out and follow me."

We bolted out of the car and followed him.

The building was a series of several small offices connected to one larger one. The office we had entered had six desks and a number of book cases. As we burst through the door one of the agents by the name of Bob leapt to his feet. When he saw it was Del, he hollered, *"What in the hell is going on here?"*

"Bob, we have just escaped with our lives." Del barked back. "We found Anthony's hidden book. We also found out who the missing link is."

Bob, still somewhat startled, muttered, "Whoa, one thing at a time."

Del who had not stopped moving since entering the office moved quickly towards the copier machine.

"We may not have much time. I need you to dispatch some agents immediately to the bus station. There's a very large man there who may be in seriously trouble, maybe even shot."

Bob grabbed his cell phone that was sitting on the corner of his desk and dialed the number of another agent who was not far away from the station.

"We have had an incident at the bus station. I need you and Frank to get there as quickly as possible and you may need to call in an ambulance. Be very careful because there could still be some armed men there. I will give you more information as soon as I get it. "He put his phone down and turned to us, "Okay guys, I need you all to sit down and fill me in."

Del was now standing by the copy machine. "Bob, I want you to meet two good friends of mine, this is Hammer and this is Billy. He walked up to us and shook both of our hands.

"Del has told me many good things about the two of you."

"Billy come over here and hand me Anthony's book."

I un-tucked my shirt and the book slipped out which I immediately handed to him.

Del looked at Bob. "You don't mind if we make some copies do you?"

"No, be my guest."

As he made copies of the book, he began to tell us the story of his friendship with Bob.

"Over thirty years ago, Bob and I went to college together. We played on the school's baseball team. I played second base and he played third base. We started every game for four years and won two divisional titles. We also studied law enforcement and had quite a few classes together. Now we were good at baseball, but not good enough to go pro. We had good grades and were in great shape so the FBI recruited us. I spent twenty-five years with the Bureau before the State of Idaho offered me a position at the state prison. Bob is still with the Bureau. His main assignment is working illegal drug trafficking cases. He was assigned to work in Eastern Idaho after substantial rumors made their way to the main Bureau office in Washington DC about illegal trafficking in Idaho."

Although Del was busy making copies, he paused every now and then to continue with his story.

"Bob is the individual who has provided me with most of the information I have obtained. He also orchestrated your rescue last Saturday. Now that you all know one another a little better, let me cut to the chase. Bob, we found Anthony's book at the bus station and were in the process of leaving with it when the county prosecutor and two detectives tried to take it from us at gun point. We were rescued by a very large man who basically tackled the bad guys, giving us the opportunity to escape. At the press conference this afternoon, we want to turn this information over to Governor Stevens. I just wanted to make several copies beforehand, one of which will be stored here for safe keeping."

Bob shook his head in disbelief. "You and your friends sure have been busy. We have been trying to stop this drug ring for years. If this information is what you say it is, you will have the bureaus gratitude."

He paused for a few moments and then in a tone of scorn continued. "I always despised the county prosecutor. Whenever we had what we would consider a solid lead, he would do something to screw it up. There were several trials in which we should have won the case, but for unknown reasons, we lost each and everyone. I always felt the prosecutor was inept, but I never once thought he was part of the gang."

Del finished making two copies of Anthony's information and handed one complete set to Bob, who without delay took it over to a vault marked 'Evidence.' Carefully twisting the combination lock several times, the big door opened. He placed his copy of the book in the vault and shut the door. With a quick twist of his wrist, he rotated the dial several times and then checked the door handle to make sure it was secure.

Looking back at us he asked, "What are you going to do with the other copy?"

Del smiled. "You know how the system works. This is a backup copy just to be safe."

Bob grinned and shook his head in agreement. "Boy do I ever know how the system works.

He took several steps toward the rear wall and grabbed a set of car keys from off of a key rack. "Let me escort the three of you back to the hospital. I also want to have some backup. This is a major bust, and I don't want to do anything that will screw it up."

He then walked over to one of the side doors and opened it. In the adjoining room were several other agents working on various assignments. He asked two of the men to stop what they were doing and join us.

After we made the trip back to the hospital, Hammer and I returned to our rooms in order to rest up a bit before the afternoon press conference. We were entering our rooms when the same nurse who was on duty when we left, came running up to us.

"Wow! That was some walk. You have been gone for over four hours. You had me worried."

We both started to laugh and I politely looked at her. "Yes it was a long walk, but we our glad to be back."

"You must be hungry, I'll bring you both some sandwiches."

She turned towards the nurse's station and walked away. Once in the room, I took off my shoes and jumped into bed. I was tired, but excited, and a sandwich sounded pretty good.

CHAPTER THIRTY

Del remained with the FBI agents on the main floor of the hospital. Bob made various calls to the state, county and local police, informing the authorities to be on the lookout for the county prosecutor. He also provided them descriptions of the two detectives that were with the prosecutor. The two agents that were sent to the bus station found the large man tied up in the locker room. He was unhurt, as were the various drivers of the cars that crashed when we made our hasty escape.

At two o'clock, there was a quick knock on my door. Doctor Epperson came into the room with an orderly pushing a wheelchair.

"I can walk to the conference room, I don't need a wheelchair."

Doctor Epperson frowned. "That's just what Hammer said when we picked him up a moment ago. But I told him like I'm telling you, you both have had enough exercise for one day. So hop in the chair and enjoy the ride."

I did as the doctor ordered and jumped into the chair. The orderly wheeled me out of my room into the hallway where I was met by Hammer and his orderly.

"Let's enjoy the ride while we can."

He turned to his orderly, "To the conference room James, and spare no expense!"

I began to chuckle as we were pushed to the elevator. The doctor pressed the down button and fifteen seconds later, the elevator door opened and down we went.

When the doors opened to the main floor, we were greeted by about twenty-five reporters and their camera crews. As we exited the elevator, flash bulbs went off from every camera around. As the orderlies pushed us towards the conference room, we could hear the music of the Idaho Falls High School marching band coming down the hallway. The orderlies continued to push us down the hall past the receptionist desk towards several men dressed in suits. One man dressed in a beautiful light gray suit walked up to us, shook our hands, and introduced himself as Governor Stevens. During this entire time, cameras were flashing and reporters were excitedly talking into their microphones. The major networks, as well as local TV and radio stations were providing live coverage to millions of viewers.

The governor escorted us to the conference room. The room was large and could easily seat over four hundred people and every chair was filled. In the center of the room was a stage, a podium, a table and a row of chairs. The room had been decorated earlier that day and banners were hanging everywhere welcoming Governor Stevens and us. As they wheeled us through the door, everyone stopped talking and stood up. An announcement boomed from the podium.

"Ladies and gentlemen, the honorable Governor Stevens."

The room erupted with applause.

The governor climbed the steps to the stage and walked over to the podium. Raising his right hand into the air, the multitude that had assembled stopped clapping and took their seats.

"I want to invite the following people to join me here on the stage," he began. "Would you please hold your applause until all who have been invited joins me here on the stage! Please welcome the Mayor of Idaho Falls, the Superintendent of the Idaho State Police Department, FBI field officer Bob Carson, and Captain Del Montgomery

The four gentlemen came up on stage and took their seats. He then introduced Del.

"I want all of you to meet Captain Del Montgomery. A former agent of the FBI, he is currently serving as the Captain of the Guard at the Boise State Prison and is a key reason we are meeting here today. He has provided valuable information to our local and state authorities that resulted in the seizure of almost a million dollars worth of illegal drugs and the arrests of key members of an international smuggling ring that has plagued this area for years."

Mr. Stevens was a true politician. Del stood at the podium with the governor who placed his arms around Del as if they had been longtime friends.

"We will have the opportunity to hear from him in just a moment." He shook Del's hand and motioned for him to take his seat.

"Finally, I want too introduce to you our two main heroes. Mister Billy Lee and Hammer..." The governor paused for a second and looked over at Hammer.

"I guess up to this point Hammer, I have not been told your last name."

Hammer yelled back, "Just call me Hammer!"

The crowd clapped their appreciation for his sincerity. The governor raised his hand and the room fell silent.

"With that said, I would like to introduce Mister Billy Lee and Hammer."

We began the short walk up the steps while everyone in the room stood up and applauded and cheered. Governor Stevens motion to us to come and join him by the podium. He placed me on his right side and Hammer on the left. He then put his arms around us while everyone holding a camera snapped pictures.

Several minutes passed before the governor raised his right hand and motioned for the crowd to sit. Once the room was quiet, he asked us to take our seats next to Del and Agent Carson and then began his speech recounting the events that took place over the past ten days. The governor went into great detail on the importance of this drug bust and what it meant for the State of Idaho. After what seemed an eternity, he announced that the three of us would receive a reward of one hundred thousand dollars each for providing information that led to the successful capture of several key drug dealers.

When he said how much money we were going to receive, Hammer looked over at me. "Now I can buy my boat."

All I could do was nod my head. I was dumbfounded. I had no idea what I would do with so much money. As I was thinking about the money, the governor asked for Hammer and I to come to the podium to address the group, asking Hammer to speak first.

Hammer looked out over the auditorium and saw hundreds of faces that he'd never seen before and probably would never see again.

In a very sincere voice, he said, "Thanks for all of your support today. It means a lot to us. But I really only have one thing to say. No one messes with the Hammer."

The audience rose to their feet and gave him a standing ovation. He smiled and clasped his hands together. There was so much excitement in the air that he got caught up in the moment and raised both of his hands high above his head and shook them. The crowd went wild. He then stepped back to his chair.

The governor raised his left hand and restored order.

"Looks like we have a born politician amongst us." The room exploded with laughter.

"Now let's hear from Billy."

He motioned for me to take the microphone. I looked out over the throng. It was very intimidating.

Standing at the podium, all I could think of saying was, "Thank you all for making this a day I will remember for the rest of my life."

I returned to my seat. Again, everyone in the room jumped to their feet and began to cheer and clap. Governor Stevens was in his element now.

"Ladies and gentlemen, our two heroes, Mister Billy Lee and Hammer!" he yelled into the microphone. The noise level rocketed.

He let the crowd express their appreciation for about a minute when he finally raised his hand to silence them. The horde took their seats.

"I now want Mr. Del Montgomery to say a few words to us."

Del walked up to the microphone. "I want each and every one of you here today to know that my part in this was insignificant. If it wasn't for Billy and Hammer, we would not be here today. They stumbled into a mystery and rather than just walk away, took it upon themselves to solve it. They were brave when they had to be, coy when it was necessary. If all young men could be like these two, the world would be a better place."

The group roared their appreciation for what he had just said. Del raised his hand and the group fell silent.

"Governor Stevens, Billy and Hammer have a very special gift that they would like to present to you in front of all of these people."

He motioned for us to join him at the podium. I brought Anthony's black book of information with me. Del continued,

"It was rumored that there was a book of information written by Mr. Anthony Jackson of the Chicago Herald. This book has the names of key individuals involved in the illegal drug trafficking throughout the State of Idaho and several other surrounding states. Furthermore, it was alleged that this book contained key dates and places relating to their operation and would seriously damage three major drug cartels if this information ever got out. Well, it is my pleasure to announce that this book is not fiction. It does exist and Billy and Hammer at this time will present it to our Honorable Governor."

The crowd sprang to their feet for the fourth time and roared their approval.

Now, it was my turn to raise my hand to silence the crowd. As I did, the mass of people sat back down. I guess I was becoming caught up in the moment because I took my hand and motioned for the crowd to stand back up. They did as I spoke into the microphone.

"Wow. What power!"

The entire group roared with laughter. For the second time, I motioned for them to take their seats.

"Governor Stevens, Hammer and I want to present this book of information to you. It came at a great price. A father from Chicago lost his son to the evils of drugs. He decided to make a difference and spent five long years gathering solid evidence that would place the guilty behind bars. He gave the ultimate sacrifice, his life. As you all know by now, I am referring to Mr. Anthony Jackson. We may be getting the glory and the reward, but he truly made this day possible."

I turned to the governor and handed him the book. The assembly jumped to their feet for the fifth time and celebrated by clapping, whistling and stomping their feet.

I stepped back from the platform to allow the governor to say a few words of gratitude. At the same time, I noticed three people in the back of the room. The first was the large man from the bus station, who we found out to be a close friend of Anthony's. He was easy to pick out of the crowd because of his sheer size. The other two, a man and a woman, were standing right by the exit. Both were wearing Seattle Mariners baseball caps and dark sunglasses. If I didn't know better, I would swear it was Lynn and Sheriff Thompson. I guess I must have stared at them too long because I noticed the man tap the woman on the arm, making a motion for them to leave. As I watched them turn to exit the room, the lady stopped and removed her sunglasses. She quickly turned back around and smiled at me. From that distance I could not be sure, but if I was a betting man, I would place three to one odds that it was Lynn.

I took my elbow and nudged Hammer. "Look quickly at the exit. I think I just saw Lynn and the sheriff."

He looked, but it was too late. They were gone.

"Are you sure?"

"I think so, if not they were certainly identical twins."

"Should we go after them?"

"No, we wouldn't make it in time. They will be long gone before we make it through this crowd. I guess they just wanted to see if we completed the task."

Hammer smiled. "Yes Billy, they wanted to see if we were able to "Reveal the Truth".

CHAPTER THIRTY-ONE

Several days later, Doctor Epperson was reviewing my chart.

"Well you look like you're ready to leave the hospital. Your bruises are all healed and the incision looks great. I can't think of a single reason to keep you here."

"How about Hammer? Is he ready to leave as well?"

"Oh, yes, he's doing fine. I may want to see the two of you in a couple of weeks, but other than that, you both have my permission to leave."

"Wonderful! It's been a long time since we went fishing."

The Doctor grinned. "So tell me, what, has it been a week or so since you went fishing?"

"No, more like two weeks, and it's killing me."

"Spoken like a true fisherman. In that case, you and Hammer have my permission to go fishing. Just don't wade out in the water too deep."

The doctor shook my hand. "It has been a pleasure to get to know you, Billy. Perhaps one day you and Hammer would care to join my wife and I for dinner?"

"Oh, we would love to do that."

"Good, then next Saturday I want you both to come by." He took out a piece of paper and wrote down his address and home phone number.

"We will expect to see the two of you around 6:00 pm. Plan on staying the night. We have extra rooms." He then pulled me towards him and gave me a hug. "Until then my friend."

I was thinking about how lucky I was to have such a good doctor when Del came into my room.

"Hey, Billy. The doctor just told me that he has given you and Hammer the green light. You know the warden called me this morning and told me that the prison can't run without me, so, I guess it's time for me to head back to Boise. Do the two of you want to come back with me?"

"Not yet. We thought we would spend another couple of days fishing."

"Well, you and Hammer are always welcome to stay with me. Oh by the way, I bought you this newspaper. There's an article in the Sports section on where the big ones are being caught this year. I thought you might want to check it out."

"Thanks, Del. You have been a great friend."

"Well, I have already said goodbye to Hammer. You have my cell phone should you need anything."

"Yes, I do, and don't worry about us. We'll stay out of trouble."

He then gave me a big hug.

"I'm not worried about you getting into trouble. I'm more worried about trouble finding the two of you."

He hugged me one more time and I felt a tear forming in my eye. It was good having him around. He knew a lot about most everything, but he knew even more about bringing out the best in people. Del released his grip on me and turned to the door.

As he started to walk away, I yelled, "If it's alright with you, I would like to call you often."

He stopped. "It's more than alright with me."

Pointing his finger at me, he said, "See you later." and left.

Right after Del left, Gladys walked into my room. My heart started beating a little faster.

"I've heard that you're checking out today, I hope you and Hammer take care of yourselves."

She walked up to me and gave me a huge hug.

"I will miss you."

As she let go and turned to the door. I anxiously said, "Gladys."

She wheeled around. "Yes!"

"I was wondering, would you like to go fishing one day with Hammer and me? It's so beautiful this time of year. The leaves are changing color and the fish are easier to catch. We might even see some deer or moose."

She smiled. "I would love to go fishing with you."

She took a pen and a piece of paper from her pocket and wrote something. As she handed it to me she blushed.

"You know, you're the first patient I ever gave my phone number to."

She hastily turned around and left the room.

I kicked myself. *'Gladys, would you like to go fishing with Hammer and me?' Why couldn't I ask her out to a movie or something more romantic? Oh no, instead, I say, 'Gladys do you want to go fishing?' Oh well, perhaps she really does like to fish. I guess time will tell.*

I walked over to the table where Del had put down the newspaper and picked it up. I was in the process of turning to the sports page when an article on the front page caught my attention. In big bold print it read, 'Killer at Large'. Without delay, I read the entire article. It talked about how the authorities were baffled. They had found a third body along the Snake River but had no clues to work with. Whoever was responsible was clever and would probably continue to kill. They were hoping that if anyone had any information, they would contact them right away.

Immediately I shut my eyes. In my mind, I visualized the beauty of the Snake River and the ugliness of the crimes that had been committed. I saw three beautiful young ladies dressed in a stunning shade of white. They anxiously walked up to me and started to speak in soft whispers.

"We need your help. We have been murdered by a very cruel individual and our families cannot rest until this person is brought to justice."

The second young lady grabbed my left hand.

"Billy, please listen with your heart and help our families."

Finally, the third young lady reached out to me. She had something that she wanted to give to me. I reached out to take what looked like a flower from her, but as I did so, she bowed her head. I could see she was crying and I wanted to comfort her somehow, but all I could do was watch. She suddenly raised her head.

"Please, oh please, won't you help us?"

She dropped the item in her hand. As it fell to the ground, I could see that it was a yellow ribbon of some sort. As I bent over to pick it up, it disappeared before I could take hold of it. I gradually stood back up and looked at the three young ladies. I was about to speak when they slowly faded away.

I opened my eyes and laid the paper down. I felt a great sadness within my heart. I knew that something must be done to bring this monster to justice. As I was still thinking about what just happened, I heard Hammer's voice in the corridor. He was talking to Gladys. An idea unexpectedly came to me. The two of us are good at solving crimes. Perhaps this will be our new profession; we'll become private investigators. We have plenty of money to open our business and a reputation as heroes. I could see the headline now. Hammer and Billy assist local authorities in capturing *The Snake River Killer*.

I went out into the hallway to tell Hammer my plan…

Billy and Hammer's Next Adventure:

THE SNAKE RIVER KILLER

Chapter One

All she could think of that day at work was how long it would take her to get from Pocatello, Idaho to Jackson Hole, Wyoming. She had planned this vacation for over a year. Since moving to Pocatello from Los Angeles to work at the Bannock Memorial Hospital as a licensed Registered Nurse, she had heard much about the beauty of Yellowstone National Park. Most of her coworkers had visited the park at least once. Several of her coworkers had been there over a dozen times. They enlightened her on Old Faithful and the countless other geysers in the park. She could hardly wait to take her fist pictures of this majestic place.

When the clock struck 3:00 p.m., she headed straight toward the main exit. Today, she had no time to stay after and chit-chat with the others. It was a semi-hot August afternoon with the temperature pushing 85 degrees with some dark gray storm clouds off in the distance. One coworker noticed her and yelled before she reached her car.

"Now you be careful Cindy. There's a lot to do in Yellowstone, but there's also bears."

"Oh, Sally, don't worry. I brought a couple of bells and whistles to chase away any bears."

"Alright, I look forward to hearing about your trip next week when you return."

Cindy unlocked her car and rolled down the windows. She was driving a brand new dark green Toyota Rav4 which offered her all the comforts of a fancy car and plenty of room for all of her hiking gear. She waved goodbye to Sally and as she was driving off yelled, "I will take plenty of pictures."

Sally smiled and continued her trek to her car.

Once out of the hospital parking lot, Cindy drove straight to the freeway. She had already packed everything she needed for the trip; extra clothes in case it rained, her camera, binoculars, suntan lotion, power bars, several bottles of water, a bright red backpack and a pair of new hiking boots, purchased specifically for this trip. She even bought a compass and several books on hiking the National Parks of America. This was going to be a trip of a lifetime, just her and Mother Nature. Getting on the freeway, she turned on her CD player and loaded a disk. Two days earlier, she had visited the local library and checked out several CD's on the history of Yellowstone. She took a quick moment and adjusted the volume and then reached over and set the cruise control to 77 mph. Nothing was going to interrupt her now.

The miles flew by and before she knew it, she had driven through Idaho Falls and was heading north on Highway 26 to Swan Valley. When the first CD ended, she decided it was good time to take a break. Just up ahead was a small rest stop just outside of the Ririe area. She pulled over and got out to stretch her legs. The rest stop was situated high above the Snake River and presented some breathtaking views. This delighted her, so she took her camera over to the fenced walkway and snapped several pictures of the river below. As she did, she noticed a large nest off to her left that appeared to have a very huge bird sitting on top of it. She aimed her camera and took a picture. All of a sudden the bird began to stir, turning towards her and leaping out of the nest. The bird soared down into the valley below. Cindy recognized it immediately as a bald eagle. Gliding back toward her, it was no more than 50 yards from where she was standing. She stood there watching this great bird for a few minutes and then said aloud, "What a beautiful start to my vacation!"

Cindy walked around the rest stop for several more minutes and then returned to her car, resuming her journey north on Highway 26. Instead of listening to the CD on Yellowstone, she searched for a local radio station hoping to hear the weather forecast. Earlier in the day, she had checked the weather on the Internet. The forecast called for mild weather for the next several days with a very slim chance of rain. Noticing several dark clouds off in the distance, she thought that the chance of rain was a little greater than what the report had offered.

Taking a left at the junction, she began her ascent on Hiway-31 to Victor. This part of the road was steeper and winding and several times she found herself behind pickup trucks pulling large trailers. Whenever she had the opportunity, she would quickly pass. She was on a mission and wanted to check into the lodge before 7:00 p.m, looking forward to a peaceful dinner and then a stroll through downtown Jackson Hole. Her friends had told her about the park located in the center of town with pillars of elk antlers. She had heard that during the summer months around 8:00 in the evening, there was a skit performed in which a couple of gunfighters would call one another out. She had visualized this performance so many times that she could hardly wait for the actual event to take place.

At the top of Jackson Pass, there was an awesome view of the valley below. Cindy decided to pull over and took several pictures. While she was snapping a few photos of the valley below, another lady, probably a tourist, who had already been there for quite some time tapped her on the shoulder.

"Look over there just below that ridge. Do you see those two dark brown figures?"

Cindy stared for a few seconds.

"Where exactly are you pointing?"

"Over there, just below that far tree. The one with the large bare spot at the top."

She finally saw what the other person was pointing at.

"Yes, I do see those two dark brown objects. What are they?"

"If I'm not mistaken, I believe that they are two grizzly bears."

"No way, you're kidding me?"

"No I'm not. I've been watching them for about twenty minutes now. They have been moving slowly down the hillside."

Cindy turned towards her car. "I've got some binoculars. Let's check it out."

She swiftly ran to her car and grabbed the binoculars.

"Let's see if I can make them out."

She took the binoculars and scanned the hillside. When she found the two dark brown spots she adjusted them.

"I don't think they're grizzly bears. They look more like big deer."

The tourist said, "Do you mind if I look?"

"No, go ahead."

Cindy handed the binoculars to her. She scanned the hillside until she saw the two dark brown figures.

"Yes, you're right. They're not bears, but they're not deer either. They're two moose. It looks like a mother moose and her calf."

She gave the binoculars back to Cindy. Cindy again focused on the two figures.

"This is fantastic! I have never seen a moose before, let alone two at the same time."

The tourist asked, "Is this your first time here?"

Cindy lowered the binoculars. "Yes, I was born and raised in Los Angeles. I have been working as a nurse at the Bannock Memorial Hospital in Pocatello, Idaho for the past year. I've planned this trip for quite some time."

"Well, you won't be disappointed. This is my third trip to this part of the country. Each time, I've had the opportunity to see a wide variety of wildlife. I actually hate it when I have to go home. I'm from New York. The only animals I ever see there are the ones at the bar near my apartment."

Both of them began to laugh.

"I'm sorry, I should have introduced my self sooner. My name is Alice."

"Nice to meet you Alice, I'm Cindy."

For several minutes, they talked about New York. Alice, looking at her watch, said, "I have to be off. My plane leaves early tomorrow morning from Idaho Falls. I sure will miss these beautiful mountains.

Cindy nodded her head.

"I know what you mean, I'm just getting here and I'm already in love with the place.

The two of them said goodbye and went their separate ways. Cindy returned to her car and commenced with the descent to the valley below.

It was just about 7:00 p.m. when she pulled into the lodge at Jackson Hole. 'Right on time,' she thought to herself as she went to check into her room.

The attendant on hand introduced himself as John. He was very handsome and friendly and asked Cindy,

"Is this your first time to Yellowstone?"

"Yes, and I plan on doing a lot of hiking. I look forward to seeing all of the natural beauty this park provides." Cindy replied,

"Well if that's the case, be sure to see De Lacy Lakes. There's a trail head just off the main road and the scenery is to die for."

Cindy and John talked for several more minutes until they were interrupted by another hotel staff member.

John then turned to Cindy and said, "It appears that I am needed in the kitchen, so here are your keys and enjoy your stay."

Cindy looked at the keys and found the room 1245 printed on the main part of the key. Using the hotel map that John had given her, she was off to find her room.

It was a beautiful suite with a king-sized bed. Cindy quickly dropped her luggage in the room and hurriedly spruced up. If she was to make it to the shootout on time, she would have to hurry. She left the hotel and walked the four blocks to the downtown park. The main actors for the skit had already shown up and were working the crowd by acting like tough old cowboys. When they saw her, they swaggered up to her and began to speak.

"Well looky here. We have ourselves a city slicker."

"Yeah, she sure does look pretty with those fancy Levi's. What do you say little gal? Are you looking forward to some fun tonight?"

Cindy was blushing and giggling. It was what she hoped for.

She was about to say something to one of the cowboys, when all of a sudden he said, "Not now little lady, look over yonder, there's Black Bart." He tipped his hat to her and sauntered towards him.

The show lasted ten minutes with the two cowboys eventually shooting Black Bart. The entire park was full of vacationers and Cindy was enjoying herself when she felt a strong hunger pain. She hadn't had anything to eat all day so she left the park in search of a restaurant. Two blocks from her hotel, there was a quaint old restaurant offering a genuine western chicken dinner for $8.99. For the next hour she relaxed and enjoyed her meal. Every sightseer walking by that night seemed to have a smile. Just being away from the rat race of life brought her great joy.

The waiter noticing that she had finished with her meal asked, "Would you like a slice of our homemade peach pie? You can have it served with two scoops of authentic vanilla ice cream."

She was tempted by his proposal.

"How about a slice of peach pie without the ice cream?"

"Sure thing, I will be back in a minute with your pie."

The waiter hurried off to get the pie. A couple minutes later, he came by with the pie and a copy of her bill.

"Is there anything else you would like tonight?"

"No, thank you. You did an incredible job."

"Well thank you very much, and have a nice evening."

"You too."

She finished her pie and looked at the bill. All together, it was fifteen dollars for a rather nice meal, her drink, and a delicious piece of pie. Opening her purse, she grabbed a twenty and left it on the table next to the bill. Leaving the restaurant, she walked back to her hotel, reminiscing back to what a wonderful day she had had as the evening sun was setting off in the west. It was the perfect ending to a wonderful day.

Cindy went back to her room and got ready for bed. After she jumped into bed, she opened one of her hiking books and started reading about the De Lacy Lakes trail. Some considered it the beginning of the great Snake River. There was a trail that crossed the divide several times and the book made it sound very doable so she decided to start off her adventure with this trail and would begin early in the morning. She planned where she would start and at what time she would head back. She took a moment and said a quick prayer and then turned off the light. Within a short period of time she was fast asleep.

CHAPTER TWO

The next morning came early and her alarm clock went off as scheduled. She reached over and hit the snooze button and quickly fell asleep again. Ten minutes later, the alarm was buzzing again. This time she sat up in bed and switched off the alarm.

With great effort she made it to the bathroom, took a shower and prepared for the rest of the day. After getting dressed, she went to the lobby to take advantage of their free breakfast, helping herself to a large plate full of eggs, toast and bacon. There was a wide choice of drinks, but she settled on a cup of hot tea. Just as she was about to sit down, she grabbed a sweet roll. *One wont hurt.* As she sipped her tea and took a nibble on the roll, she thought to herself, *Wow, spending a night out here sure helped me work up an appetite.*

After finishing with her breakfast, she sipped the last bit of tea. She stood up and quickly made it back to her room where she applied some suntan lotion, put on her hiking boots, grabbed her book on hiking and headed towards her car. Everything was perfect for a great day of hiking. Driving out of the parking lot, she headed through town and north on highway 191 towards Yellowstone Park.

Five miles north of Jackson Hole, the beautiful Grand Teton Mountain range ascended into the sky and made its presence felt; its beauty was beyond comparison to any other mountain range she had seen before. She wanted to stop and take a few pictures but felt she needed to start her hike early enough to avoid any potential problems.

"I will take pictures of them on the return trip." she thought.

Thus she continued down the road for several miles, taking a left on Highway 89 towards the Moran Entrance Station. She approached the entrance to the Grand Teton National Park and pulled up to the park entrance.

"Its twenty-five dollars for a ten day pass," the ranger on duty informed her. "However, for fifty dollars, you can purchase a yearly pass that will allow you access to all of the National Parks."

Cindy knew that she would be back so she reached into her purse and removed two twenty's and a ten.

"I'll take the yearly pass. By the way, how far to De Lacy Lakes?"

"Around sixty miles. Be sure to turn left at the West Thumb/Grant Village junction."

Handing her a plastic entrance pass, he said, "You'll have to sign the back of this, and be sure to show your I.D. each time you use it. Would you like a map of the park as well?"

"Yes, please."

The ranger handing her a map, smiled and said, "Have a nice day."

She nodded her head and drove off.

Around thirty miles later, she saw a big sign, Yellowstone National Park and another ranger station. She pulled up and handed the ranger her new card.

He smiled. "I'll also need to see some photo identification."

"Oh, I'm sorry."

"Here you go sir," she said, handing him her driver's . license. "By the way, has anyone seen a bear today?"

"There have been several reports of a grizzly bear around Canyon Village, next to Wolf Lake. Other than that, I haven't heard of any other sightings. Would you like a map of the park?"

"No thanks, I have one. Can you tell me if Wolf Lake is near De Lacy Lake?"

"No, Wolf Lake is about twenty-five miles as the crow flies from De Lacy Lake, or around fifty miles if you take the park highways. How come?"

"I'm going to take the hiking trail near Craig's Pass and head towards the lake."

The ranger smiled. "That should be a great day hike. Be sure to register at the trail head."

"Thanks, I'll do so. Have a nice day."

The ranger tipped his head and looked at the next car in line.

Cindy entered the South Entrance of the park and headed north along highway 89, driving past Lewis Lake and came to the first sign indicating that she was passing by the Continental Divide, a sign indicating that the elevation was 7,988 feet. The temperature was a brisk forty-seven degrees, with a slight breeze, but felt pleasant because of the abundant sunshine. She passed Grant Village and at the West Thumb junction, hung a left. For the second time, she passed the Continental Divide. This time, the elevation was 8,391 feet. Two miles later she saw a sign that read 'Craig Pass Hiking Trail', elevation 8,262. She pulled over and took a picture of the sign and then looked for a place to park in the small lot. Two other cars were already parked in the lot.

Cindy thought, "Oh well, I guess I won't be the only person hiking today."

She put on a light jacket and her backpack. She felt red would be a great color and allow others to be able to see her in case she got lost. Her backpack was loaded with snacks, bottles of water, extra socks, a few medical supplies, and her cell phone. She slung her binoculars around her neck and placed her camera into the front pocket of her jacket. Finally, she took her hiking book and studied the trail for several minutes. Her plan was to follow the divide north, crossing it several times until she reached the north shore of De Lacey Lake. Cindy knew from studying the map that De Lacy Creek emptied out of the lake and flowed south to Shoshone Lake. From there, the water continued its journey south to Lewis Lake, into the Lewis River, on to Moose Falls, and from Moose Falls, it emptied into the Snake River.

Cindy felt that making it as far as De Lacey Lake was equivalent to making it to the mouth of the mighty Snake River. She knew that there were other tributaries off to the west of Heart Lake, but as far as she could determine, the furthest point north was De Lacy Lake. All the water on this side of the divide would flow towards the Pacific, and the water on the other side of the dived flowed towards the Atlantic. She was ready for her adventurer and grabbed a ski pole from out of the trunk of her car. She had bought it earlier in the week to use as a walking stick. The last item she took from her trunk was a Los Angeles Dodger baseball cap. It was time to start the hike.

Even though there were two other cars parked in the lot, she saw no one. It was what she hoped for, a hike with nothing but her and Mother Nature. Forty-five minutes into the hike, she found the going fairly slow. The trail kept switching back and forth and for the most part, was not very well maintained. The elevation also made it difficult to go very far without taking a break, however, she continued for another hour before stopping to take a rest.

She removed her backpack and took a sip of water, studying the hiking book for a few seconds. She was on track and according to the book, should be nearing her destination in another hour or so. Up to this point, she had seen several squirrels and three chipmunks, but no large animals. She put her backpack on her back and resumed her journey. For the next sixty minutes she allowed her mind to relax. The beauty of the trees and the silence of the forest were very uplifting. Occasionally she would hear the cawing of a crow or the slight rustling of the trees in the gentle breeze, but other than that, she was alone. She had not seen another soul since she pulled off the main road and parked her car. She continued her hike until she came upon a small clearing.

At the clearing she saw her destination, De Lacy Lakes. They were two fairly small lakes nestled amongst the trees. The first lake was about the size of five football fields and the other the size of two fields. She was at over 9,000 feet and the temperature was in the mid fifties. Near the lake were several small tree stumps, perfect for sitting on so she decided to rest. She removed her backpack and was in the process of opening it up when she heard a loud noise coming towards her from the other side of the lake. She stared in the direction of the noise for several seconds when all of a sudden, a large grizzly bear came wandering out into the open within two hundred yards from where she sat. Cindy had two thoughts.

'Oh no, I should have been wearing those bells I purchased for this hike.' and 'What a beautiful creature.'

Now she didn't want the animal to continue coming towards her so she slowly stood up and made a loud clapping sound with her hand. The grizzly stopped dead in his tracks, stood up on his hind legs, and sniffed the air. He then looked over at her.

Cindy was somewhat concerned at this time. She didn't know what to do. From all of the stories she had heard, you should never sneak up on a bear, but in this case the bear appeared to be sneaking up on her. She wondered if she should head back the way she came but didn't want to do this until she had finished her hike. After all, it had been close to three hours of hard work to get to this point and she wanted to dip her feet in the lake, but not at the expense of potentially being mauled by a bear.

Fortunately for her, when the bear saw her, it dipped to all fours and slowly lumbered back into the woods. As it did, Cindy felt relief but then frustration set in.

"Damn it! I had the chance to take some pictures of a wild bear. Well if this happens again, I'll be ready." she said aloud,

She took her camera out of her pocket and loosened the strap, carefully wrapping the strap around her wrist.

"Now I am prepared, should this happen again."

Cindy followed a small trail to the edge of the lake. As she did, she noticed a small porcupine by the water's edge. She took her camera and snapped several pictures. The porcupine did not appear to even notice her, sipping water from the lake several times and before slowly returning back towards the woods. It took about thirty seconds before it disappeared between two large trees. Cindy gently took off her hiking boots and socks and dipped her feet into the water. The water was extremely chilly, yet refreshing. The day was warming up very nicely and she was getting hot with her jacket still being on. She observed a nice spot about twenty yards away in which she could soak her feet as well as sit down. Carefully she walked barefooted along the edge of the lake until she reached the spot.

Cindy had hiked well over five miles and the entire time still had not seen any other hikers. It was as if she had the forest to herself. She opened up her backpack, grabbed another power bar and took out the bottle of water that she had been sipping from throughout the morning hike. The weather was perfect so she placed her backpack on the ground as if it were a pillow and cautiously brushed away some pine needles that had fallen off of the near by trees. Laying down, she shut her eyes, thinking that she would only rest for about fifteen minutes.

Several hours later, she awoke to the noise of a low growl. The grizzly that she had seen earlier had her backpack in his mouth and was trying to get at the food inside the pack. When she saw the bear, she froze with fear, having no idea what to do. He was no more than five feet from her. Quickly she began to say a silent prayer.

"Oh God, please make this bear go away."

She said this prayer to herself numerous times, but the bear was not going anywhere. It became obvious to her that she would have to do something. She felt the best thing to do was jump up and yell at the bear. She was ready to when she heard a man yelling in the distance. He was shouting at the bear.

"Hey, Hey, get away from there."

He clapped his hands several times. The bear pawed at the ground and then took off running in the opposite direction of where the man was standing.

The man came running up to Cindy yelling, "Are you alright?"

Cindy sat up. "Yes thanks so very much. I was scared to death."

He came over to her and grabbed her by her hand and helped her up.

"I thought the bear had attacked you."

"No, I guess I must have fallen asleep. The next thing I knew, he was tearing up my backpack.

"You're lucky he didn't tear you up. He must have thought you were dead or something. Are you out here all alone?"

"Yes. I've heard so many stories about how beautiful this place is and I had to find out for myself. I sure am lucky you came along. I haven't seen anyone else out here all day long."

Cindy quickly brushed herself off and went to see what remained of her new backpack.

She turned to the stranger, "Do you know what time it is?"

"Yes, it's 4:30 in the afternoon." He said as he looked at his watch,

"Four-Thirty! I must have fallen asleep, I've got to get going."

The man asked her. "Do you have a campsite around here?"

"No, I'm staying at the lodge in Jackson Hole."

The man nodded his head. "I know the place well. Do you have someone there waiting for you?"

As he said this, Cindy had a strange sensation come over her.

"Why is this person so interested in who is or who isn't waiting for me. And why does it appear that he mumbles when he talks?"

Cindy became concerned and felt that she might have been safer with the bear. So she told a quick lie. "Yes, my husband is waiting there for me."

This stranger was uncomfortably close to her. This made her feel even more anxious. He pointed at her left hand. "You don't have on a wedding band?"

"Oh I left it at the hotel."

Cindy felt extremely uneasy with the way he had now started to stare at her. She blurted out, "Well thanks again, I have to be off."

She picked up her ripped backpack and hurriedly started to walk down the trail back to her car. But before she could take a third step, the man reached out and grabbed her.

"Ouch, that hurts. Let go of me, my husband will hear about this."

The man did not say a word. Instead, he jerked Cindy to the ground.

"Help! Help!" she began to scream.

The man slapped her violently across her mouth. "Scream all you want, there's no one else out here."

He placed both of his hands around Cindy's neck and started to choke her. She couldn't scream, so she desperately scratched at his arms. Her fingernails tore into the strangers left arm and he shrieked liked a woman in pain, but didn't loosen his grip from around her neck. She tried for a second time to break the man's grip, but she was tired from the long hike and her strength was slowly slipping away from her. Desperately, she looked into the strangers eyes. She could see that he was wearing contacts, but even more than that, she could see pure evil. As she gazed at this stranger, she felt something was very eccentric about this person. With all of the energy she could muster up, she tried for the last time to loosen his grip, but could not.